MERCI SUÁREZ CAN'T DANCE

Talk about awkward: Wilson and I had nothing much to say as we waited. I only knew him from PE and earth science, the quiet kid with freckles across his nose and reddish hair he wears natural. I had noticed his walk, too. He swings one hip forward so his right leg can clear the ground. He says it doesn't hurt or anything. He was born that way, he told us last year during one of those annoying icebreaker activities we're all subjected to on the first day of school. Anyway, we hadn't really talked much this year. The only other intel I had was that his family is Cajun and Creole from Louisiana. He told us that when he brought gumbo to the One World food festival when we were in the sixth grade, and it was pretty good, if you didn't mind breaking into a full-body sweat from the spices.

Miss McDaniels grabbed her key ring and made us follow her down the hall toward the cafeteria, our loafers squeaking in the quiet halls.

A few minutes later, we stood in front of the Ram Depot, formerly known as the custodial supply closet before Mr. Vong and his equipment got upgraded to a bigger room near the gym. That's where she told us the lousy news.

We'd been drafted.

"I think you two would make a fine management team

CHAPTER 1

IT WAS MISS McDANIELS'S IDEA for me and Wilson Belle-vue to work together in the Ram Depot, a job that nobody wants. For the record, I applied for an anchor spot on the morning announcements with my best friend Lena. But wouldn't you know it? Darius Ulmer's parents decided it was time he addressed his "shyness issues," so he got the job instead.

Anyway, when Miss McDaniels called Wilson and me to her office, neither one of us had any idea what she wanted, which should have been a big warning right there. We sat on the wooden bench near her desk at 8:15 sharp, just like her note said, since being late is the quickest way to get on her bad side. It's why some kids call her Stopwatch behind her back.

FOR MERCI FANS WHO WANTED TO KNOW
WHAT HAPPENED NEXT . . .

Copyright © 2021 by Margaret Medina

First edition 2021

Library of Congress Catalog Card Number pending
ISBN 978-0-7636-9050-2

21 22 23 24 25 26 LBM 10 9 8 7 6 5 4 3 2 1

Printed in Melrose Park, IL, USA

This book was typeset in Berkeley Oldstyle.

Candlewick Press
99 Dover Street
Somerville, Massachusetts 02144

www.candlewick.com

A JUNIOR LIBRARY GUILD SELECTION

MERCI SUÁREZ CAN'T DANCE

MEG MEDINA

CANDLEWICK PRESS

at the school store," she said as she unlocked the door to the tiny space. A box of pencils labeled INVENTORY was stacked against one wall near the dust bunnies. A metal cashbox and calculator sat on a cast-off desk with uneven legs. "You can hone your business and math skills right here and get real-world experience."

I tried to keep my glare of death to a minimum level. First of all, if my business skills were any sharper, I'd have to register them as weapons, thank you very much. Who does she think helps Papi figure out job bids and write ad copy? Sol Painting, Inc., doesn't have five stars on Yelp for nothing. As for Wilson, he was already a math whiz. I hear he computes circles around the other kids in the algebra class he takes with ninth-graders.

But the bigger thing is how unfair this all was. Lena had morning announcements. Hannah was assigned to be the supply aide in the cool makerspace that's new this year. Me? I was facing a dungeon where fun goes to die— and with a boy as my only company no less.

Wilson seemed just as appalled. "Isn't there anything else?" he asked. "Maybe the Earth Club? I wouldn't mind rinsing out recyclables."

I sneaked a glance at him, secretly agreeing. Even washing out juice boxes and plastic Snackables trays seemed better. What was there to do at the Ram Depot except sell pens and pencils to kids who forgot theirs at home?

She pursed her lips. "I'm afraid not. Dr. Newman is very interested in improving the school store this year, and I need especially strong student helpers for the task."

She was buttering us up like biscuits. The question was, Why?

Then she handed over a brochure from the Poxel School in North Palm Beach. The Pox, as we call them around here, is our archrival in everything from soccer to landscaping. You want to drive a stake through our headmaster's heart? Tell Dr. Newman that the Poxel School is better than Seaward Pines at anything. The brochure showed photos of their recently finished building project. Smack in the middle was a picture of their new school store, looking like it belonged in the Gardens Mall. Clothes, electronics, coffee bar, beanbag chairs, you name it. There was even a web link for online orders.

I gave her a grim look. "You'd need miracle workers, miss, not us."

Wilson nodded, backing me up. "She's right, Miss McDaniels."

I could practically feel the air around us grow colder as she narrowed her eyes, digging in.

"Perhaps I can persuade you another way. I have been authorized to offer you a significant perk if you will both agree to take the job," she said.

"Perk?" Wilson said.

"Let me guess," I said, my soul already on life support. "Free pencils for life."

Wilson started to chuckle, but her sharp look turned my joke into ash. *Being churlish*, as she says, is at the top of her list of no-no's, especially for seventh-graders.

"Not that pencils aren't useful," I mumbled.

"Better than pencils." She lowered her voice, her eyes steady on ours. "What would you say to eating free dessert from the cafeteria every day. Mrs. Malta's key lime pie, in fact."

My mouth watered.

Graham cracker crust. Tart filling and whipped cream. That's my lunchroom Kryptonite, and she knew it. From the look on Wilson's face, it was his, too.

Maybe we could be business partners after all.

"Free?" I always bring a bag lunch thanks to Mami. No sugary treats are ever part of it.

She nodded slowly to let it sink in. "Every. Single. Day."

Wilson and I exchanged looks.

"It's settled, then," Miss McDaniels said, victorious.

Sometimes you have bad options, but you still have to pick, like, do you eat the yucca or the quimbombó at Lolo and Abuela's house for dinner? You just make the best of it. So that's what I did.

"I'm in," I said. If I was going to die of boredom with a kid I barely knew, at least there would be pie. And Wilson, shrugging, said he was in, too.

CHAPTER 2

"HEY, WHERE Y'AT?" WILSON SAYS. That's *hello*. He doesn't know, but I kind of like how he talks. He puts no *r*'s on the ends of words, which makes him sound like Mr. Finley, who's from Boston and teaches American history. *Cah. Bah. Fah,* instead of *car, bar, far.* Wilson isn't from Massachusetts, though. He's from New Orleans, which is hot and steamy just like here in South Florida. He says it's not *evah* pronounced New Or-leenz. If you say it that way, he corrects you—even if you're Miss McDaniels. I've heard him do it with my own ears.

I'll be honest. At first, I wasn't crazy about working with a seventh-grade boy in close quarters, especially because of their annoying jokes about farting and body parts. In sixth grade, most of the boys were relatively normal, but not anymore. Now the lunch menu can't list chicken breast sandwiches without them elbowing one another and convulsing. Some of them punch other boys in the privates to be funny, like that guy on YouTube. Michael Clark went down like a tree and had to go to the nurse when Jason Aldrich got him after hiding under his desk. And God forbid if one of the boys likes you. He'll spend a whole class saying obnoxious things so that you'll look at him, even if it's with murder in your eyes. More than one girl has had to tell the teacher or scream "I hate you!" to get them to stop. It's so confusing. I mean, if you want someone to like you, shouldn't you act nice? But no. They act so badly that the kids they have crushes on dream of beating them to death with a shovel.

Wilson, it turns out, is not like that at all, and this job is not the worst thing that could happen to a person. His top qualifications so far: He doesn't make mean comments about my lazy eye and then complain that I can't take a joke. He doesn't copy off my tests in earth science and take credit for smart answers. He doesn't hog the basketball in PE so he can make the shot himself. Plus, he's basically a human calculator, which is good when you're trying to revamp a total disaster of a business like we are.

He hangs his backpack on the hook behind the door

and looks around for a place to sit. We only have room for a table and two chairs in here, and today it's even more cramped than usual.

I look up from the poster I'm making on the floor. "Careful. You're going to stomp me," I tell him.

His shoes are badly scuffed, especially his right one, the one that's wider on account of the brace he wears to keep his toes from dragging down. The soles are caked with wet grass, too, a telltale sign that he didn't stay on the walkways like we're supposed to as per the gazillion signs about keeping our campus beautiful. That's a level-one offense in Miss McDaniels's book. And I would know since I'm more or less a regular on walkway infractions.

"Wipe those off if you know what's good for you," I say. "I got hassled again just yesterday." Miss McDaniels saw me run across the grass because I was late for English.

Wilson pays me no mind. "What's all this?" He fishes out his sandwich and offers me half. Ham and cheese, same as every day, and his mom uses full-fat *máyo-nay-is*, so I'm in heaven. At least it's better than Mami's healthy turkey breast with alfalfa sprouts "for fun," which she says are "nutrient dense." I looked it up and found out sprouts are full of vitamin K, which helps your blood clot. Useful in case I'm stabbed, I guess.

"I'm making room for new stock, of course," I tell him,

taking a swig from my water bottle. "We have to unload those dumb erasers before the new inventory gets here. So, we're having a winter clearance sale."

We've been waiting weeks for the bobbleheads we ordered. Hunky Jake Rodrigo, hero of the gene-spliced-universe bobbleheads. It's a million-dollar idea. No one will be able to resist them.

"We are, huh?" he asks. "Did we have a meeting to decide that? Let me think . . . NO."

I push the hair off my face and roll my eyes. He's such a stickler about things. "We didn't need a meeting. We needed action. So, I took it." I cap my marker and hold up the sign.

Fix your mistakes in style.

Two-for-one erasers! Wile supplies last!

"What do you think?" I ask.

"I think you spelled *while* wrong. I thought you were good at English."

I look at it and grimace. Then I add a few words and hold the sign up again. "How's this?"

Fix your mistakes in style.

Two-for-one erasers! Wile supplies last!

(See? An eraser would have helped!)

Wilson grins and crosses his arms. "Erasers don't work on marker."

"You're nitpicking again," I say. But I don't mind when

he teases sometimes. I let my tongue roll around on *mah-kah*, just the way he says it.

"And have you run the numbers on this so-called sale that I didn't co-sign for? What if we lose money at that price, woadie?" That's another of his New Orleans words I like. It means we're friends. "Stopwatch will get cheesed, you know—"

"I will get *cheesed* about what, exactly, Wilson—aside from those grassy shoes that have created a mess along the hall?"

Miss McDaniels stands at the door with our custodian, Mr. Vong, in tow. He's pushing a hand truck stacked with a pile of cartons that's taller than he is. He glances around it and gives Wilson a steely look.

"Thank you, Mr. Vong," Miss McDaniels says. "I believe the students and I can manage from here."

Then she folds her hands and turns to us again as Mr. Vong unloads. "You were saying, Wilson?"

Wilson goes mute, of course, a common side effect of encounters with Miss McDaniels, especially since his footwear is about to earn him some time, just like I warned. When we both stand up, he takes the merest step behind me.

Luckily, I've had plenty of practice with Miss McDaniels, so I can save him from his sorry mess this time.

I go right to what I learned in the "Sound Management Principles" chapter from *Peterson's Guide to Building Your Business,* sixth edition, which I've been reading at night.

"Oh, hello, miss," I say. "Wilson and I were just talking about how to make things tidier in here. Clutter makes us seem very unprofessional."

"Oh?" She glances around at our mess.

"I'm sorry to say this, miss, but those snowflake erasers that you ordered aren't selling, and we're coming up on February already. Luckily, I have a plan to fix the loss— and clear some space in here."

"We," Wilson says, peeking out from behind me. "*We* have a plan."

I try not to roll my eyes. "OK. We."

She looks over her glasses at us, waiting, so I hold up my sign. "Ta-da! A clearance sale! What do you think?"

She reads the words and arches her brow. "You've worked out the finances, I hope."

Wilson squeezes my elbow in an "I told you so" move.

"Yes, miss. They're right here." I crouch back on the floor to riffle through the scratch papers where I've done all my figuring. Numbers are scrawled all over the place because sometimes it takes me a few minutes to work something out. It's not automatic like it is for Wilson or my brother, Roli. I'm never sure at first how to solve a problem.

Do I add, subtract, divide, or what? I find the paper and squint at my own horrible writing.

"The way I see it, we bought two thousand erasers for only a dime a piece, which is . . . a two hundred–dollar investment. If we sell them *two* for a quarter, we'll be selling them at . . . at . . ." I hold the paper close, trying to read my messy handwriting.

Wilson sighs and steps in to help. "Twelve point five cents per eraser. That's two point five cents' profit per eraser. Which, if you multiply, gives you two hundred fifty dollars—or, specifically, a fifty-dollar profit."

"Um, right," I say.

She looks from Wilson to me. "Impressive," she says at last. Then she gives a quick nod. "Very well. I'll allow it." In Miss McDaniels–speak, that means *What a genius idea!* I beam a smile at Wilson. This joins my other successful suggestions: the emoji stress balls in time for exam week, which everyone liked squeezing to make the emoji's eyes bulge to the size of eggs; and the secret spy decoder pens that sold out in only two days thanks to the fifth-graders who liked the disappearing ink.

Miss McDaniels turns to me and hands over a fat roll of red tickets. "We have other, more pressing matters to discuss, anyway."

I look at the roll. "What's this, miss?" I ask.

"The ticket roll for the Heart Ball, of course. Valentine's Day will be here in a few weeks. I need you to sell the dance tickets here at the Ram Depot during lunch hours starting next week."

My stomach sinks. I hate the Heart Ball. At Seaward Pines, each grade has a special assignment to build teamwork and class spirit. Sixth-graders run the games for the carnival night. Eighth-graders go on an annual class trip to Saint Augustine. But what do we seventh-graders do? We're in charge of the silly middle-school dance for Valentine's Day. What kind of special treat is that?

"I thought you'd be pleased," Miss McDaniels says. "It will drive customers to the store."

True. But please, dancing is just not my jam, at least not in public where people can see me flailing around like a fish dying on a deck. And more important, I've heard rumors that some kids are planning to kiss at this thing. Just the thought of that gives me hives.

So, no gracias.

I look down at the tickets glumly.

Miss McDaniels crosses her arms. "Is there a problem?" She asks in a tone that tells me there shouldn't be, so I stay mum.

She heaves a sigh. "Might this have something to do with what we discussed last semester?"

"Maybe, miss," I say. "You have to admit, it would have been more fun."

Way back at the beginning of the year, I started a petition to change the seventh-grade project. I suggested our own version of *American Ninja Warrior* right here on the quad. I provided detailed diagrams of the challenge course and everything. I got fifty signatures of kids who wanted to rappel down the science building, but still she squashed my dream flat.

"The Heart Ball is a fine Seaward Pines tradition," she says. "It builds teamwork and social graces."

It's also being run by Edna Santos.

She and I have agreed to a truce, but it's not been that easy, mostly because neither one of us has had a total personality transplant. After she got in trouble for wrecking my costume last year, she tried being a little less bossy, but it was as temporary as a wash-off tattoo. Not many people hang around with her anymore. Not even Rachel walks with her to class. But now that Edna is the Dancing Queen, she doesn't seem to care about that. She walks around with a clipboard and won't talk about anything except that silly dance. It's thanks to her that every square inch of this school has been plastered with posters for the Heart Ball. They even have her picture on them! You can't tinkle in the bathroom without her watching you and telling you to buy tickets. Wilson claims it has made peeing at school difficult for him.

I guess my face is communicating all of this, the way Mami says it does, because Miss McDaniels zeroes in.

"Some tasks require us to put aside our past personal differences, Merci. We take them on for the general good of the school community, even if they are not our favorite thing. Wouldn't you agree?"

No, I would not, but I keep my lip buttoned. I, for one, am *not* going to any silly dance, even if I *do* have to sell tickets. My plan is to watch an Iguanador Nation movie that night and gorge on the big box of assorted Russell Stover chocolates that Mami and Papi always give me for Valentine's Day.

Wilson clears his throat. "Will the dance committee pay the Ram Depot a handling fee?"

Miss McDaniels looks at him over her glasses, but he stays calm. "It's just that the store runs on a pretty slim staff, and tickets sales will take up time. Not to mention that we're expecting a busy month in here with new merchandise, remember?"

"I have no doubt that two capable students like you will find the proper way to multitask."

"Still, it seems fair to give us a slice," Wilson says. "Maybe just ten percent?" He does a quick calculation.

"That's fifty cents a ticket. We could use the funds to make improvements around here."

I turn around and look at him, shocked at his hard-knuckle negotiating skills. Is he reading *Peterson's*, too? And all at once, my heart sort of warms to him.

Miss McDaniels folds her hands. "Fine. If that makes it more amenable for the two of you, we'll do that. The accounting will reflect your participation and support."

Wilson gives me a triumphant smile as Miss McDaniels turns to the stack of cartons that Mr. Vong left for us.

"Now that we've settled *that*," she says, "let's get to these boxes. Those lizard items you ordered won't put themselves away."

"*What?*" I run over to the boxes. Sure enough, the delivery we've been waiting for has finally arrived. I grab a pair of safety scissors and pierce the tape on the first box. Then I make a snowstorm of packing peanuts as I dig through to find my treasure.

"Ooh," I whisper as I pull out the first precious bobblehead. Those reptilian eyes. The pale green skin. Even with skinny plastic arms and a wobbly head, Captain Jake Rodrigo of the Iguanador Nation's eastern fleet makes my heart pound. I've got his newest poster on my closet door so he's the last thing I see every night. Sometimes I dream that we zip around the galaxies fighting enemies together and planning ways to save the universe from the likes of Rotz and other villains. Maybe he'd be my first boyfriend—a good one who wouldn't tell fart jokes.

Wilson flicks his finger against Jake Rodrigo's chin to make him move. "I thought these would never get here."

He tries to ping the little captain again, but I stop him.

"Don't," I say. "You might damage him."

"What are you talking about? A bobblehead is made for bobbling, Merci. It's more or less the whole point."

I turn my back away as heat creeps up my neck. Even I know I'm being weird.

I clear my throat and turn to Miss McDaniels. "We should definitely up our price for these," I say. "The new movie tore up the box office, so everybody's going to want one. We could charge anything we want! Thirty bucks, even fifty!"

"We'll do no such thing," Miss McDaniels says primly. "They might price gouge at Poxel, but we're not here to take advantage of people."

"But, miss—" I give her an exasperated look. "What about charging what the market will bear?" She must know what I mean. Does she not see the new cars in the senior parking lot? People around here can bear a lot. "This is a business, remember?"

"Yes, and one with ethics. I think ten dollars is appropriate." She holds the box toward me and motions toward the bobblehead.

Reluctantly, I drop it back in.

Meanwhile, Wilson is looking over the invoice. "Don't worry, Merci. It says here that they cost us three dollars each. That would be a profit of about three hundred and thirty-three percent," he says. "We can live with that."

He's beaming, even as I give him a withering look. *Traitor.*

Miss McDaniels hands me the box. "You can start recording the new inventory and price tagging those lizard things—"

"Iguanador Nation—" I interject.

"I'll have them featured on the morning announcements along with the Heart Ball tickets for next week," she continues, "so we'll need script copy for Lena and Darius to read as soon as possible."

Wilson is taking notes as she talks. Suddenly, Miss McDaniels freezes, studying something across the cafeteria. Her next urgent priority has surfaced. I can tell by the quiver of her nostrils. I follow her gaze and see that one of the boys in the lunch line isn't wearing his tie.

Her heels click like little chisels as she makes her way across the room.

CHAPTER 3

WHEN I GET TO EL CARIBE after school, Tía is already plugged into her earbuds as she wipes the counters clean. The snowbird lunch crowd has thinned, and it's too early for the dinner people, so my aunt is here with the regulars, who are reading the paper near the coffee bar. I take a deep breath. It's what I imagine heaven smells like: little biscuit angels floating around with the scent of vanilla and brewed coffee baked right into their wings.

I climb onto Lolo's old stool—the one with the red duct tape on the seat—and put Mami's twenty-dollar bill on the counter. She's waiting in the car, checking email about her physical therapy patients while I put in our order. I've been coming to El Caribe forever, but it's not really the same without Lolo parked here for the afternoon the way he used to be. He always kept Tía company while she worked, drinking his favorite kind of fruit shake, batidos de mamey, on the house. Since he can't walk here on his own anymore, it's up to us to bring him his treats.

Tía doesn't notice me at first. She's smiling and has her eyes closed as she swings her hips left and right to whatever song is playing in her ears. I know she had the early shift today, so she's already been here since five a.m. But even in bright-green support socks and with swollen feet, she can't help dancing. Abuela says Tía Inés was born that way. It's a gift, like round hips from all the women on Abuela's side of the family. When she was still in Abuela's belly, Tía would squirm and kick whenever Abuela had the radio on. I guess I'm more like Mami's side of the family. Abuela says they're Gallegos, even though they're not Spanish, on account of their cement feet. Not that I mind. Twirling skirts? Shaking my colita? Please. I get my workouts on the field, thank you very much. But Tía? Her dance class at the community center on Wednesdays always fills up fast. If she could, I bet she'd teach there every day.

"Tía!" I call, waving my arms. When she doesn't notice, I hit the bell on the counter a bunch of times to get her attention. "Hello? Helloooo?"

She startles, like I've interrupted a dream, and pulls out her earbuds.

"What did I tell you about that thing?" She scoops it off the top of the display case and puts it away. "I am not a bellhop, you know."

"You couldn't hear, and Mami's waiting!"

She checks the time on her phone. "¡Ay! Four o'clock already? Where did the day go?" She tosses her rag into the sink. "The usual?"

"Yep. Plus a few pastelitos de carne for dinner. Mami doesn't want to cook."

"Which reminds me: I'm going to be late," Tía says as she starts gathering my order. "Don't wait."

I give her a look. Abuela will make us wait to eat anyway, and she knows it.

"Again?" I try not to sound too bitter, but I've had to help the twins with homework three times already this week. I don't want to circle anymore *at* words on worksheets. First grade was bad enough once. I shouldn't have to relive it.

"Yes, *again*," she says, straightening. "Berta called in sick, so I'll be here until five, at least. And it's parent conferences at the school." She walks over to the blender to mix Lolo's drink.

I heave a sigh. A school meeting means she's going

to be even later than usual. Teachers always have a lot of notes about the "experience" of having Axel and Tomás in a classroom for six long hours every day. The twins' latest habit is hiding when it's time to come in from recess, something that throws their teacher into a teary panic. They've even talked their little friends into the game, too. Last week, the school security officer had to help their teacher round up all the kids who'd seemingly vanished into thin air. They were curled inside volleyball bins and supply closets, just like Axel and Tomás told them to.

When Tía's done getting our food, she waves at Mami through the window and hands me the box and the batido. "Just give me twelve bucks," she says, ringing it up. "Lolo's shake is on me."

"Generous," I say.

"Why break tradition?"

I stuff a dollar in the tip jar on the counter and walk outside.

"Tía's working late again." I buckle in and put my nose to the box of pasteles. It's going to be hard to resist opening it. "She said not to wait."

Mami gives me a knowing look and shakes her head. "Make yourself a sandwich to hold you off until dinner," she says.

Then she places her phone in the stand and glances

back through the window at Tía, who's plugged into her music again while switching out the menus.

We pull away, the box of treats warming my legs as we go.

There's a ladder leaning up against our house when we get home. Papi is perched on the top step, squirting something at the rust spot on the stucco.

"At last!" Mami says. She's been complaining about a stain that looks like a map of South America on the side of our house for months, but Papi hasn't had time to do anything about it, or about the big crack in the stucco at Tía's house—compliments of the twins' recent hammer-tossing contest. The sun has faded the paint color, too, so our three houses aren't the bright pink that Las Casitas used to be.

Not that it's his fault. Seemingly everybody in South Florida needed a paint job before the holidays, so he was super busy, even with brothers Simón and Vicente helping six days a week. Papi looked beat when he came home every night, but he insisted he didn't mind. "Paid work before free, Ana," he told us every time Mami asked him about our place. "We have to eat, and pay Roli's tuition. Plus, my men need the hours."

I know he didn't have spare time for the repairs

because of my soccer games, too. This year was my first season on the school team, and let's just say it wasn't the best. I thought I was going to be a starter, but I only played left wing when Emma Harris, an eighth-grader, needed a break. And our team wasn't very good, either. I spent a lot of time wondering if I should quit and just stick to playing with Papi's team, even though Mami doesn't like it. She says it's dangerous for me to play with grown men. Ha. For them maybe. I can run circles around some of them, except maybe Vicente, who has chops.

Anyway, Papi wouldn't let me quit. He said Suárezes don't stop trying when things are bad. Instead, he showed up to every game after work, sometimes still in his painter's pants. I had to look carefully to spot him. Papi isn't a sideline yeller, for one thing. And he doesn't talk much to the other parents, either. Instead, he likes to stand in the shade of the nearest tree and watch. On the drive home, he'd tell me where he thought our strategy could improve and how not to give up even with the odds against us. When we lost, he'd toss me a Jupiña from his mini cooler, too, and tell me corny jokes to cheer me up.

Anyway, with soccer over, it looks like Las Casitas is finally getting a makeover.

"I was wondering where you two were," he says, smiling down at us.

"Where else?" I tell him. "Waiting for my eight hours of daily bondage to be over." I hold up the bakery bag. "And picking up dinner."

"I can smell it from here." He wiggles his eyebrows. "Did you get the papas rellenas?" Stuffed potato balls are his favorite.

"Yep."

Mami walks over to the ladder and shields her eyes against the sun. "Looks like you're going to be a while, though," she says.

"Not too bad. I've got help."

That's when I notice Simón near the shed at Lolo and Abuela's house. He's lugging a bucket of pink paint and stir sticks. Vicente has the rollers and extension rods. Confession: I used to think Vicente was cute, a little bit like Jake Rodrigo, even. But not anymore. He's around here a lot, and now it feels like he's my cousin. Besides, he's a lot older than me—almost eighteen like Roli—and he has an annoying habit of calling me his little pal.

Simón and Vicente work every day that Papi can afford to hire them. It's not so they can pay for a car repair like last year, when the transmission in their Corolla went kaput. Now they need money for a lawyer in Miami who's trying to convince a judge that Vicente should stay with Simón, who's his oldest brother. I'm not allowed to ask them about that, though. Mami says it's strictly private. "I don't understand why," I told her. "People ask me private stuff all the time. What I want to be. If I have a boyfriend. God. Nobody seems to mind their invasion of *my* privacy."

She gave me that irritated look when she thinks I've been thoughtless. "Por Dios, that's completely different, Merci. Now, give those brothers some space and respect. They have enough to worry about."

I started to argue. I mean, I have things I worry about, too. Don't they matter? But that night, I thought about how I don't have to worry about never seeing Roli again. I know he'll come home in the summer. It's different for Simón and Vicente.

I drop my backpack in the grass. "I'll give you guys a hand."

Papi stops swiping off the rust spots and looks down at me. We both know the rule. School is always first. He glances at Mami and asks what he knows she wants to hear. "Don't you have homework?"

"Only a little," I say, which is, of course, not true. I have a ton, as usual, because seventh grade is a heartless killer, especially if you have Mr. Ellis for science. "And don't I deserve a little break? You don't want me to have anxiety issues, do you?" I give Mami a knowing look. I saw those flyers she brought home from the PTA meeting last month. It was all about the warning signs of stressed-out kids. She made me drink chamomile tea before bed for a week.

Mami softens a bit. She knows how much I like helping Papi—and I'm good. Aside from Simón, I'm his best worker.

"Fine," she says. "But only for an hour. And don't ruin another uniform blouse, please. That's the only one that still fits, and you still have five months of school to go."

My cheeks get red as I cross my arms over my chest. My growth spurt is not a topic I like talking about in front of Papi, or anybody else for that matter. I'd gladly stop growing, but everything inside of me has gone haywire. I wear a size eight shoe, which Mami tells everyone is bigger than hers, and I've started getting pimples on my forehead, even when I scrub my face at night with a washcloth until my skin shines. I guess I should be thankful I don't have it as bad as Marie Perillo, who basically had a growth explosion this year. From behind, people confuse her for a teacher all the time. Everything is full-size on her now, so much so that people whisper and sneak stares at her in the locker room after gym.

"I got her covered," Papi says quickly. He climbs down the rungs of his squeaky ladder and kisses Mami's cheek, lingering a little too long until she smiles.

"Kissing in front of me is awkward, you know," I say.

They exchange a look before Mami heads inside. Papi rummages through the rag pile for one of his old T-shirts and tosses it to me so I can pull it on.

"You're in charge of rust stains on the south side," he says. "There's more cleaning fluid in the shed, top shelf. Wear gloves."

"Can I use the drywall stilts?" I love those things. It's house repairs and Transformers all rolled into one.

Papi isn't listening. He stretches his back as he watches Mami walk into the house, probably wishing he could sit down for a while and watch TV, holding hands with her the way they sometimes do when they think I'm not looking. I used to plop myself right between them to feel cozy, but not anymore. Somehow, the couch just feels too small with all three of us on it. It's like they become Ana and Enrique, not just Mami and Papi, the way they're supposed to be.

"Well?" I say, snapping him back. "Can I use the zancos or not, Papi?"

"Talk to Simón," he tells me as he steps up again. "And be careful with your shirt, muchachita," he says, "or we're both in for it."

"Got it." I tie my hair up and run to Simón for the stilts.

CHAPTER 4

IT'S BEEN A WHOLE YEAR since I found out that Lolo has Alzheimer's. He takes new medicines now, so some days he's almost the same as always. Like today. When I finish helping with the house repairs, I wash up and go over to Abuela and Lolo's, where we're going to eat dinner. I find Lolo in his recliner working on a puzzle with the twins.

"Hey, Lolo," I say.

"¡Preciosa!" he says.

They've spread out the pieces on his folding snack table, trying to build the picture of a cat that looks like ours, except with two blue eyes instead of just one, like Tuerto has. The box has twenty-five pieces, so nobody gets too confused by the colors or shapes. It's one of my old ones from elementary school. That was Mami's idea. Lolo can fit the pieces together if there aren't too many of them, and Mami says it's important for his brain to keep working things out. That's why she's always telling me to go over to play dominoes, bingo, and even my *Wheel of Fortune* app with him. I used to love playing games with Lolo, since we could be by ourselves and talk about stuff. But it's not as fun this year, to be honest. Lolo talks a lot less now, for one thing, and sometimes he forgets what I just told him, so I have to start my story all over again. And if he's having a hard day, he starts thinking about pretend stuff—and not the fun kind like when I was little and we played post office. Take last week. We were trying to play Uno, but he kept looking up from his cards, sure that someone was spying on us from the patio. "Espías," he whispered to me, looking scared. "Hide." We sat with the lights off and the blinds closed until he finally fell asleep in his chair. I felt afraid the whole time. Not of spies, though. Of Lolo.

"She's finally home." Abuela comes in with the box of pastelitos from the bakery and a big salad bowl perched on top of it. Oil spots have seeped through the cardboard. We waited for Tía, just like I knew we would, no matter how many times I said I was starving.

"People get worked to death," Abuela mutters. "If she's not careful, Inés could leave behind orphans. Then what would become of these angelitos?"

Angels? I love my cousins, but geez, that's a stretch.

"What's an orphan?" Axel asks suddenly.

Mami puts down the *Vanidades* magazine that she's reading and widens her eyes at Abuela in alarm. "Teresita!" she says. "Por Dios. You'll scare them." She hates when Abuela goes full-on drama, like the time she explained to me what could happen if Papi fell from a roof while on the job. I cried for a week dreaming of him nearly lifeless, his brain bleeding inside his skull.

Thankfully, Tía comes through the front door before Abuela starts in on the finer points of dead parents.

"Mamá!" Tomás runs to Tía and buries himself in her legs. Axel isn't far behind.

Tía looks even more worn-out than when I left her this afternoon, but she covers their heads with kisses anyway. Then she bends down to unlace her black work sneakers that are splattered with powdered sugar and oil. "Go wash your hands," she tells them. "And use soap. I'm going to sniff your palms to check."

They race down the hall, elbowing each other to see who gets to the sink first, as she kicks off her shoes and winces.

"Dios mío," she says. "I thought this day was never going to end."

My stomach gurgles loudly. "And I thought you were never going to get here."

"You waited?" she says, looking around. "I told you not to."

"Who listens to me, Tía?"

I try not to sound bitter, but I wish Tía didn't work so much, either—and it's not because I think it's going to kill her. It's more that it's killing the rest of us. When she's not around, somebody—usually yours truly—has to watch the twins and help them with homework and keep them from burning down the house or some other travesura. And now there's Lolo to keep an eye on, too.

"Well, maybe El Señor will help us all," Abuela says. "I'm going to play a Lotto number tonight. I dreamed some pretty digits last night. Who knows? Maybe we can become millionaires. Then no one will have to work long hours."

Just then, Papi, Simón, and Vicente come in dragging the extra plastic chairs from the patio.

"Lottery millionaires? Where do I sign up?" Papi says.

"Imagine if we got rich! So many things would be possible." Simón places a chair near Tía's usual spot at the table and glances shyly at her. "Buenas noches, Inés," he says, smiling. "It's good to see you."

Tía stands a little straighter when she sees him. She smooths her uniform, and her eyes flit down to her support socks with a small hole in the big toe. Her feet don't exactly smell like roses, either. "Simón," she says, really formally, like they've barely met. "I didn't know you were here this evening. ¿Qué tal?"

Oh brother. The goo between them is like hot taffy as they stand there gawking at each other. If heart bubbles could really float out of someone's head, Tía's would be going on full steam.

I cannot have it.

"I'm starving," I say loudly. "Can we please eat?"

"Sió, niña. Where are your manners?" Abuela surveys the table to make sure nothing's missing. "All right. I think we have everything. Siéntense."

The twins rush to their seats, so I click off the TV that's been on for no one in particular and get up from the couch to help Lolo, like I do almost every time we eat together. It's the only one of my chores that I don't mind. I move the snack table out of his way, so I don't disturb the puzzle they've gotten done so far. Only the tail is still missing. Then I unfold his walker and click the sides into place, the way Mami showed me.

"Ready?" I say.

My grandfather's eyes are bright behind his big, round glasses. "Ready, preciosa. Let's see if we can get this motor running."

"Scoot to the edge and lean forward like I taught you, viejo," Mami reminds him.

Lolo grips his walker and gets into what we call launch position. He looks like a swimmer hunched on the diving block, except, of course, he's starting from a recliner. I stand next to him and start our countdown as he rocks back and forth to get some momentum.

"Three, two, one . . . liftoff!"

He struggles to straighten his knees, breathing hard and wobbling a little as I hold his elbow.

I pretend I don't see how hard this has gotten for him, even with Mami's trick. *Focus on abilities,* she always reminds us, *not on what he can't do anymore.* But sometimes it's hard not to keep a list of all that's gone. Bike riding with me. Walking us to the park. Asking me about my day. It's like he's fading, vanishing from the inside out a little bit each day, even though his body is still here.

"Start eating!" Lolo tells everyone as he makes his way to the table slowly. He pulls his arm away from me. "Go sit."

Papi winks at me and motions to my seat. So, I take

my place as Lolo inches his way to the head of the table, opposite Papi.

My stomach lets out another loud gurgle.

Lolo's chest is rising and falling like he's in a race. "I said don't wait for me," he scolds.

But not even the twins reach for their forks. Hungry and tired, we all wait, hands in our laps, until he finally drops into his chair. No one starts without him. We never do.

How long, I wonder, before that disappears, too?

CHAPTER 5

"GOOD MORNING, SEAWARD PINES RAMS! Lena Cahill and Darius Ulmer here with your morning announcements. Please stand for the Pledge of Allegiance."

Wilson and I flash Lena a thumbs-up sign through the glass door of the TV studio. Then, because Miss McDaniels frowns at us, we quickly face the flagpole in the corner and put our hands on our hearts until the pledge and the moment of silence finish.

Our TV studio—WSPA, pronounced *double-u spah*—is in the front office, inside a glass cubicle right behind Miss McDaniels's desk. It's off-limits to anyone but the anchors, which means that Wilson and I have to watch the whole thing through the window out here in the waiting area.

We're sitting on the dark wooden benches that are usually reserved for kids who've gotten in trouble, so we're getting stares from the nosy stragglers who need late passes.

It has taken Wilson and me almost a week to come up with our ad campaign for the Heart Ball tickets, but we finally did it. Mostly it took so long because Wilson is epically stubborn. I tried to explain—nicely—that I was delegating the ad-writing duty to him.

"Nah," he said. "Technically, you can only delegate to employees. I'm your co-manager."

"So?"

"So, I'm delegating the job right back to you, woadie."

We texted back and forth forever to work it out, and let me tell you, it was tough with Wilson being so ridiculously picky about everything I proposed.

He did not appreciate my first attempt:

> Buy a Heart Ball ticket if you don't mind holding germy hands with somebody you barely know

> 😡 THIS is the best you can do?

> I refuse to engage in deceptive advertising.

The second one didn't go any better:

> Buy a Heart Ball ticket if you have absolutely nothing better to do in this sad life.

We finally compromised with the help of a book called *Jokelopedia*—a companion volume to the twins' favorite resource, *Prankolopedia*. I found it lying on the floor of my room, which the twins have started to use as their criminal lair. Turns out, Wilson is as mad for knock-knock jokes as they are. He doesn't care if they're dumb; in fact, the cornier the better, he says, which is weird. Lolo used to say the same thing.

In no time we wrote some jokes for our ads that we could both live with.

Lena shuffles her notes and pushes up her new glasses. I like them. A lot of the girls in our grade got contact lenses this year. Now they just have red eyes instead of glasses. But not Lena. She went straight-up nerd with a pair of specs that make her look even smarter than usual. They match her hair, too, which she dyed a new color that would look good on TV. It's called Hey Gurl Passion Purple No. 5. I guess I didn't get the memo that people were changing things about themselves in seventh grade. I mean, even Hannah got bangs this year to "bring out her eyes"—who knows what that means. Anyway, all I did was ask Mami to trim my ends in the kitchen, same as always, which nobody ever notices. I'm the same Merci as always except taller. Boring.

Lena begins.

"Today is Monday, January twenty-fifth, and you know what that means, right, Darius?"

Darius sits in the chair beside her and stares straight ahead. He's a slim white kid, with blond hair and terrified blue eyes. This whole anchor business isn't really helping his shyness at all, if you ask me. What were his parents thinking? Maybe they're just monster parents, the kind that pushed him into the deep end of the pool to teach him to swim. All I know is that his face is as red as his blazer, and his temples are beaded with enough sweat that I can see it through the window. He's wrung his script cards to bits, too.

Lena gives him the slightest nudge with her elbow as she smiles steadily at the camera. "Darius?"

He swallows hard. "Y-yes," he says. "It's . . . It's . . ."

Lena doesn't rush him as he tries to form words, but it doesn't help. Darius has once again become the rusted Tin Man with no oil in his jaw. I feel for the guy. I still shudder when I remember the time I got a singing solo in the second-grade play. I forgot all the lyrics and started to cry right there onstage, with parents snapping pictures and calling me adorable the whole time. Beasts.

Anyhow, it's Lena to the rescue. She looks right at the camera and grins slyly. "Why, Darius! What a clever way to build suspense for . . . National Opposites Day! Thank you!"

"So *that's* why she walked to class facing me," Wilson whispers.

"Shh," Miss McDaniels says.

Lena asks for sign-ups for the Earth Club's beach cleanup this Saturday—she's the president—and then ticks through the other news items pretty quickly. Today's lunch menu. The basketball scores for JV. News about an upper-school SAT something-or-other that's due. Then the weather map flashes on the green screen, and Darius manages to tell us that it will be much cooler than normal this weekend, near freezing at night, which we already know. Everyone at school is wrapped in our fifty-dollar Seaward Pines hoodies and jackets, and for once I don't mind my itchy knee socks or wearing Roli's hand-me-down sweatshirt. The temperature has dropped into the high forties, which hardly ever happens here in Florida. It's almost like those other states up north that have actual seasons besides *wet* and *dry*. The downside of cold weather, though, is that Papi can't paint outside jobs for a couple of days, in case it freezes. No work, no money— which makes him moody about stuff like socks on the floor or my bike in the driveway.

Finally, it's time for our ads. Wilson and I exchange looks.

"And now we have a few announcements from the new and improved Ram Depot, your home for school supplies. Ready?" She looks hopefully at Darius, but even from here, I can see that his hands are still shaking.

Don't wreck this for us, Darius! I think darkly.

> Lena: Knock-knock.
> Darius: Wh-who's there?
> Lena: Felix.
> Darius: . . .
> Lena: *Felix.*
> Darius: F-Felix who?
> Lena: Felix-cited about Valentine's Day?
> Buy your Heart Ball tickets starting next
> week during lunch at the Ram Depot!

She presses the sound-effects buzzer for the drum rim shot. *Ba-dum-TSSS!*

Wilson leans over to me. "Is it the green screen or does Darius look a weird color to you?"

Miss McDaniels shoots us another warning look.

> Lena: Knock-knock.
> Darius: Wh-wh-who . . . ?
> Lena: Bob.
> Darius: . . .
> Lena: *Bob.*

Darius: . . .

Lena: Bob who, you ask? Why, BOBbleheads
for Iguanador Nation are finally in!
(*Ba-dum-TSSS!*) Ten dollars gets you one
of these beauties at the Ram Depot while
supplies last! Competitive prices!
All sales final!

Darius's eyes are wide now and fixed on the camera. His
lips quiver, and his blazer looks wet around the armpits.
I remember feeling like that last year when I had the
stomach flu.

Lena must notice the warning signs. She slides the
wastebasket with her foot to his side of the table. Then
she takes over for the rest of the broadcast, doing our last
knock-knock bit on her own at lightning speed.

"Knock-knock. Who's there? Clair. Clair who? Clair-
ance sale on all glitter snowflake erasers! Two-for-one,
while supplies last! Hurry in during your lunch period!

"Well, Rams, that wraps up today's news. Happy
Opposites Day! And have a terrible, terrible week. This is
not Lena Cahill and Darius Ulmer signing off!"

The red button flashes, and the screen goes to our
school crest.

Darius reaches for the wastebasket just in time.

CHAPTER 6

THAT AFTERNOON, LENA AND I are in the seventh-grade hall waiting for Hannah, who's still finishing up her unit exam in Mr. Ellis's room. Hannah is always the last one done on tests because she likes to check her answers three times before she hands anything in. Not me, of course. What's the point of all that? The more I check, the more confused I get, especially in advanced earth science. I ran out as fast as I could after the exam. Forty multiple-choice questions weren't enough for the man. He tacked on a twenty-point essay, too, to give us "writing practice." I cracked my knuckles so much, I'm pretty sure I'll have arthritis by nightfall, just like Abuela always warns.

"The present is the key to the past." Please explain who made this statement and how it applies to early geological science.

"What did you answer for the essay?" I ask Lena. "Was it James Hutton or John Smith?"

"Hutton," she says. "John Smith is the Jamestown guy from social studies."

I rest my head against my locker in disgust. "Are you positive?" She types into the search bar on her phone and shows me the screen. *James Hutton (1726–1797). Father of modern geology.*

I heave a sigh as soon as I recognize the guy's mug from our textbook. Naturally, I panicked at the last second and changed my answer to the wrong one. Twenty points, *pfft!*

It's turning out to be a long year in science, and we're only about halfway through. It's bad enough that we've been studying rocks for a month—for heaven's sake, *rocks*. But the real killer is that I have Mr. Ellis. I mean, he's one of our younger teachers, with his hair in dreads and AirPods in his pocket and fun posters on his walls. But do not be fooled! All that chill goes right out the window when you're in his class. He's a drill sergeant. Three pages of homework daily. Graded labs. Tests every other week. Pop quizzes whenever the spirit moves him. He even

counts spelling on the hardest scientific words. *Detritus.*
Metamorphosis. Speleologist.

But worst of all is that he was Roli's teacher a few years
back, not to mention his senior adviser last year. Mr. Ellis
thinks my brother is "one of tomorrow's most promising
scientific minds." At least, that's what he wrote on one of
Roli's college recommendations.

Which means that I am a big disappointment.

"Oh, are you Rolando Suárez's little sister?"

The question froze me in terror when Mr. Ellis first
asked. I'm always cooked when teachers find out I'm
related to one of the biggest brains to have ever graduated
from Seaward Pines Academy. Roli got a full scholarship to
study biology at the University of North Carolina, where
he wants to study neurology. And even though Drew
Samuelson, who didn't get into UNC, told everybody
that Roli got in because he's poor and Latino, I know it's
because my brother is crazy smart. Anyway, Mr. Ellis called
on me nonstop at first, assuming I must be a genius, too.
It took him almost a month to figure out the sad truth.
Before him sat an ordinary girl. A not-so-special brain.
Maybe one day, Roli can figure out how to fix *that*.

Lena puts her hand on my locker to dull the sound of
my head banging. "I'll bet a lot of people got that question
wrong. Maybe he'll grade on a curve."

"And maybe the moon is made of cheese," I say.

"Basalt, actually," Lena says.

Just then, somebody shoves past me.

"Excusez-moi." Edna Santos bumps me with her fancy red leather backpack and steps between us to get to her locker. "That test was a breeze," she says. "N'est-ce pas?"

I glare at her as she starts working her combination. Hannah and Lena are in my science class this year, which is great. But so is Edna, and every so often we end up as lab partners, which I hold as another strike against Mr. Ellis. No one ever volunteers to be her partner, even though she's one of the smartest kids in there. Let's just say Edna puts a capital *E* in *Extra*. And worse, she's taking French this year, too, which is even more annoying. It's *bonjour* this and *au revoir* that, all day long. The one thing I haven't heard is *merci beaucoup* for the fantastic ads Wilson and I wrote for her silly dance. *Please*, *thank you*, and *I'm sorry* are still not in her vocabulary.

When Edna opens her locker, a whiff of cinnamon hits me. It's the car air freshener she's got in there. She has mirrors, bookends, and even little shelves. It's all neat as a pin, not like mine, which occasionally dissolves into an avalanche if I'm not quick with the door.

She grabs a folder covered in heart stickers and looks at me irritably. "Do you know what's keeping Hannah?

We're going to be late for the dance committee meeting this afternoon."

"Meeting?" I say. "Hannah said she was coming over after school today. She's helping me and Lena babysit the twins."

Edna shrugs. "Well, she can't go. I've called a mandatory meeting to go over last-minute things for the Heart Ball."

"Who decided that?" I say.

"I did. I'm in charge of the dance, remember?"

"Really?" I say bitterly. "I hadn't heard."

Lena jabs me in the ribs with her elbow. She and Hannah both promised to help me with my Edna skills. I rub my side. Seriously, how could we *not* know? It's all Edna talks about these days. What she's going to wear to the Heart Ball. Who she thinks she'll ask to the Heart Ball. What songs they'll play at the Heart Ball. Who she thinks will kiss at the Heart Ball. Heart Ball, Heart Ball, Heart Ball. I'd like to free-kick the Heart Ball into outer space.

But here's what really eats at me. I don't understand why Hannah ever agreed to be on Edna's committee in the first place. Dance planning is eating up all of Hannah's spare time—specifically, the time she used to spend with me and Lena. I thought that's what best friends did: hang out with each other. Hannah and Lena are the only ones who come over to Las Casitas. I mean, you can't just invite anyone from Seaward Pines home with you. Some moms look up your address, and if they don't like how your block looks, they invite you over instead.

But I guess I should have known Hannah was a goner as soon as Edna told her she could be in charge of decorations. Decorations means arts and crafts, Hannah's favorite thing. Her eyes got all dewy once she thought about heart-shaped balloons and disco balls and, most of all, the glitter, glitter, glitter she could use to make all that stuff.

"Come on, Edna. Hannah was supposed to come home with Lena and me today. We're going to take the twins to the park to try out Lena's new scooter. Can't she take the day off?"

Edna glances at Lena, who's holding her Razor Beast, folded, in her arms. "You can ride that thing another day."

"That's not the point. You're hogging all of Hannah's time."

She holds up her hand to stop me. "If you want a perfect event for our school like the one *I'm* organizing, you need to have every detail in place. No offense, Merci, but planning a dance for the whole middle school isn't like selling pencils and toys during lunch."

My blood boils. "And selling *Heart Ball tickets*, you mean?" I say pointedly. "You're welcome for the ads, by the way."

I get another of Lena's elbows to the ribs.

Just then, Hannah comes racing up the hallway.

"Sorry, sorry, sorry!"

She's out of breath as she reaches us. Her cheeks are flushed, and her shirt is untucked. Always a nervous test taker, she's pulled the hairs on the side of her head all hour long, so now they're sticking out all over the place, and her ponytail is lopsided. She looks like she's escaped from a lion attack.

She twists the dial on her lock as fast as she can, but it won't budge when she tugs on it. She tries again. Another fail. Poor Hannah. It took her most of the fall semester to even memorize her combination.

"Agh!" she says.

"Allez!" Edna mutters in French.

"Here, I've got it," Lena says, taking over. "I know your combination." When Hannah had the flu in September, Lena and I took turns bringing home the books she needed. I even sat on her bed with a germ mask to help her study for social studies. Did Edna do that for her? No, she did not.

Hannah looks over at me and heaves a sigh. "That test was a killer," she says. "Am I right?"

"The worst," I say. "I felt my brain leaking out of my ears."

"Me too."

"Will you two please zip it and hurry?" Edna checks her hair in her locker mirror one last time. "We start in three minutes."

That's when I spot the picture Edna has taped at the very back of her locker. It's one from her mission trip to the Dominican Republic last year. She went with her dad, who's from there, and a team of doctors and nurses. Edna helping humanity. Go figure.

I have to admit that I like this shot, even though Edna is in it. She's under a palm tree holding a little kid, who's sucking his thumb. The sky is bright blue all around them, puffy clouds overhead. I don't know. Maybe it's the expression on her face or all the color that makes me like it. What I remember most, though, is that she told us the boy's mom had lost one of her legs to a sickness called gangrene. Her father and the other doctors were helping to keep the other leg healthy. For the life of me, I can't imagine Edna on a trip like that. She's a germophobe, for one thing. She won't drink out of a water fountain here at school on even the hottest day.

Edna catches my eye in the mirror and then slams her locker closed.

"Dépêche-toi," she tells Hannah. "We have a busy agenda!"

Hannah digs through her locker as Edna marches off. "What is she even saying through those puckered lips? All I hear is *zz-zz-zz*!"

Lena giggles.

"Why don't you skip today?" I whisper to Hannah. "The Evil Dance Queen will live."

"*Merci*, I made a commitment. Plus, she's not *that* bad," Hannah says.

I brush her words aside. "But we were going to take the twins to the park and do tricks on Lena's scooter. Remember?"

She pauses, looking from me to Lena.

Lena smiles. "A day off isn't so bad," she says.

Hannah looks doubtful, and for a second I think we've freed her from Edna's clutches.

But no. Hannah would rather eat dirt than let someone down or break any rules. She starts down the hall. "I wish I could, Merci, but I'm on the committee, and I still have a ton of paper flowers to make." She walks backward a few paces.

"Wait—"

"We'll hang out soon! Tell Axel and Tomás I said hi."

Before I can argue, she turns and dashes down the hall after Edna, who's already sprinting around the corner on the gangly legs that she's gotten this year.

Lena peers through the exit that leads to the car loop. "Your mom's here." She holds open the door for me and lets in a chilly gust. I hitch up my backpack and follow, but my mood has fouled.

"How was school?" Mami asks as we buckle in. It's the same question she asks every day, but right now I don't want to answer it. What part does she mean? School was a gazillion ways. It was boring in English because we worked on grammar, and awful in science thanks to that dumb test. It was fun in PE because I hit all my layups. And it's horrible right this second because one of my best friends in the whole world won't come over. Who has time for a conversation about all of that?

Mami holds her eyes on me in the rearview mirror. The car engine is still humming in park. My ride is being held hostage until I communicate like a proper unstressed child.

"Good," I mutter.

I look out the window as we pull out. It's not a big deal, I try to tell myself. Hannah is just volunteering after school.

But there's a little voice way inside my head, and it won't stop taunting me.

Hannah picked Edna instead of you.

CHAPTER 7

HERE'S HOW IT WORKS AROUND our house.

If you need permission to do something even remotely fun, it pays to know who to ask. For instance, you can ask Papi to show you how to use power tools because he'll say yes. But don't bother asking him to drop you off at the mall with your friends because he'll interrogate you about who you're with and where you're going and all that. Tía Inés will let you stay up late to watch a scary movie at her place, but she hates video games and won't ever play them with you. If you want extra dessert, forget Mami; all you'll get is a boring lecture on the effects of too much sugar on your metabolism. Abuela is the one who will slip you another piece of cake and tell you it's good for you.

So, you see, it's complicated, which is why I knew

better than to wait to ask Abuela about bike riding this afternoon. I asked Mami last night and got the green light the way I knew I would. She's keen on "cardiovascular exercise."

So, I'm ready when Lena and I get to Lolo and Abuela's house to find the twins.

Lolo is on his porch glider when we get there. Even though it's chilly, he's watching Vicente power-wash the stucco as if it's a riveting TV show. Until last year, Lolo always did the power washing. I can tell by the way he's fidgeting that he'd like to be there helping now, too.

"Hey, Lolo. Hey, Vicente," I shout over the noise.

Vicente shuts off the washer and checks his phone. Girls are always texting him. Simón teases him about it all the time. Good thing his glam has worn off for me, especially since I sometimes have to step in to supervise his work for Papi. Like now.

"You're not going to spackle in this cold, are you?" I tell him. "It won't dry."

Vicente glances at Lena shyly. He doesn't like to talk in front of people he doesn't know well, especially if English is involved. "I know, chera," he says in Spanish. "I'm just finishing the prep like your dad told me. We're trying to wrap up early today. There's a game tonight in Loxahatchee. Are you playing?"

I shake my head miserably. It's a school night, and Mami has been putting her foot down.

"Not tonight," I tell him in English. "You'll have to slaughter Manny's team without me."

"My pleasure," he says in English.

Abuela comes through the screen door just then, pulling her sweater around herself tightly and shuddering. The frog thermometer outside her window reads fifty-five degrees, which is what she calls pneumonia weather. We're not in coats and gloves the way Roli has to be in North Carolina, of course, but it has been cold enough to wear pants. Personally, I love it when the weather is like this, especially since it only happens once or twice every winter. The sky is so blue that it hurts to look at it, and when the wind blows, it makes my eyes water.

Abuela feels Lolo's hands and gasps. "Practically frostbitten! You, señor, need to come inside and away from the power washer's mist. Look at that runny nose!"

"Hi, Abuela," I say.

Lolo pays her no mind. Instead, he beams a sleepy smile at Lena and me and adjusts his glasses. He's still in his windbreaker and baseball cap from the walk home from school with Abuela and the twins, but his drippy nose is bright red and his eyes look glassy from the cool wind. Little beads of water cover his pants. Abuela might be right this one time.

"Preciosa," he says, his voice a little froggy. Then he smiles at Lena. "And who's this?"

My heart sinks a little. Lolo loves Lena and Hannah, but lately he thinks he's meeting them for the first time. That's how it is with Alzheimer's, though. You start to forget kind of obvious stuff. Your friends' names. The steps to getting dressed. Your address. What year it is.

Luckily, Lena is used to it. She sits down next to him on the glider. "It's just me, Mr. Suárez. Lena Cahill." She digs in her pocket and hands him a tissue.

He pats her spiky hair and smiles. "Pointy." He blows his nose.

"Gracias," she says.

"We're here to get the twins," I tell Abuela.

She looks relieved, even though she'd never say so. Abuela likes to sew in the afternoons when the sun is bright enough to help her see. But it's hard to do with the twins around, not to mention the fact that she has to keep Lolo company in case he wants to wander. If she's not careful, he walks down the street and out of view. Then the neighbors start phoning.

"Boys!" she calls.

•

A few seconds later, Axel and Tomás burst through the door, cookie crumbs all over their faces.

"Grrr!" Axel says, clawing his fingers up near his eyes as he approaches me.

"Hello, Axel," I say.

"I want blood, blood, blood!" He's got a loose front tooth that's hanging at an angle, so he looks deranged enough that I sort of believe him.

"We're monsters," Tomás explains. "We're going to eat your faces off now."

"Oh," I say, eyeing my cousins carefully. "Well, that's sad. You'll miss a chance to ride your bikes to the park."

"The park!" Tomás shouts.

They rush at us, hooting. Tomás jumps on Lena's back and Axel on mine.

"¡Muchachos!" Abuela says, trying to pull them off. "That's no way to say hello! You'll crush the girls if you squeeze them like that!"

I drag Axel off my back and bring my face close to his. His loose front tooth is barely hanging on.

"Get your jackets fast," I tell him. "We don't have much time before dark."

In a flash, they're racing each other toward Tía's house to get their things.

Abuela's face twists into a rag of worry as they go.

"Don't you think it's better to watch some TV?" she asks. "There's a canal in that park, isn't there?" She doesn't add the rest of what she's imagining. *Where they'll drown. Where an alligator will eat them. Where they will get salmonella from a wild duck.*

"There are canals all over Florida, Abuela. Three hundred seventeen miles of them in Palm Beach County alone, according to Mr. Ellis," I say. "We won't go near it. Promise. We're just going to ride bikes and scooters on the main path."

What I don't say is that Lena is also planning to teach me how to make sparks come off the back of her scooter when you ride it, just like Jake Rodrigo's aeris zoom. If I do, Abuela will lecture about falls, about clothes igniting, maybe even about spontaneous human combustion like we saw on that TV show *Supernatural Science*. People exploded into flames—*pouf*—for no reason, even though Mami insists that's nonsense.

Abuela hesitates and tries again. "But it's too cold to be outside. The boys will get sick. Think of the doctor bills!" she says. "Why don't I make you all hot chocolate instead?"

"Delicious!" Lolo says, smacking his lips. He loves chocolate, same as me.

I learned in science last year that we don't catch colds from weather, but I know better than to argue. Instead, I just go for the big guns. "Mami said I could go."

Silence.

Abuela's lips press to a thin line as I walk to the shed to get the bikes, but she doesn't go down easy.

"Make sure you take the side streets, then. People drive like maniacs," she calls to me, pulling her sweater around her even tighter.

"OK."

"And keep your eyes on the boys. Don't leave them alone for a minute. You know how they are."

"Walk faster," I whisper to Lena.

"And make them get off their bikes to cross the busy streets."

"Check!"

"And look both ways at the corner."

"Of course."

"And text—"

"—when I get to the park."

"And don't forget—"

I turn around, exasperated.

"Abuela," I say, "I'm in the seventh grade! Besides, Lolo is getting cold out here."

She frowns at me. We both know I'm not supposed to talk back to grown-ups.

"Esta juventud . . ." she says, shaking her head. Then she reaches for Lolo's chilly hand and helps him inside.

Lolo has always done the bike-riding instruction in the family, but not for the twins. That was one more thing that changed.

Last summer, Lolo and Papi called me over to the porch. They'd been watching the twins ride the path around Las Casitas, wobbling on their uneven training wheels that were already worn thin.

"I think you're the bike expert around here now," Papi told me. "Plus, you're the oldest kid at home. It's time to get those guys on two wheels."

At first the twins balked. Lolo helped cheer them on, but it was me who ran alongside them instead of Lolo. It was me who let go and picked them up when they crashed. After they got the hang of it, we all ate paletas together to celebrate, the way Roli and I did when we learned. I was happy for them, I guess. And I was proud that I'd done it. But it wasn't really the same as when Lolo was in charge.

The twins are pretty good on their two-wheelers now, if I do say so myself. The park is only a few blocks away, so it isn't too far for the twins to ride, either. It's nothing fancy like Sugar Sand Park in Boca, where we took them on their birthday last year to ride the carousel until they were dizzy. But at least we can bike here on our own when we want to get out of our yard. When Lolo used to come, he'd bring a big bag of stale bread to feed the Muscovy ducks, even though the sign says not to. But it's been a while since he's felt strong enough to walk here. And now there's a Suárez rule that there has to be another adult with us, too. No one—not Mami, Papi, Abuela, *or* Tía—ever says yes to him going out with us by himself anymore.

A few kids are already here, hanging out on the benches near the kiddie basketball courts when we get there. They're from the neighborhood, but we're not really friends except to say hi. I don't know when it happened, but I've basically become a stranger to the kids around here. It started when Mami and Papi decided a few years ago that Roli and I needed the "wonderful educational opportunity" that Seaward Pines Academy offered in Palm Beach. So, I don't know their teachers or their mascot or anything about them now. Today I only recognize one little kid in the group—the girl in a thin windbreaker. I think she dances at the after-school center where Tía teaches.

I wave as I ride by. My bike's looking sharp as always, and they stare, which sort of makes me feel worse. At Seaward, I'd love it if kids stared at my ride, but the truth is their bikes are better than mine. Whenever I ride around here, though, someone compliments me on my bike or else they just watch me—like now. I try not to look like

I'm showing off because their bikes are mostly rusted from the salt air like my old one. Papi is always telling me to lock up my bike in the shed to keep it nice, but I still forget all the time.

I lead us all to the banyan tree on the other side of the path and park my bike.

"Let's race," Tomás says to Axel.

"Wait." I channel my new-oldest-kid-in-the-family mojo. "Stay away from the canal and ride where I can see you," I tell them.

Axel sticks his tongue out.

"I mean it."

When they take off, I watch for a minute to make sure they're doing what I said. Then Lena and I get to work on the important stuff.

"Watch first. It's pretty simple," Lena says.

She starts off on her scooter and glides smoothly along the path like she's surfing. Then she turns back toward me and pushes a few times to gain speed. Just when it looks like she's going to ram into me, she shoves her weight back, and a sweet stream of sparks flies off the back of the metal board like a meteor shower. She's right. It's almost like Jake Rodrigo when he hovers over an intergalactic criminal he's about to arrest.

"Sweet," I say. "Let me try."

I put my right foot where Lena says and push off. At first, I'm fine, but when I try to spark the brakes, I wobble and have to hop off.

"You're wiggling the handlebars," Lena calls from where she's standing. "Keep them straight, and relax your shoulders and hands."

I try again and after only one minor wobble, I'm zooming along. *High command to Captain Rodrigo,* I say to myself. *Come in, do you read me?*

Is it dumb to pretend when you're twelve? Does anybody still do that? I push and push as I steer back to Lena, imagining that I'm coasting along with Jake Rodrigo as his second-in-command. When I'm a few feet away from her, I lean back on the brake as hard as I can, just like she did. Sparks fly, and it looks like fire is streaming off the board.

"You're a beast," Lena says, grinning.

"I want another try!"

And so it goes. I don't know how long we take turns on the scooter after that. But the fun doesn't last. A bloodcurdling scream makes us turn.

It's Axel.

He's on the other side of the bike path, howling on the ground. He and Tomás have somehow both wiped out on their bikes.

I take off on foot, and Lena follows me on her scooter. By the time we reach them, Axel's face is covered in blood. Bright red streams drip from his mouth and onto his shirt. He's got a big scrape on his chin, too, and it's filled with dirt and pebbles that are going to hurt to pick clean. A big bump is rising along his cheek. Tomás looks scared, but at least he's not hurt.

My heart pounds in my chest. Blood always makes me feel faint. When kids at school get nosebleeds, I get a watery mouth and buzzy ears. At home, it's Mami who patches people up with her first-aid kit.

"What happened?" I ask, trying to look away.

But Axel can't hear me over his own screams. He slaps at my hand as I try to unclip his helmet and spits a clump of blood on the ground near my shoes. "Stop swatting at me!" I say as he bawls. "I have to look."

Lena checks out Tomás's hands and squirts water on them to wipe them clean. "Not a scratch," she says. "But I think I see what happened." She points to his handlebars, where the twins have attached their bikes using the sleeves of their jackets.

"Were you playing rancheros again?" she asks.

I look over at the evidence, exasperated. "What did I tell you about pretending to calf rope on bikes?" I yell.

Axel howls even louder. Clearly, I'm not the calming

influence that Mami is in an emergency. I take a deep breath, trying to think.

Then I spot something on the ground where Axel spit. It's a bloody incisor.

"Look, Axel. Your tooth came out when you fell." I pick it up off the ground to show him.

His chest is still heaving with hiccups, but he quiets a bit. He moves his tongue in the now-empty space.

"The Tooth Rat will come," says Lena. "You'll get money."

He's trying to calm down, but his eyes are red, and his lip is swelling larger by the second. "Raton-cito Pé-rez?" he says between spasms.

"I think so," she says, giving me a careful look to be sure. Her family's from the Philippines, like Lolo's father was. Pérez is just called the Tooth Rat there.

"Of *course*, Ratoncito Pérez," I say. It's amazing how fast you have to think when it comes to keeping up with all the stories for these two. I've had to explain that the Tooth Fairy, the Tooth Rat, and Ratoncito Pérez are all distant cousins who collect teeth as a team. Don't even get me started on how Santa Claus and the Three Wise Men hang out.

"He'll definitely come tonight," I say, "but only if you

stop crying. His ears are very delicate. Loud noises scare him."

"Will he leave me something, too?" Tomás asks.

"Did *you* lose another tooth?" I ask.

He bares his teeth, but his pearly whites are all where they belong.

"Sorry, Tomás. You already got paid for your tooth when you lost it last year, remember? Pérez has strict rules."

Instantly, I see I've said the wrong thing. His lip starts to quiver, and he kicks a few pebbles at Axel.

"That's not fair," he says.

"No kicking," I say.

"No fair!" he says again, kicking harder. And then, he spits at my feet.

"What do you want, Tomás?" I snap. "I could loosen a few of your choppers right here and now, if you like!"

"Merci," Lena says.

I take a deep breath, the way I'm supposed to when I want to strangle one of them. I'm not calm the way Lena always is. I'm not good with little kids like Hannah. I'm just fed up. This is when I hate being the new oldest kid in our house. How am I supposed to know what to do?

"We have to fix Axel's busted chin, Tomás," I say. "Ratoncito Pérez won't like it if we leave him here bleeding."

He scowls at me, but then Lena asks him to help her untangle the jackets from the bikes. "Let's round up the ponies before they get away," she says. I get Axel to his feet and prop him on the scooter, still whimpering. Then I go fetch my bike.

The walk home feels like a death march. All that's missing is that funeral doom music by Chopin that we learned in band. Axel's chin has ballooned. Tomás won't quit whining. I have a big bloodstain on the only sweatshirt that still fits me.

Just wait until Abuela sees this.

CHAPTER 8

MY EARS ARE STILL RINGING.

Abuela yelled at everybody in the whole world. Me, for not watching the twins the way I was supposed to. Mami, for saying yes to letting me go to the park. Tía Inés, for working too many hours again. Even Lolo, for clapping when Axel showed him the empty spot where his tooth was. She grumbled all through dinner until Papi finally told her that going on like that was bad for everybody's digestion, especially Lolo's. "¡Basta, Mamá!" he said. "You want us all to get sick?"

Now, all these hours later, Tía Inés stares miserably into the water that's swirling in the foot spa she borrowed from Mami. If she'd been home, none of this would have happened. I don't want to mention it, though, because Tía's toes look like Vienna sausages, and she has another long shift tomorrow.

"Maybe Abuela is right about your long hours," I tell her. "Why don't you look for another job? Like, maybe you can become a stuntwoman in Hollywood or something."

"Too dull," Tía says, smiling.

"I'm serious. What did you want to do before you worked at the bakery?"

Tía stares into the water and shakes her head. "Ay, mi amor, that was a very long time ago," she says. "I was a kid then. What did I know?"

"Kids know plenty, but whatever," I say. Does growing older kill dreams or what? I mean, I want to take over Papi's company one day. I hope I don't stop wanting that when I'm Tía's age. I can't even imagine such a thing.

She flips off the switch and sighs as the water stills. "I'd better say good night to the boys and tuck them in."

It's going to be another long night for me. Since the twins can't wake up alone, they sleep here when Tía works the early shift. Lately, that's been a lot. If I'm not careful, they're going to think Roli's old bed is theirs or, worse, that they share a room with me. ¡Dios nos ampare!

I check over my shoulder to see if they're still in the

living room watching TV with Mami. Papi is at his soccer game, and since he hasn't texted me with the score, I'm assuming they either lost or are still in the heat of battle. But Mami has things under control. The twins are still side by side on the sofa, and Axel has a bag of frozen peas pressed against his face.

I nudge the napkin on the table toward Tía. Axel's bloody incisor is wrapped inside. "Leave me some money, Tía," I whisper. "He's expecting Ratoncito Pérez tonight."

Tía opens the bundle and stares at the tooth like it's a pearl. "They're getting so big," she says quietly. "I'm working so much that I'm missing it."

I roll my eyes. "All you missed today was a lot of blood and yelling."

She reaches for the towel. Her skin is red, and the veins in her feet look like yarn. "I know they can be a lot to handle," she says, "but they're still ours to love." Then she hobbles out to the living room to kiss them good night.

It's 12:02 a.m.

Tuerto is doing his nighttime prowl of the house, occasionally taking a swipe at the cord from the window blinds or pouncing on a shadow. He hops on my dresser and gives me a scary nighttime stare where the street light reflects from his single eye. It always makes him look like a Cyclops, one that yowls like a spirit to go outside.

OK, so here's something new. Lately I've been scared of the dark again. I don't know why my room feels scarier in the middle of the night, but it does. Maybe it's the quiet, with just the toads croaking outside, waiting to shoot their poison at anything that chases them. Or maybe it's that my room is just so different now, lonelier. It doesn't look anything like it used to when Roli was still here. For one thing, his smelly socks are missing from all over the floor, not to mention his extensive lab equipment. It took six moving boxes to pack all the science junk he didn't want when he went to college. Cracked petri dishes, owl pellets and rusted scalpels, skeletons with moving mandibles, a chipped plaster bust of Marie Curie—you name it. We hauled all of it to Goodwill in Papi's truck. If mad scientists happen to shop there, they're going to be in luck.

Roli's bed, where the twins are sleeping now, is one of two things that survived the purge. I kept his glow-in-the-dark constellation stickers, too. Papi offered to scrape them off the ceiling when we painted, but I decided to let them stay. Whenever I couldn't sleep, Roli would pull back the curtain that divided our room and tell me the

Greek myths that went with the stars, until my eyes closed again. When I can't sleep, like now, I stare at the stickers and think about him all the way in North Carolina.

I turn over, hoping the squeaks don't wake Axel and Tomás, who are finally asleep. I know better than to doze off before they do. Last time I did that, they drew a twirly mustache on me with permanent marker. Mami had to scrub my face with hand sanitizer and baking soda to get it off before school.

Sometimes I think life would be easier without these two. There are kids at school who see their cousins only once or twice a year. I get an overdose every day.

I wonder if Tía ever feels that way. Probably not. Maybe moms aren't allowed to think that. Not that I could ask. She feels bad enough about working all the hours she does. Do the twins feel sad about not seeing her, or are there enough of us here at home that they don't even notice? Maybe they don't care at all. They never say. All they ever tell me are things like "You're a poopy head" or that they're going to grind up my bones. Yeah. They're real conversationalists.

I pull the comforter up to my chin. It still smells of lavender from the closet where we store our winter gear. Papi turned on the heat in Abuela and Lolo's house after dinner, but we kept ours off tonight, so we could enjoy snuggling under our blankets for a change, instead of just sheets. It won't stay cold for long. Seems like nothing fun lasts.

I look over and listen to make sure the twins are sound asleep. Then I flip back my covers and walk across the room, the tiles chilly against my bare feet. They're in Spider-Man pajamas, wrapped around each other like puppies. The twins have never looked exactly the same to me, but now for sure they're different. Maybe that's what was bothering Tomás so much. Axel's hair is all points, and his lips hang open a little bit, still bloated and crusty. Up close by the glow of the night-light, I can see the dark and gummy space inside his mouth and the lump on his chin. Just looking at him makes me feel bad all over again. I wonder if this is how Roli felt the time he let me slam down on the seesaw, and I got a big bump from the fall. "Shh," he said, "please don't tell," and then he let me look at his Famous Scientists deck of cards.

Anyway, Tía didn't remember to give me the dollar before she left, even after I reminded her. Maybe her customers were cheap with tips today and she just didn't have it. I'll have to take care of it, so the twins will still believe in a cash-paying rodent. They don't know that our baby teeth—Roli's, mine, and soon Axel's—are all in a breath mint tin that Abuela keeps in her underwear drawer. She says she's saving them to make a necklace one day, like the gold flower pin she has with Tía and Papi's first teeth in the middle. Former human body parts as jewelry— the whole idea sends a shiver along my spine. Imagine if I wore that to school? People would call me a freak.

I cross to my dresser and find the money that I've been saving for the bobblehead. It's been hard watching kids plunk down cash, easy-peasy, and walk off with them while I have to wait. But that's how it is, I guess, and there's no use complaining to anyone around here about it. "Be satisfied with what you have, which is plenty," Abuela always says when I ask for something that she thinks is too expensive. That's when I get the lecture about how she never complains about sewing clothes for people who bring her fabric she could never afford for herself. And then there's Papi, she says, who sometimes paints houses large enough that there's an echo even with furniture inside them.

I tuck a dollar under Axel's pillow and take his tooth to put in Abuela's tin. Then I look over at Tomás. As best I can with only a night-light, I feel around for a pen and my notepad, so I can write him a message.

I leave him the slip of paper and two quarters under his pillow.

Don't worry. I'll be back when you lose your next tooth.
Tu amigo, RP

Then I climb back in bed, and for a long while after, I lie awake, thinking about impossible things and studying the stars.

CHAPTER 9

MY EARTH SCIENCE FLASH CARDS are still in an untouched stack near the sugar bowl, where Mami put them last night. She tosses me a look and then slides two scrambled egg whites with rubbery low-fat cheese on my plate and Papi's. "Concentrate, Merci," she says.

I'm at the table, staring at my reflection in the back of a spoon as if it's the most interesting thing in the world. My nose looks big, like in a funhouse mirror.

"I *am* concentrating. I'm doing my eye exercises." I fix my gaze on the tip of the spoon and move it back and forth from my nose like a trombone. I hate these, but I'm supposed to do them every day, even though they make me look cross-eyed and silly. Dr. Tate says it's like push-ups for my eye muscles to keep them strong.

"I meant concentrate on your science work," she says. "You have another quiz coming up, don't you? And you said you didn't do so well on your last one."

As if I need a reminder.

"There should be a law against so many tests," I say. "Why do we need one *every* week?"

"To keep your skills up." She peers out the window and frowns. "Merci, didn't I tell you to put your bike away last night? It's going to rust out there or get stolen one day, and you'll be sorry."

"I'll get it in a minute. I forgot with all that drama at the park yesterday," I say. "It was kind of traumatic for me, too, you know. All that blood . . ."

Mami is barely listening.

I turn my glance toward the twins, suddenly a little jealous. I wish it was me who got to watch cartoons before school instead of doing flash cards and eye exercises. They always get a break. Not one person except me called them out for playing rodeo on their bikes yesterday.

On top of everything, we also have to get them to school today. Normally Abuela and Lolo walk the twins to school together, but not today. Lolo woke up with a cold, just like Abuela warned. She knocked on the screen door this morning, even angrier than she looked last night, though all I could see were her eyes above the germ mask she was wearing. She told us we'd have to drop off the twins. Then she quarantined Lolo and smeared him in so much Vicks VapoRub that I can practically smell him from across the yard.

"Pack your things. It's almost time to go." Mami checks her watch and takes the last swig of her coffee standing up. Then she grabs clean shirts and jeans out of the twins' backpacks and heads to the living room, where the fifth cartoon in a row is about to start.

"OK, caballeros," she says. "No more television or you're going to be late for school."

Tomás and Axel don't even turn their gaze from their show until she walks over and turns off the TV. Then she lays their clothes and sneakers in front of them.

"Here you go," she says.

Good luck is all I have to say. Convincing these two to get dressed fast is useless, especially when they're plugged in. You end up having to help, and it's like putting socks on an octopus. Still, Mami's big on being independent, even when it's reckless. I mean, she insisted last night that they cut their own steak. Who in their right mind would arm Axel and Tomás with knives?

They reluctantly start changing, but, of course, they get it all wrong.

"I want Lolo to come with us," Tomás says as he tries

to stuff his head through the armhole of his shirt.

"He's not feeling well today," Mami says, stooping to show him the space for his neck. "We can visit him on the way home."

Axel rolls on his back with his pants still bunched around his knees and his Spidey underwear on full display. His chin is bruised but not as swollen as yesterday, I notice. His nose is scabbed, too. Somebody is bound to make fun of him.

"But I want Lolo . . ." Axel whines.

I know what you mean, I want to say. *Me too.*

Tomás joins in. "And where's Mamá?"

"At work, remember? She's baking the breads this morning." Mami's voice is getting pinched, and she's broken into a sweat, bending down to help them here and there.

Papi walks in just in time. "I have an idea. How about your favorite uncle takes you to school today?"

Everyone perks up at that one, especially Mami, who gives him a grateful look. The twins' eyes also go glassy. Papi's van makes funny squeaks that they love. They can touch all his brushes and pound on the empty buckets like drums.

"Yes!" they yell.

Mami walks over and plants a kiss on his cheek. "You sure?"

"I can handle these two."

"You have no idea," I mutter.

"It's no problem. I'm going to check something out down on Dixie Highway," he says. "It's on the way."

"What's there?" I ask.

"Not your flash cards," he says.

Smart aleck.

He gets up and squeezes the top of my head gently. Then he glances at Axel, who's still tangled in his trousers. "Hombre, turn those pants around, so the zipper is on your private parts. We can't send you to school looking like lunatics."

Axel starts to whine, but Papi knows just what to do next. He grabs a twin in each arm and lets out a roar as he lumbers like a giant to the sofa.

"Careful with them, Enrique," Mami warns. "Axel's had enough bumps for a while."

But Papi has morphed into the best kind of play monster. With each stomp of his foot, Mami's set of demitasse cups rattles on the kitchen shelves and the twins screech. He lifts them high as they point to what they call the lava pit of our couch, the flattened space where Papi naps. I watch for a second, remembering when it was me squealing in that game, breathless as Papi held me over his head, staring into my pretend doom.

When exactly did we stop? I can't remember. I stand there blinking, wishing I were still small and in the game, only having to pretend to be scared.

"Ready?" Mami says, startling me.

I toss my flash cards inside my backpack and go outside to store my bike.

CHAPTER 10

I HATE HAVING PE SECOND period this year. You go through all the trouble of washing your face, combing your hair, and getting into your school uniform in the morning, only to get sweaty after an hour at school.

But here's a secret.

Most of the girls do not shower after class, even though we're supposed to, as per the student health manual that we all signed at the beginning of the year. We dry off and overload on body spray and call it a day. I use those disposable body wipes Abuela has for the days when she can't convince Lolo to take a shower. It was bad enough to risk having someone see me in my underwear at school. But Edna, whose father is a podiatrist, told us you can get foot fungi from public showers, even fancy ones like Seaward's. She showed us pictures of feet with pustules and everything. Nope. Oozing toes are not for me.

I wonder if it's the same for the boys in PE. Probably. Some of them smell a little like onions after gym, except maybe Wilson, who somehow always smells like laundry detergent. Not that I go around sniffing him, of course. It's just that the Ram Depot is small. If he stank, I'd have no choice but to use a gas mask. I think Wilson smells good because he doesn't get too sweaty, especially if we get split into teams for a basketball scrimmage, like we did this morning. Even when he's in the game, he doesn't play that much. The trouble is that Wilson doesn't run fast because of his foot, and he has to square up to get his balance before he shoots. I've seen him sink a shot better than plenty of other kids around here, but *some* people, aka one Jason Aldrich, don't even bother passing to him.

Anyway, Wilson was standing right under the net today, with Edna barely guarding him since she recently got a manicure. It was the perfect scoring position. But Jason, who was captain of our team this time, didn't even do a bounce pass to him. Instead, with the score tied, he looked around for any other boy. Finally, in desperation, he hurled the ball at me so I could sink it from the three.

Naturally, the other team had their toughest guy on me since everyone knows I'm quick on the court. That was Michael Clark, who I'm pretty sure grew two more inches since yesterday. I tried to fake him out, but what could I do? The guy has arms like an orangutan now. In the end, all I managed was a desperate rim shot. The red-pinny team got the rebound and scored.

"Ooh. Denied!" Michael called out as he high-fived his teammates.

Jason rolled his eyes at me in disgust. With him, it's win—or else.

"You suck, Merci," he muttered.

"I play better than you any day," I hissed. "And you had a guy right under the net—the perfect high-percentage play. Why didn't you pass?"

"Teamwork!" Mr. Patchett called out to both of us. Then he pointed to our bench. "Subs!"

I was still fuming as we made our way to the bleachers, but Wilson stayed pretty cool.

"Jason is pure butt cheese," he said as our replacements jogged onto the court. "Good try."

By lunchtime, I've forgotten all about Jason and his mean mouth. That's because Wilson and I have been slammed with customers again. *Cha-ching!* We're so busy that Lena, who usually reads outside during lunch, offers to help. As I predicted, the bobbleheads have been flying out of here. Or at least they *were* until Edna parked herself in front of the line to pester me.

"The answer is no," I say. "Now, is there anything else I can help you with today, Edna? You're holding up the line."

Kids are clutching their ten-dollar bills and craning their necks to see what's wrong. Darius is right behind her giving silent death glares as he waits, but Edna does not care.

She and Hannah are here on what she calls "a grave emergency." Miss McDaniels informed them that the photographer they lined up for the Heart Ball double-booked and has to cancel. Now they've got no one for the job, and the dance is only two weeks away. Guess whose help they want?

"Why can't you take some pictures for us?" Edna asks for the tenth time. "You're good enough with a camera and an obvious choice for backup photographer."

I wiggle my index finger inside my ear. Maybe I heard wrong, but for a second, I thought Edna gave me a compliment. That hasn't happened in the three years that I've known her. I waver inside. I do love taking pictures, but still it means I'll have to actually go to the dance. God. It's like smearing cod liver oil all over my favorite candy bar. I can't get past it.

"Sorry," I say. "But I'm not going to the Heart Ball."

She rolls her eyes. "Of course you are. *Everyone* is coming. Do you need a free ticket or something?" She asks this loud as can be. "I can arrange that, you know. The PTA has a special fund for the less fortunate."

Wilson looks up from counting a wad of bills near the cashbox and shakes his head. He's on scholarship here, too. His mom works at Lowe's.

"I don't need a free ticket," I say. "I just don't dance, that's all."

Edna breaks into a big smile. "So, what's the problem?" she says. "No one's going to ask *you* to dance."

I close my eyes and imagine Jake Rodrigo slamming her with a roundhouse kick right to the choppers.

Lena steps forward to stand next to me, but she doesn't elbow me this time. Her purple hair spikes are practically quivering like quills. If only she could shoot them like a real porcupine.

"We're done here," I say. "Next."

I signal to Darius, who starts to step forward, but Edna only puffs up into a bigger dragon.

"Step back," she hisses at him. "I'm *not* done." Then she glares at me. "Be selfish, then, Merci Suárez, but I'm telling Miss McDaniels that you won't help us. She's not going to like that one little bit."

"What are you talking about?" I say. "We're selling your dance tickets!"

"And writing funny ads for you on the morning announcements," Wilson adds from the back.

Grateful, I look over my shoulder. "That's right—and they're working. In fact, what's the tally sold so far?" I ask.

"One hundred eighty-seven," he says.

"See?" I say. "We *are* helping—in one hundred and eighty-seven ways, to be exact."

"You're taking a cut of the tickets!" Edna says. "It's not like you're working for free."

I glare at her. She does have a point, but still. Is it a crime to make a buck—especially when you have to do something against your will?

"Are you going to buy something today? Because if not, I have paying customers behind you."

She folds her arms and stares me down.

That's when Hannah finally steps in.

"All right, everybody. Let's not fight." She leans over the counter and gives me a pleading look. "We could really use your help, Merci. Won't you do it for me?"

I look at her, wondering what to say. Best friends are supposed to help each other. That much I know.

"Besides, Edna hasn't even told you the best part yet," she continues. "If we promise to be careful, her dad is going to lend us his selfie booth equipment." She gives me a knowing look and leans farther in. "It's the IMA Paparazzi 10 Selfie Station. Remember it?"

I feel my knees wobble. How could I forget it? That primo photography kit was part of last year's spring auction. It has a professional background screen and a big iPad stand with an LED light so people can take all the selfies they want. Best of all, if you know what you're doing, you can make GIFs and Boomerang photos. You can add custom edits to each shot, too. Last year Hannah and I played around with it. I'd just figured out how to put ballerina tutus and pig snouts on our headmaster's picture when the bidding closed. Edna's dad won the bid at $3,000. What was Dr. Santos going to do with all that stuff, I wondered. Take pictures of his patients' ingrown toenails?

Edna leans in and grins like a cat who just ate a canary. "Think you can handle it?"

I look to Hannah. Is this fair? She's my friend. She

knows how much I like to take pictures. But is it worth helping Edna?

"When else will you get to work with equipment like that?" Hannah asks.

I heave a sigh. "I don't have to be inside the gym?"

Hannah shakes her head. "Nope. Your booth will be right outside in the hall. I'll help you set up and break down." She takes my hand and squeezes it. "Please," she says. "Do it for me."

I glance at Lena, who gives me a shrug.

Just then, the bell rings. A chorus of groans rises up from the kids who got stuck in line. Wilson tries to calm them all down.

"Relax. We'll still have stock tomorrow," he calls out to the crowd. "You'll be first in line, Darius," he adds.

I turn to Edna. "Happy, now? You've made everyone mad at you as usual."

She blinks, startled for a minute. And maybe I'm a little surprised, too. The words sound meaner outside of my head.

But then she crosses her arms, looking even more determined. "So, is it a deal or not, Merci Suárez?" she asks. "I have to let Miss McDaniels know."

Hannah gives me puppy-dog eyes again.

"Fine," I say. "I'll do it."

Hannah breaks into a huge grin and pulls me and Lena into a group hug. Edna just watches us for a second, her arms still tight across her chest.

Then she turns on her heels and walks away to find Miss McDaniels.

CHAPTER 11

MAMI SAYS THAT FEELINGS ARE tricky because sometimes they get disguised. Like when Roli was packing for school and the twins wouldn't talk to him all week. On the day he was leaving, they called him a doo-doo head and put a dead frog they found flattened on the sidewalk inside his duffel bag. As soon as he left, though, they fell in a heap, crying. Sad got disguised as mad.

I don't think grown-ups have feelings figured out, either. At least, that's what I find out today.

"Is Tía sick?" I give Mami a careful look from inside my closet, which she calls a black hole. I tried to tell her she was wrong because Roli already explained black holes. But she just held up her hand and said I had to clean it out today or else.

But here's what's strange. Today is Saturday, the bakery's busiest day, and I can see from my bedroom window that Tía's car is still in the driveway. My stomach flutters. People around here sometimes keep secrets about important things. Exhibit A: they didn't tell me about Lolo's Alzheimer's until I half figured it out myself last year. What if they're keeping another secret, this time about Tía?

"No, not really," Mami says, tossing one of my old T-shirts in a pile.

"Well, *what* really? Is she skipping work for no reason?"

"She took a break today, that's all. A person can feel sick in spirit, too, like when you feel lonely or overwhelmed. Does that ever happen to you?"

Every day, I want to tell her, but I shrug instead because she's prying and I don't like that. Besides, there are just too many annoying things to name. Mr. Ellis calling me by my full name instead of Merci, the way I like. Jason saying that I suck. Hannah hanging out with Edna. Missing all the stuff Lolo used to help me with. Plus, I don't understand why it's OK for Tía to take a pass, but not me. I mean, the last time I had a science test and wanted to stay home, Mami yanked my sheet off and ordered me to get dressed— "¡Inmediatamente!" Did she care about my sick spirit? No, she did not.

I cross my arms and stare at the car some more. "Be serious. How is staying home with the twins a break?"

"She's their mom, and she wants to be with them," Mami says. "She misses them when she's at work."

I'm practically speechless. Missing Axel and Tomás? What a concept!

"They drive her crazy, Mami. She always says so. 'They are going to send me straight to the insane asylum!' Those are her words exactly."

"All children drive their parents crazy." She gives me a pointed look. "And we still can't get enough of them. One day you'll understand."

I always hate when she talks about things that will happen *one day* as if nothing that I know now matters.

She kisses my forehead and takes a deep whiff of my hair the way she sometimes does. "Now, finish cleaning out your closet. I'm dropping stuff off at Goodwill this afternoon."

It takes most of the morning to empty out my trophies and best cleats and next-to-best cleats, and third-best cleats, and all the clothes that are too tight now, even my old Mets jersey that Lolo bought me in Port St. Lucie a few years ago. The dust makes me sneeze like crazy. But in the end, all my work might be worth it because as I'm tying up the last garbage bag, I get an idea for some quick cash.

I walk over to Tía's, hauling my bags of clothes like Santa Claus. To my surprise, she's not in bed nursing her soul back to health. Instead, she's swishing a mop over every inch of her kitchen floor as Shakira sings on the radio. The twins are playing with their plastic dragons in the next room.

"You're cleaning?"

Even on her best day, she's not much for housework. "What's the point," she always says, when Abuela accuses her of keeping a sloppy house. "The twins will have it wrecked ten minutes after I do it!"

"Scoot up on the counter, please, Merci. I missed a spot near your foot."

I climb up near the sink, where the twins' cereal bowls are still soaking. Tía looks like a sailor on deck detail as she pushes the scattered Matchbox cars and plastic toys to the baseboards with strong, sure strokes.

A vaguely familiar scent rises from the bucket. Berries and honey or something. What is it? I grab the squeeze bottle that's on the windowsill to see what it is.

Uh-oh.

ABRE CAMINO. OPEN YOUR PATH TO
JOBS, LOVE, AND HAPPINESS!

Tía has been to the botánica on Forest Boulevard again. She goes whenever she has a problem she can't solve without divine intervention, like last November when she was saving for the twins' Christmas presents and her house needed a new air conditioner. She bought Abre Camino bath salts and soaked in the tub so long that her fingertips got pruney. It worked, too. One of Papi's guys volunteered to fix the air conditioner for cheap. Anyway, I guess Abre Camino has expanded into floor cleaner now.

I open her tin of animal crackers and eat a broken zebra as I watch, sulking. "You should have told me you were going to Señora Magdalena's," I say. "You know I like to go."

The botánica is like a bodega, a church, and an art shop all rolled into one, depending on what you're looking for. There are urns and candles like the ones Abuela keeps in her bedroom for Lolo. And the display of bath oils near the register reminds me of the vials that Hannah and Lena like to sample at Lush, only instead of things being called You've Been Mangoed—whatever that means—these say Romance, Fright, Finances, Safety from Evil Eye. My favorite is Lost Items. I've found my house key a bunch of times thanks to that little vial.

Here's the thing, though. Not everybody in our family is on board. Namely, Mami. She insists that everyone can believe what they want, but she still shakes her head about the products Señora Magdalena sells. Mami says things should have *proof of efficacy*. That's the no-fun scientist in her talking. That's why she hardly ever burns the Richer in Business candle I bought for her and Papi the last time Tía took me shopping over there. It's a shame, really. I even sprang for the jumbo size with the glitter dollar signs in the wax and everything.

"You busy today?" I ask.

"Depends on who's asking," she says.

"I was thinking that since you're home, we could go shopping."

Tía stops what she's doing. She stands her mop in the bucket and tiptoes over to feel my head. "Are you sick? Maybe you've picked up Lolo's bug."

I push her hand aside. Normally, going shopping is about as appealing as having my fingers chopped off one by one, even when it's with Tía. Everyone knows that. But this is business.

I point to the bag of outgrown clothes that I left near the door. "I was just thinking I might sell some things I've outgrown at the Red Umbrella and make a few bucks. I've got my eye on some new decor for my room, and I could use the cash." (By decor, I mean a new bobblehead, of course.)

Tía hesitates. The Red Umbrella is her favorite consignment shop.

"I'll bet the twins will want to go, too," I add.

"Why not?" She yanks the chain on the ceiling fan to dry things faster. "Boys!" she says, heading to the living room. "Time to get dressed! We're going toy shopping!"

In no time, we're out the door with our bags and the twins in tow.

CHAPTER 12

YOU CAN FIND EVERYTHING AT the Red Umbrella, from video games to ball gowns, just like at a pulguero, only it's inside and the merchandise is nicer. Still, Abuela always complains about us buying used things.

"Why buy someone's old clothes?" She claims it reminds her of when she first got to this country and had to wear clothes from the refugee center. And don't get her started on germs. When the twins brought home matching toy firetrucks from here, Abuela snatched them away and bleached them until the plastic turned pink, just in case they were carrying the plague.

But Tía doesn't care. She says the price is right for buying clothes on a budget, especially for the twins, who are in a growth spurt.

The shop is small and cluttered, and it smells like the inside of a musty closet. A few people are ahead of us, so we have to browse while we wait our turn. Tía already has three dresses on hangers slung over her shoulder, and now she's looking over the shoe selection, checking for sneakers in the right size for the twins and heels for her. I'm sitting on my bag of clothes, checking my phone to pass the time. Hannah texts that she's about to start her piano lesson. Lena is picking up trash at the beach with the Earth Club.

Just then, Tomás runs up the aisle with his hand stuffed inside a single inflatable boxing glove. It's jumbo-size so it makes him look like a cartoon since his arms are so skinny. Axel comes up behind him wearing the other one. Two halves of a bad sandwich. Without so much as a warning, they each wind up and give me a hook in the back. My phone goes flying.

"*Pow!*" Tomás says.

"You're going to get us tossed out of here again," I warn as they wind up for the next hit.

"*Pow! Pow!*" Axel replies, giving me a one-two. Then he turns to Tía. "We want these!"

Tía looks up from a pair of heels she's been considering. They're red patent leather and have bows on the ankle strap.

"Boxing gloves? Mi amor . . ."

"Please!" he says.

Tía glances at the price tag that's stuck on a thumb, considering. "Fine," she says.

My mouth drops open as I rub my flank. Kidney damage, here I come.

"Do you even know what that toy is going to mean for me?" I give her a pleading look as they run off to pummel each other some more. "In case you don't know, their current favorite game is called Slay Merci the Ugly Giant. Plastic bats are involved."

She shoos off my concern. "Relax. They'll forget about those silly things in a day." Then she holds up the shoes. "Verdict?"

I snatch my phone from the floor. A few of the girls at school say they're going to wear heels to the Heart Ball since we don't have to wear our uniforms. I wonder if their shoes will be like these, all pointy and hard to walk in so that they'll have to move like Tuerto that time he stepped in wet spackle. I have no idea how anyone balances in tacones like these, let alone dances. Drywall stilts would be easier.

"Bows," I say, shaking my head. "Not really my thing. And where are you going to wear them, anyway? The bakery?"

"You never know," she says quietly. Then she glances at my empty hands. "Don't you want to pick anything out for yourself?"

I look at the long row of clothes and sigh. It's overwhelming, which is how I always feel when I think about clothes or makeup. Also, should I even buy clothes here? I've heard that some kids at Seaward buy some of their clothes at Goodwill. Rich kids! They do it on purpose because they've made it cool to wear ugly plaid pants that belonged to someone's grandpa. But I don't think it would be the same for me. I'm pretty sure if anybody knew I bought clothes secondhand, they'd just say I look cheap.

"I don't know how," I say.

"What do you mean, you don't know *how*?"

When I stare at her blankly, she walks over and slides a few hangers back.

"Mira."

She pulls out a pair of white skinny jeans and checks the size. Then she finds a T-shirt, knotted at the hip, and holds it up in front of me.

"Add a pair of Jordans and cute hair, and you got yourself a look," she says.

Cute hair? A look? I stare at the reflection of us in

the full-length mirror and try to imagine myself in these clothes. All week long I wear a blazer and a kerchief at my neck. On the weekends, it's strictly shorts and tees, except on cool days, when it's leggings.

"Go on," she says, motioning toward the dressing room curtains. "Try them on. It's something you can wear when you go to the mall—"

"You want me to dress up for the *mall*? That's dumb."

But even as I say it, I think of the girls Lena, Hannah, and I sometimes see when we go to the Gardens Mall. Some of them are from Seaward. They post about what they buy on Insta. Outfits, earrings, lip gloss.

"It's just an example, niña. You can wear these clothes when you go out somewhere nice."

"I don't go anywhere nice."

"Well, how about that dance you're going to?"

Mami must have told her. As usual, there is absolutely zero privacy to be had in this family. You can't have a cold or start wearing a bra or flunk a quiz or get drafted into going to a dumb dance without it becoming breaking news that they whisper about behind your back.

"The Heart Ball?" Just saying it aloud makes me squeamish. "It's in the gym. What's the big deal about dressing up for that?"

She grins. "This outfit would be perfect. In fact, I'm so sure of it, that I'll buy it for you." Then she gives me a sly look. "Who's your lucky date?"

I'm instantly annoyed at her. What is it with adults messing with your love life? They either say you're too young, or else they ask you questions like these and grin at you in that uber-creepy way. Plus, they have nothing useful to explain, such as if someone does ask you and you say yes, would that mean you'd have to be willing to kiss them, too? I think no, but it's not like I can ask her. Because then she'll say, "You're too young!"

"Don't get ideas," I say. "I'm going with myself, Tía. I'm the photographer, plain and simple. Besides, I don't dance, remember? I'm not like you."

"What are you talking about? You're twelve. How do you know what you do and don't like?" she tells me.

I narrow my eyes at her. "I know plenty—especially that I don't like to dance."

I consider myself in the mirror again when one of the salesclerks waves at us from the top of the aisle.

"We're ready for you, ladies," she says. "Thanks for waiting."

Just then, a foam dart flies through the air and hits her in the temple. The twins race up the aisle, shrieking about making a hit. They've found Nerf guns in the bin.

"Sorry," Tía says.

"Aren't they so big now?" the saleslady says through gritted teeth. I can tell she's disguising some feelings of her own, but only barely.

Still, Tía smiles brightly. "They definitely are," she says. "Come on, boys. Our turn."

CHAPTER 13

I DON'T KNOW HOW I didn't see it coming.

Simón is already at Las Casitas when we get back. He's here to repair the stucco on Tía's place since the weather is warming up enough to be able to work again.

Or so he says.

Mostly, he's been talking to Tía.

I'm in Abuela's sewing room, which I'm supposed to be straightening up, when I hear his voice. Mami and I always come over on the weekend to help with the chores she can't quite manage anymore: picking up dropped pins, folding big blankets in the laundry, vacuuming. I finished picking up all the pins super quick so that I could watch a YouTube video about the advanced features of the IMA Paparazzi photo app. I was just getting some good tips when they interrupt me.

He's talking with Tía Inés around the side of her house that's closest to Abuela's. The window is open to let in the fresh air, so I'm not snooping. And is it my fault I have ears?

I slip beside La Boba, Abuela's dress-form mannequin, and peek through the blinds.

His painting supplies are still neatly stacked near the wall—untouched, I notice, which isn't like him. He's always the first to start a job, always the one who works the longest hours and does the best work. What would Papi say if he saw him slacking?

I glance around and notice that the twins are nowhere in the yard, either. They're probably in a trance playing video games inside. So, it's just Tía and Simón. Alone.

I'm about to call out and ask if he and Papi were able to find an empty field for a game tomorrow like they wanted, but something stops me when I see how they're standing. What's different? It's like looking at those picture riddles where you have to find the thing that's not the same from one picture to the next. I watch carefully for a minute, detail after detail, and then I finally see it. They are standing way too close, like, a lot closer than usual.

Tía shields her eyes from the sun and beams her brightest smile at him.

"I know, but it's just that it's your day off. Don't you like to do other things in your spare time?" she says sweetly.

Simón leans against the house, smiling. "This is where I want to be—painting a pretty lady's house."

Is Tía a pretty lady? I haven't ever thought about it much. She's just my tía, the twins' mom, Inés. Tía laughs in a way that's new. She pulls a stray hair behind her ear.

"But how about you?" Simón asks. "I'll bet there are things you like to do when you're not working?"

They keep their voices low, as if they don't want anyone to hear. Simón leans closer to her, a look on his face that I don't recognize. So, I creep closer to the blinds, wedging myself between La Boba and the screen. My ears feel like they're stretching bigger as I listen. What is he saying that has to be whispered? I squint and try to read his lips.

Tía's laugh again.

My heart is pounding. It's the Abre Camino's fault. It ought to come with a warning label. *Inappropriate love spells possible. Discontinue use if the following symptoms arise: sappy glances, giggling, quickened heartbeats, lack of focus.*

"Merci! Aren't you done in here yet? I need help with the laundry."

I startle to find Mami at the door to the sewing room. I step back from the window and grab a random pincushion.

"Sorry," I say. "It takes a while to find all the pins Abuela drops."

But Mami is too smart for that excuse. There's not a pin left on the floor, so she walks over to see what has snagged my attention. When she looks out and sees Tía and Simón, she cranks the window shut and turns to me, her eyebrows arched.

"What did I tell you about giving people privacy?" she whispers. "You shouldn't be eavesdropping."

I frown at her. "I was just sitting here when their voices floated in, Mami," I say. "It wasn't like I went spying. Besides, if I give people privacy, how will I ever know what's going on around here?"

"Maybe you don't need to know every single thing. Has that occurred to you?"

"I'm not a six-year-old!" I jerk my thumb at the window angrily. "I can tell that they like each other."

"Good. Then, that's all you need to know. The rest is your aunt's personal business."

My mouth drops open. "Since when do we have personal business in this family? Abuela sent over prunes last week when she heard Papi was constipated!"

Mami walks to the door and holds it open for me. "The laundry is waiting."

All afternoon, I turn things over in my mind as Simón works outside.

It's only later, long after he's gone and the wet paint fumes are finally leaving the yard, that I find out the sickening truth. Tía and Mami are filling Lolo's pillbox in Abuela's kitchen, while he and I play dominoes in the next room. I lean over my fichas, pretending to consider my move, but really I'm growing my ears again.

Valentine's Day is coming up, Tía tells her. She and Simón are finally going on a date.

"That's wonderful, Inés," Mami says. "I think it's about time you let yourself have a bit of fun."

I don't even look up as they both burst into mad giggles.

So much for minding your own personal business.

CHAPTER 14

LOLO AND I USED TO ride to El Caribe on Sundays. It
was our job to pick up bread and desserts for our Sunday
dinners. That was our time, just him and me, without the
twins grabbing for his attention, without Abuela telling us
what to do.

Lolo doesn't bike at all anymore. He forgets when to
stop or even how to balance on a turn. On good days,
we used to let him ride at home, doing a loop around
Las Casitas. But a few months ago, he crashed into the
grapefruit tree, and Abuela has had his bike chained up in
the shed since then.

I suppose I should be glad that Abuela trusts me
to ride alone to the bakery by myself. But the truth is,

without Lolo, it feels like an ordinary chore instead of the fun thing it used to be. It feels lonely not to have him to talk to.

Especially today.

I grab my bike from the driveway and dry off the seat with my shirt. I left it outside again last night. Thank goodness that I'm up before Mami or she'd dog me about it getting stolen or, worse, about how I never take care of anything, which is not true. To her, everything I own has to last for years. School blouses. Backpacks. Sneakers. And definitely bikes. In fact, she told me they bought this one in adult size so I can ride it even when I'm a grown-up. "It will last if you take care of it," she said. I love my bike, but geez. I'll bet nobody else at Seaward Pines has to worry about theirs the way I do. If they outgrow a bike or just get tired of it, they can buy a new one like it's no big deal. I can't.

Anyway, Lolo is already awake and at the kitchen table when I stop by to pick up Abuela's list. As soon as I walk in, I have to plug my nose. The whole room still smells of camphor and eucalyptus, and his skin is shiny with VapoRub. He's still in his pajamas and wrapped in a blanket to his chin. Some sort of sludgy tea is untouched and getting cold on the table in front of him.

"Hi, Lolo," I say, and blow him a kiss.

He looks up at me and coughs a bit. "Preciosa," he says.

"One of Señora Magdalena's brews?" I sniff his cup as I sit down. Bark and something foul.

He stares at it, looking miserable as he nods.

I listen for Abuela. She's in the shower. So, I hurry up and microwave us a little milk. Then I mix in some sugar and instant coffee, the way he likes. "Toma," I say, pushing one of the mugs toward him. "But we have to hurry."

He pats my hand as I sit down next to him to have our con leches. Neither one of us says anything for a long time, but inside me, thoughts are churning, and they have to come out. So, I lean forward and whisper, hoping this might be a good Lolo day.

"Tía is going on a date with Simón for Valentine's Day. Did you hear? I mean, we all knew he had a crush, but . . ." I shudder dramatically.

Lolo takes a deep sip. "Simón?"

Cold rises at the back of my neck. Lolo used to go on jobs with Papi and Simón. He's sat next to Simón at dinner plenty of times. How can someone you see all the time disappear from your memory?

"Yeah. Simón. Papi's guy. Our friend." I scroll through

my phone and hold up a picture from last Christmas. Simón in our yard with a sparkler.

Lolo nods and takes another sip, but he doesn't say anything else.

I stare at the fruit flies dancing around the bananas in the wire basket. *Calling the old Lolo. Come in, Lolo. Do you read me?*

"What's going to happen if Tía falls in love and all that, Lolo?" I ask aloud. I don't add all the other things swirling in my mind. *What about the twins? Will he boss me like an uncle? Will Tía still have time for me?*

Lolo coughs a little and pulls the blanket tighter around his shoulders. "I don't know," he says.

I wait for more, wondering if he really understands what I'm asking.

"No sé nada," he says. Then he takes my hand in his papery fingers and squeezes.

I take a long sip of my coffee even though the heat burns my tongue.

There's a soccer game after dinner. We're playing against a team of drywall guys from Lantana. Mami let me come since the field is close by and because Papi's team was a guy short, and he begged. Now I wish she hadn't.

"Get your head around what you're doing, Merci," Papi tells me.

He and Simón have jogged over after I missed yet another goal, the third one in a row. I went way too wide and high this time, like I had no control at all.

"Sorry," I tell them.

"Be aware of the field, like I told you. You could have crossed it," he said. "We had a man in position." He gives Simón a hard pat on the back. I try not to glare. Are they going to act like brothers now that Simón and Tía are a thing?

I don't look at Simón. I *was* aware that he was in position, of course. I just didn't want to pass to him. Normally, Simón and I play great together, our eyes catching a fraction of a second before I dribble past a defender and then pass off to him for the goal. But all that giggling on the side of the house has changed everything. I sneak a glance at his hands—hands that might hold Tía's. All at once he's become Tía's boyfriend and not just a soccer player. I feel cut out.

"I said I was sorry," I say irritably.

Papi checks his watch and grimaces. He worked hard to get Mami to let me play today, and what have we got to show for it? We're down three-to-four, with only five minutes left before we all have to leave. If we lose, though, Papi will have to buy the drywallers beer on the way home. That's the rule, and it's not cheap. I know he doesn't want to spend the money.

"Everything all right?" Simón asks me. "You don't seem yourself."

I give him a cold look. Nothing is all right, but I'm not about to say why, especially not in front of Papi, who is allergic to any thought of me thinking about love things. Besides, what would I say? "I hate that you and my aunt make lovesick eyes at each other?" How can you be jealous of someone who likes someone you love? I know it's ridiculous, but I can't help it one bit.

And what if there's kissing? So gross. I can't even look at his face in case my eyes get glued on his mouth.

I glance at the sidelines, where Vicente has been doing head stalls and other tricks to kill time, in between texting with one of his many crushes.

"Put Vicente in," I say. "He looks bored."

Papi and Simón exchange looks.

"Don't, Enrique," Simón says. "He was in the whole first half." He looks to me. "It's your turn. Don't you want to play?"

"We're losing," I say. "And I'm not helping."

"What did I tell you about not giving up?" Papi says. "About teamwork?"

I can see they're not going to back down, so I go to desperate measures. "I just don't feel good, OK?"

It's a dirty trick, I know. But those are the magic words to get Papi to back off me these days. He's always assuming if I don't feel good, it has to do with having my period, which, yes, everyone in my family has probably talked about. Papi is somebody who can't even hang bras and underwear on the line without feeling awkward.

He puts his fingers to his lips and whistles to get Vicente's attention. Then he turns to me. "You're out, then," he says. "Get a cold drink."

I walk off the field and sit on the cooler with my shin guards stripped off to watch the rest of the game. Vicente comes through, of course, with those fast feet and muscular legs that Hannah always notices. God. What if Simón and Vicente become part of our family? It was bad enough having to share a life with a super brain. Then I'd have to deal with being a sidekick to a supermodel soccer god.

It doesn't take long for him to score a goal. He rolls the ball and cuts right past the defender. Then he sets up Simón for the second goal, a sweet shot to the corner that dips right over the keeper's head. When we score, our guys break into cheers. Simón rubs Vicente's scalp with his knuckles, and for a second I feel bad for hating on him.

Afterward, everyone comes off the field and grabs their water bottles and towels. "Where are we stopping?" asks Junior, the drywallers' captain, when he shakes hands with Papi.

"Me? Nowhere. I've got the kid," Papi tells him. "Take my guys for a drink if you want. They've earned it."

There's trash talk about next time as everyone heads for their cars, but I don't join in. I pack up our stuff in silence.

Simón wipes off his face. He's sweated through his shirt, and his hair is dripping worse than when we have an outside paint job in August. Vicente hoists a Styrofoam cooler to his shoulder.

"Feel better, Merci," Simón tells me. He walks backward a few paces, waiting for me to answer.

Papi frowns at me and gives me a nudge. "Didn't you hear him?" he asks, low and stern. Being rude is not OK in his book.

So I give Simón a quick glance and say, "Thanks."

At least Papi doesn't talk on the ride home, the way Mami would, and I'm glad. He puts on the radio, and I stare out the window the whole way. When we finally pull in, I can see Tía through the open blinds of our front window. She's at our house, reading to the twins on the couch. They suck their thumbs, listening. Tomás has his hand on her cheek as she turns the pages of the book. Soon she'll tuck them in Roli's bed again and leave them overnight.

Would I miss them if she and Simón got married and moved away? My throat gets tight. My eyes fill.

Papi turns to me. "You don't look so good," he says. "Maybe you're getting Lolo's cold?"

"I don't have Lolo's cold!" I wipe my nose and shove open the van door with a loud screech. Then I hurry inside.

CHAPTER 15

WE'VE GOT A LOAD OF stuff in Mami's car trunk for the
Fab Lab. That's our new makerspace at Seaward Pines.
The Fab Lab has a 3-D printer and digital stuff like at
the downtown library, but it also has power tools that
you can borrow if you get trained, two sewing machines,
and a sound booth where we can make podcasts instead
of writing book reports. The shelves are piled high with
junk like PVC pipes, egg cartons, fabric, wood scraps,
and duct tape. Hannah's job is to organize it all. She's
one of the supply monitors as part of her community
service assignment, so she checks in donations and makes
sure everything is put away neatly after people work
on their projects. It's not a bad job, she says, unless the

upper-school robotics team is in here with all their circuit boards and LEGO pieces. They get bossy because they're older, like when they eat in here even after she reminds them that they're not supposed to. She had to tell Miss McDaniels and everything, which is hard for Hannah. She hates to argue with anybody.

Mami puts the car in park and steps out when we pull into the drop-off loop, even though she knows it will bug me. She's wearing the scrubs with cupids all over them, her favorite for February.

"Did you have to wear those?" I ask.

She looks down at herself. "What's wrong with them?"

"It's just that there are perfectly decent scrubs without naked angels slinging arrows. Valentine's Day isn't for two weeks."

She looks at the sky and takes a deep breath. "What's wrong with you these days?"

I just know she and Papi have been talking about my so-called moods.

"Nothing!" I tell her. "I just think wearing naked cherubs is kind of dumb."

"I'm sorry to hear that." She hands me the box from her trunk, her lips pressed to a tight line. "Here you go." When she leans forward to kiss me, the way she always does, I take the box and turn away fast. PDAs with your parents are OK for lower school, but not anymore. Why doesn't she know that?

"Bye," I say, and hurry along inside.

The box is full of CDs that she found mixed in with her old night-school stuff. She's been on a cleaning binge lately. I wonder what this junk is going to become. The Art IV students made mosaics with broken CDs last year. A few of the really good ones are still hanging in the gallery near the front office. Maybe these will become something like that, too.

Hannah, Lena, and I love to work on projects in the Fab Lab when no one else is around, which is usually after school. Our best invention so far was the Recycle Bot for the Earth Club. Lena wanted to make sure people would recycle their cans and bottles instead of tossing them in a trash can in the cafeteria. The signs reminding us that an aluminum can takes 200 years to decompose in a landfill weren't enough, apparently. So, we made a huge bin that looks like a space robot. We used an old metal garbage can for the body and a pail for the head. Flexible foil ducts (from Papi) became the arms. The best part? When the mouth opens, a little recording says, "The Earth thanks you." The robotics pests helped us with that part after Miss McDaniels told them they had to, on account of breaking the eating rules.

Unfortunately, Lena, Hannah, and I haven't been there together lately. I can't go during lunch because of the Ram Depot. Hannah's been busy in the afternoons with the Heart Ball. And Lena sets up for the morning announcements as soon as her dad drops her off. We have to wait for a study period or a special pass to come to the lab now.

The door is unlocked when I get there, and I hear voices.

"Hello?" I step inside. Light is coming from the last space that's around the corner, behind the screens, so I walk over.

It's Hannah.

She's standing at a worktable with Edna. They're each armed with a shaker full of glitter that they're aiming at an enormous cardboard heart, which I suppose is for the Heart Ball. But they're laughing together so hard that they don't hear me when I come in.

"Hi," I say again.

Hannah turns. "Oh, hi, Merci," she says, trying to catch her breath. Her cheeks are flushed, and little dots of glitter are stuck to her arms. Edna stays mum.

I step closer. "What's so funny?"

"Nothing," Hannah says, but she turns pink in the face and snorts a little.

"Kissing," Edna blurts out.

Hannah tosses some glitter at Edna. "Gross." Then they burst into giggles again.

How is kissing funny? I think back to the two options that Edna explained to us in gory detail in the locker room not too long ago. It almost made me sick. Her sister had told her everything, she said, as we huddled near the unused showers to hear. There's wet and dry, depending, and tongues could be involved. This year Edna likes a kid named Brent from the eighth grade, who has muscles and the start of a mustache like a high schooler. It's kind of scary to look at him. Maybe now she knows about kissing for real.

"Who's kissing?" The box in my hands feels heavy all of a sudden as I keep my eyes on Hannah. I'm thinking of Tía and Simón all over again.

"*Not* me," Hannah says, and relief washes over me.

"Of course not," I say.

Edna shrugs. "Well, you have to kiss somebody *some* time," she says. "We all do. We're nearly thirteen."

I stare at her, thinking, *Is that a real rule?*

Hannah keeps her eyes down on the heart she's decorating, considering the bare spots. Her cheeks are blotchy. "What's in the box?" she asks me suddenly.

I hold it out as she peeks inside and pulls out a CD.

"Ooh. We could make mobiles. They'd sparkle on

the dance floor!" She looks at me. "You want to stay after school today and work on that with me?"

Edna pipes up before I can answer.

"Don't you think we have enough decorations, Hannah?" she says. "Besides, those CDs would look too small and cheap hanging from the gym ceiling." She glances at me. "No offense."

The warning bell rings, and Edna grabs her backpack. She puckers her lips at Hannah and makes big smoochy sounds as she heads out the door. "Bye, Hannah-Hannah-Bo-Bana," she croons.

Hannah laughs. Then she looks at the clock and gasps. "*Agh!* We only have a few minutes to get to homeroom. Can you help me put some of this away, Merci? I don't want to be late."

I glance after Edna, wondering why *she* didn't stay to help and why Hannah doesn't seem to mind.

Hannah hurries to place my box of CDs on the shelf while I move in what feels like slow motion putting the glue bottles back where they belong. She grabs the broom and dustpan and begins sweeping. All the while, I'm thinking back to last year when Edna tore up the costume that Abuela helped make for Michael Clark. How Edna invited everyone to a sleepover party except me. Why does Hannah like her? Why is she on this stupid committee?

"Are you and Edna friends now?" It sounds like I'm accusing her. *Are you going to start kissing people?* I want to ask.

Hannah puts down the broom and moves the hearts to the drying rack. Then she turns to me.

"We're on the dance committee. That's all."

"She's bossy and horrible," I point out.

Hannah says, "Sometimes, yes. But not always. Besides, we declared a truce, remember? You have to try, too."

I dig in. "Almost no one likes her anymore," I say. "Not even Rachel."

Hannah plucks at her hair nervously. "Merci, that's mean."

"But it's true."

Before Hannah can argue, Lena's voice comes over the loudspeakers to start the morning announcements. Hannah turns off the lights, and we hurry down the hall.

"Good morning, Rams. This is Lena Cahill and Darius Ulmer. It's National Tater Tot Day!"

She asks everyone to stand for the pledge. Hannah and I freeze in our spots like we're supposed to. I can't see a flag anywhere, though, so we have to pretend. We put our hands on our hearts and promise our allegiance to thin air.

CHAPTER 16

RIGHT BEFORE THE LUNCH BELL, I push open the Ram Depot door and hang my backpack next to Wilson's.

"I had an idea for more merchandise," I tell him. "Flash drives. We can have them in a few days if we order by this afternoon."

Wilson is sitting on the edge of a chair in the corner with his back to me, like he's in time-out. One of his shoes is off. His sock is balled up inside, and his brace is on the floor.

I walk over. "What are you doing?"

He startles and reaches for his sock quickly. "Nothing."

I try not to stare at the brace. It's not like I haven't seen one before, though. Some of Mami's patients use orthotics, too. Wilson's has a black strap that wraps above the ankle with Velcro; the other strap wraps around his foot arch. An adjustable clip attaches them together, like on a backpack.

I cross my arms. "Nothing? You're just airing out your footsies?" I glance at his feet. He has long, skinny toes.

"Why are you up in my business?" he asks. "It's ugly."

"Not as ugly as foot odor." I wave my hand in front of my nose.

"Which I do not have," he says. "Unlike some people I know."

He's probably right. I'm wearing yesterday's socks, and I didn't even change them for PE. "All right, fine," I say. "But seriously. What are you doing?"

He sighs and checks to make sure we're alone. "My exercises, OK? I didn't have time this morning, and I have to take my brace off to do them. They're supposed to make my ankle and hip stronger, so I'm steadier."

"Oh." I think about him in gym, how he sometimes looks like he might teeter over when he's moving too fast. Now I feel like a dope for prying.

So, I offer an olive branch. "I do stupid exercises, too," I tell him. "*Really* stupid."

He gives me a doubtful look and glances at my loafers.

"No lie," I say. "Mine are for my eye. Like this." I take

a pen from my backpack and demonstrate the trombone move, making my eyes cross and straighten.

"That's ridiculous."

"Yes. I said that already."

"Every day?"

"Yeah. And it's not something I can really do at lunchtime, either," I tell him. "So, what do yours look like?"

Wilson lets out a breath. He unclips the brace he had already put back on, and his foot drops forward. Then he holds out his leg to show me. "You do the alphabet," he says. He makes an *A*, *B*, and *C* in the air, as if his toe is a pencil. "Who wants to do this in front of people? It's guaranteed mocking material."

I nod. Grim but true. Any imperfection can be used against you. Sometimes kids complain that they can't tell if I'm talking to them because my eye strays.

Slowly, I lift my leg in the air and I try to make an *A*. Wilson stays very still and watches me until I'm at *D*.

"Technically, you should be barefoot," he says.

I slip off my shoe and sock, praying my feet don't stink too much like vinegar. Only a little, I decide.

We start moving our feet to make the letters. I start singing the ABC song like I do sometimes with the twins. The letter *W* turns out to be hard to do sitting up, so we decide to lie on our backs and try it with two legs at the same time. It's like conducting an orchestra with your feet.

Soon we turn it into a game. One of us writes and the other one guesses the word or sentence.

He writes, *Hi Merci.*

I write, *Waddup Wilson.*

He writes, *Boogerhead.*

I write, *Moosebreath.*

We're laughing hard and having fun until we hear the scrape of the metal chairs. Wilson sits up and straps on his brace. I yank on my socks and stuff my feet back inside my loafers, too. We both know it's time to stop without saying a word. We're twelve, the last year before we're teens, like Edna said. What if someone sees us? They might point at us and make fun of worse things than my eye or his foot.

Look at them, they'll whisper. *Still acting like babies.*

Or else: *They're talking. She likes him. He likes her.*

And that's bad because . . . Well, I just don't know why.

CHAPTER 17

BACK IN FOURTH GRADE, MAMI gave me the big talk about love and bodies and babies. She had diagrams and everything. I was horrified, especially at all the body parts inside me that I didn't know about and what they're supposed to do together with someone else's.

"Do I *have* to do that?" I asked. My stomach was heaving.

"No," she said. "But one day, you'll be grown and in love, and it won't seem terrible at all."

One day? When was that?

But here's the thing that drives me nuts about Mami. She didn't say a thing about the stuff I wanted to know about, like holding hands or kissing for the first time or going out and breaking up over and over again the way Michael and Rachel do all the time. Or about liking boys or girls or neither or both. It's like she skipped the most important part of the story and went all scientific with words like *ovum* and *sperm* that made my hair stand on end. Then again, what can Mami possibly know? They did things different way back when she was young. I mean, they had to talk on the phone with people they liked. There was no texting. Awkward.

Anyway, now I'm finding out that "one day" doesn't arrive all at once. It creeps up on you a little bit at a time, like a skilled assassin. You're minding your own business in the school store, and the next day you're staring at somebody's key-lime-pie-crusted lips, wondering if they've kissed anyone.

"What are you looking at?" Wilson asks me. He's been reading aloud our most recent sales figures and sneaking bites of my uneaten pie. I didn't realize I was staring into space again, but my mind has been looping back to what Edna said yesterday. She said I *have* to smooch somebody sometime. But who would that be? And now I wonder if Wilson is on that list of candidates. The whole thought makes me feel like I'm sitting at the highest drop on the Iron Gwazi at Busch Gardens—terrified that I'm about to free-fall but somehow thrilled just the same.

"Me? Nothing!" I slide my chair away from him and scowl for good measure. "And back away from my pie, sir. You had yours already."

"Yeah, but my piece was smaller," he says.

"Tough break." He's sitting close again in a way that makes me jittery, so I take a swipe. "And eat a breath mint, will you?"

He grins and exhales in my direction on purpose. Sometimes he forgets to brush his teeth in the morning, and his mouth smells like a soft-boiled egg. Not now, though. It's just limey and nice.

"You are so gross sometimes, Wilson," I say.

"I try, woadie." He snags another forkful of pie.

I glare at him.

Does anyone want to kiss *me*? Does Wilson?

He better not.

I hate on Edna and her rules all over again.

Mr. Ellis must have sensed that we were slipping into a jumbo-size coma. What did he expect? We're reviewing our quizzes on identifying minerals.

A lot of people got question six wrong. They listed the *characteristics* of minerals, instead of how you *identify* them. But not me. The right answer is *color, luster, streak, hardness, and cleavage*, although I kept my hand down when he asked who knew. Who wants to say *hardness* or *cleavage* with the likes of Jason in the back row? He's obsessed with jokes about people's body parts these days, especially private ones. Last week, he held up two plastic yogurt cups to his chest in the Fab Lab and called it a bra. He got a detention for that.

Anyway, just when I was sure that my brain was fossilizing like one of his displays, Mr. Ellis announced our last unit project. We're going to make toothpaste. I have to admit, the project sounds strangely fun. There's a good payoff, too. When we're done, our entries will get judged by kids from Miss Kirkpatrick's class across the hall. The best and most marketable toothpaste wins a no-homework pass for a week. That would be like getting an entire semester of no homework in Miss Kirkpatrick's class. Her students don't know how lucky they are. She doesn't assign half the work Mr. Ellis does.

I have my hair pulled up and my goggles on securely because Mr. Ellis is serious as a corpse about procedures. No loose hair. No backpacks on the floor. No loud talking in case there's an emergency and he needs to give us directions. Absolutely no touching glass if anything breaks. And we *have* to be neat about all our supplies. "No one likes a messy lab partner," he claims. It's all a little over the top, but at least the goggles are cool. He used some of his supply budget to buy neon colors. Mine are bright orange and they're big enough to fit over my regular glasses so I don't have to work blind.

Wilson lines up the supplies as Lena reads over the directions again.

"OK, where's the sodium bicarbonate?" she asks, looking up from her tablet.

"Here." I reach for the box of baking soda without batting an eye. A lifetime with Roli has taught me the fancy science vocabulary for almost everything.

"Then, I guess this is the calcium carbonate." Wilson grabs the roll of unflavored Tums. "Hey, my mom eats these all the time."

"We need to crush them up and make a pasty mix," Lena says.

Wilson drops the tablets into the mortar and pestle and grinds them down. Then Lena fills her dropper with some water.

That's when Mr. Ellis stops by for what he calls a "spot observation," which means that he's snooping to make sure you're not goofing off or sneak-texting. He's in goggles, too, with his locs tied back like the rest of us. Having him around instantly makes me uncomfortable. Part of it is that some of the girls have a not-so-secret crush, even though that's twisted. He's a teacher. But mostly it's because he likes to grade our lab skills as we're working. He claims he likes to see how we're "problem solving as scientists." Forget about kicking back like you can do in Miss Kirkpatrick's class. When it comes to science labs, he does not play.

He opens his grade book just as we start mixing. Lena adds the water to our powder and stirs.

"Uh-oh," I say, when she shows us the result. Somehow, we've ended up with something that looks milky. Nothing at all like paste.

We stand there thinking for a second, as Wilson records our first results. It's a failure, but Mr. Ellis always says most of science is made up of failed attempts.

"Did you follow the directions?" Mr. Ellis asks.

That's code for "you didn't." So, I turn on the tablet's screen and reread the words. "How much water did you use?" I ask Lena.

"Four milliliters."

"That's the trouble. Four milliliters is way too much," I say. "This says to use four *drops*."

"It does?"

"Good eye, Mercedes," Mr. Ellis says.

I don't look up. I wish he wouldn't mention eyes around me, not ever, even if he's being nice. And I wish he'd call me Merci like regular people. When he uses my whole name, I can practically feel him comparing me to "Rolando."

"We probably want point two five milliliters or even less," Wilson says. He points to the first line near the tip of the dropper.

"Can I crush the powder this time?" I'm a mortar-and-pestle pro thanks to Abuela, who asks me to mash down garlic and spices all the time when her arthritis is acting up. This is much less smelly.

Lena measures out the new drops and adds them in slowly this time. We finally get a pasty mix, so Wilson pulls the food coloring out of the bin for our next step.

"Let's make it red," Wilson says. "We can call it Bleeding Gums and sell it during Halloween or something."

Lena laughs and makes that v-*lah*, v-*lah*, v-*lah* vampire sound. Edna turns from her table, where she's working with Darius and Ana, the two sacrificial lambs for this lab. She looks over just long enough to roll her eyes, like we're annoying her.

Mr. Ellis takes notes. "Innovation . . ." he says.

Wilson squeezes a few drops and starts mixing it with our sample. At first, I'm hopeful, but then we notice that no matter how much dye Wilson adds, the color stays a light pink. Lena purses her lips as Wilson keeps mixing. "It's more like bubble gum than blood," he says.

"On the bright side," I say, "do we really want bleeding gums? I mean, nobody would buy blood-colored toothpaste after October. The seasonal market is a challenge." I turn to Wilson. "Look what happened with those snowflake erasers we got stuck with."

"True," he says. "Plus, blood isn't a good taste on your lips. I got stitches in my bottom lip once." He shows us a small scar. "See?"

Lips? The kind that kiss? I stare down at my hands.

"God, Wilson," I mutter. "No one wants to see you pucker up."

"Huh?" he says.

Mr. Ellis keeps writing. "Bonus point. Good business minds," he says. "But you've got an unfair advantage, don't you? Being in housing and construction makes you something of an earth science expert, right?"

I give him a blank look. Papi and I are most certainly *not* interested in earth science, but it would be super risky to tell Mr. Ellis he's bananas, especially when he has his grade book open.

"What do you mean?" I ask instead.

He looks up at me through his goggles and furrows his eyebrows. "Well, a business like yours pretty much depends on everything you're studying this year. There's gypsum for drywall and plasters, not to mention lawn fertilizer. All the stones for foundations, roadwork, and decorative finishes. The list is endless."

I feel myself blush. Should I have known that? That seems like the kind of thing Roli would know.

Mr. Ellis stands to go but stops to push in his stool. He must be reading my mind. His voice gets quieter as he steps closer. "Been meaning to ask: How's Rolando doing up at school this year? Everything all right for him?"

I shift a little on my feet. I can tell Mr. Ellis isn't asking to be polite. He's asking the way Papi does every time he gets on the phone with Roli. *You all right, hijo? You need anything? They treating you right? Are you meeting people?*

"Good, I guess," I say, and then because it's awkward, I add, "It snowed up there. He sent a picture." I pull out my phone and scroll to the shot. Roli is outside his snowy dorm building. He's in a trapper hat, pajama pants, a sweatshirt, and boots.

Mr. Ellis pauses over the photo, his expression hard to read. Maybe he's trying to imagine Roli in that postcard town, the same way I do sometimes, a place with big columns and lawns that are blanketed in white. "Tell him I said hey. We miss him around the lab."

He adjusts his goggles, casting one last glance at our

stuff. "Good work is going on here," he says, "but watch the clock. There's time management to consider."

Then he swivels his attention to Jason's table, where they are currently flicking toothpaste samples. "Table four, you are confusing me deeply." He says it in a steely voice that makes them quit right away.

For the rest of the hour, the room has a quiet buzz that I like. Lena asks us to try a dark blue color for our paste. Her idea is to add blueberry extract and call it Berry Spacey Plaque Blaster. But after half a tube of blue gel, all we get is a pale color, like the walls of a pool. It must be the white that's keeping the colors pale. So, we have to jot down the results of another attempt and then start all over again, measuring, mixing, and dyeing.

As the clock ticks down, I get nervous. One group after another finishes, and we haven't even gotten to adding the taste yet. "Five minutes and it's a wrap," Mr. Ellis announces. "Start cleaning your stations."

We go at our project like contestants on one of those crazy baking shows that Tía watches. Heads together, we whisper our new ideas, our hands moving quickly to get it all done. I add the final dots of flavor and mix it in, just in time for Lena to walk our creation to the display table, where it will be judged. I look around at the other entries, worried.

"Time's up. All right, researchers," Mr. Ellis says. "Take your seats. Our judges are outside in the hall."

Five kids from Miss Kirkpatrick's class file in holding clipboards. They walk around the table sniffing, sampling a taste if they dare, and rubbing the mix between their fingers to test the texture. I close my eyes and send mental messages, hoping they'll pick ours. It's just stupid toothpaste, but a week without homework would be a dream.

Finally, the judges huddle to make their choice. When they're through, one of the girls whispers the final results to Mr. Ellis, who jots them down in his grade book.

"Runner up is . . . Periodontal Peppermint," he says. "The judges' notes say: 'Good consistency, pleasant appearance, familiar flavoring.'" There's mild applause as Edna leads Darius and Ana to the front of the room. "Two points on your next quiz," Mr. Ellis tells them.

"Merci beaucoup," Edna says bitterly. Second place is the same as failing in her book.

When they're back in their seats, Mr. Ellis clears his throat and pauses to send a look of doom at the kids who are whispering at the back of the room. When they quiet down, he continues.

"And now for the winners of our challenge . . . Citrus Chompers."

"Hey, that's us!" Wilson blurts out.

Mr. Ellis holds up our bright orange paste. "Judges' notes say: 'Smooth consistency, unusual but pleasant flavoring, good color.'"

I won something in science? And more, we even beat Edna's group? Who would believe such a thing? From the shocked look on her face, certainly not Edna. We head to the front of the room to collect our free homework passes. I walk by her slowly so she can soak it all in. *Take that in the kisser, Edna*, I think.

"Good work, team," Mr. Ellis tells us, and for the life of me I can't stop grinning.

CHAPTER 18

IT'S LATE SUNDAY NIGHT, AND I text Roli:

> Happy Periodic Table Day!

I don't want him to think we forgot since it's something of a high holy day for him. When he lived at home, he'd wear his favorite T-shirt—the one with the table of ele ments—under his uniform and challenge us to quiz him. He never got any wrong. I can still hear him calling out his answers. "Actinium, atomic number eighty-nine! Gadolinium, atomic number sixty-four!"

There wasn't any quizzing at Abuela's table tonight. There was nothing fun at all. Simón stayed for dinner, for one thing. Then he sat next to Tía on the porch swing soaking up all her attention while the twins showed off for them in the yard, performing like circus animals in the grapefruit tree. They aren't used to having Simón in the audience, so they had lots of extra energy.

"Go play inside for a little while," Tía finally told them.

That's when they came in and started bopping me with those silly boxing gloves she bought them, no matter how many times I told them to stop. Of course, Abuela wouldn't let me "interrupt" Tía to tell on them.

"Por Dios, niña, she's busy," she whispered, like I was going to be interrupting a surgery or something. I can't see how sitting on a swing with somebody is more important that being pummeled to death, but Abuela wasn't budging.

Finally, the twins started a new puzzle with Lolo. Then I pricked those inflatable horrors with one of Abuela's straight pins and left so I wouldn't be there when they discovered the carcasses.

My phone buzzes. Roli texts back a smiling scientist emoji but nothing else. I wanted to tell Roli about winning the toothpaste challenge this week, especially since Lolo didn't seem that interested when I tried to explain it to him. Also, I want to know if he's had any more snow, maybe tell him about Tía and Simón and see what he thinks.

> You busy?

But he doesn't answer so I lie back in bed, restless.

The whole house is quiet except for Tuerto, who's skulking around after the lizard he's trapped inside. Though it's dodging under furniture, it's facing certain doom. It's amazing how good a hunter Tuerto is, even with one eye.

I look over to my favorite poster of Jake Rodrigo. It's life-size and hangs on the back of the closet door, so I can see it from wherever I am. His burly arms are folded over his chest as he looks out bravely into the galaxy somewhere. No matter where I walk, his eyes are on me, like an intergalactic male Mona Lisa.

I love Jake Rodrigo. I know he's not real, but I can't help but wish he were. Not real like a regular seventh-grade boy, of course. Jake Rodrigo wouldn't mind my eye or that I don't know how to dance or kiss or anything.

I slip out of bed and walk over to the poster, staring into those dreamy reptilian eyes. What if one day he were real? Would *he* want to kiss me?

Yes, I decide. He would.

I step closer and lean in. When I'm only an inch away from his face, I close my eyes and plant the softest kiss I can on his poster mouth.

Flat.

Paper.

Weird.

And still my heart is racing.

CHAPTER 19

TÍA ASKED ME TO HELP her during the after-school dance program she teaches. She wants me to rein in Tomás and Axel "in case they get out of hand." *In case* were her words. I would have chosen *when*.

Anyway, she's been in a good mood lately, even yesterday when she had to switch her schedule to take Lolo in for chest X-rays. I guess all that thinking about Simón has her floating around.

Annoying.

We walk into the front hallway of the Second Avenue Church of Christ community center. It's an old building that's attached to the church next door. Tía is wearing her yoga pants and tan Zumba shoes, all ready to teach her "dancers," which I have to say is a pretty generous way of describing this crew. None of these kids looks like a dancer, at least not like the girls at Seaward who take studio classes. Those girls carry monogrammed duffel bags with satin pointe shoes inside. Tía's kids, on the other hand, are in jeans and socks. Mostly, they look like they just walked off the playground.

Lou Luchazo, who runs the place, stops us in the hallway. He looks grim.

"Can I see you in my office, Miss Inés?" he says. "We have to talk."

Tía and I exchange looks. We've never much liked Lou. For a church guy, he's kind of creepy. He's always smoothing down his thin mustache as he thinks. Plus, he also checks Tía out when he thinks no one is watching, which she hates. So, she takes my hand and pulls me into his office with her. It's cluttered, but we find two folding chairs and take a seat.

That's when he gives us the ax. He tells us the after-school center is closing. Turns out, the church doesn't have enough people to stay open as a congregation anymore, so they're going to sell this building and merge with another church down the road in Greenacres. That means no more community center—and no more dance classes for Tía.

"You mean, I'm out?" Tía asks.

"I know it's a shock," Lou says. "But we've got to vacate in a month. There's nothing I can do."

Tía looks like she's been mugged in broad daylight. Her eyes slide to the opening that leads to the gym, where the kids are already waiting for her. A few boys are playing HORSE under the net. The girl I saw a while back at the park is eating chips in the corner, right under the NO FOOD OR DRINK sign. Two girls are digging like badgers through the bin to borrow a pair of dance shoes, the ones Ballet Palm Beach sends over if they're still in good shape. Tomás and Axel are inside a crate playing Pop Goes the Weasel and laughing hysterically.

"And what happens to all these little ones?" Tía asks Lou. "What are they going to do after school now?"

Lou rubs the back of his neck. "I know it's hard, Inés. But the board has no option right now. We have to close. Their parents can hire a babysitter or something."

"You know they can't afford that," she says.

"Lo siento. They'll have to figure something out." He hands over a stack of papers. "Here are the notes that should go home today," he says. "At least you can say goodbye in person."

Tía stands up and walks out without a word.

Aurelia, the so-called receptionist, takes this as her cue. She's been sitting red-eyed at her desk, listening to every word, too upset to fix the chips in her nail polish the way she usually does when she's here. I guess she's also gotten her pink slip.

"¿Y qué me hago ahora?" she whispers as we go by. "I have rent to pay, too."

"Something will come up for you, Aurelia," Tía tells her gently. "Don't worry."

I look around. They're both acting like it's a tragedy, but is it really? I mean, this will give Tía more time at home, won't it? With the twins who supposedly do not drive her crazy. Besides, it's not like this place is deluxe. The rugs in the hall smell a little moldy. The game room is too small, with only a few tabletop games, like chess for the quiet people, and a pool table, with strict no-gambling policies enforced. There's only one screen for video games, so you have to be lucky enough to get here early. A couple of volunteers from Palm Beach State College help people with homework in an office at the end of the hall. And then there's Tía's domain: a sagging stage on one side of the gym.

Still, Tía looks pretty sad. She takes a deep breath and marches over to the doorway.

"Where are my dancers?" she says in a firm voice, like it's any other day. "Onstage for warm-ups, please!"

I take a seat on a dented folding chair at the far end and

watch as she corrals everyone into a circle for stretches. She leads them through ankle rolls and toe touches, and in between she asks how it's going in school and such. Axel and Tomás are a little too young for the group—you're supposed to be eight—but it turns out they're Romeos for the older girls, especially the one who shares her Doritos.

Tía plugs her music player into a speaker and tells them to get into position. The merengue music starts, and Tía claps the rhythm. "Five, six, seven, eight . . ."

I watch for a second before I start practicing my lay-ups. I've seen these dances my whole life at birthdays and Nochebuena parties. But it's not like any of it is going to help me at the Heart Ball. We have a few Latinx kids in each grade, but not enough that anybody's going to break out in a merengue in front of the whole school.

When the hour is finally up, Tía sits the kids in a circle again. I hear the rise and fall of her voice as I aim and shoot, the ball echoing against the loose backboard now that the music is off. I try to keep my eyes on what I'm doing, but when I get the rebound and dribble, I hear my name.

"Merci, please," she calls out.

I can see from their faces that she's telling them about the closing.

So, I stop making noise like she wants and her words fill the room. She tells them that she'll miss them, that they need to listen to their teacher at school, that they should keep busy with things that are fun. She stops to take a breath, and I can see that her eyes are watery. I've always known she loves dancing, but it's only now that I realize that she cares about these kids, who I don't know at all. Standing there, basketball tucked under my arm, I feel bad for wanting her home and to myself.

When they finally stand, there's a lot of hugging. I guess nobody minds that this place isn't nice, maybe the way I don't mind that Las Casitas isn't one of those houses near the water that some kids at school have.

The girl who was eating her chips hangs on to Tía's waist the longest.

"I'll see you around, Stela," Tía tells her. "Come visit me at the bakery, and I'll get you a free cookie."

Stela gives her one more squeeze before racing out the door.

Tía packs up her music slowly. She drops off her clipboard with Aurelia and tosses Lou a cold look on her way out.

"Tell your board that the neighborhood kids are going to miss this place."

The ride home is quiet except for the beep of Tía's horn as we drive past the kids walking home along the sidewalk. Even the twins are silent as they turn to watch them get smaller behind us.

Tía has gone mute. She almost misses the turn for home, and when we pull in, she stays in the car for a long while by herself.

I come back to check on her.

"Don't worry, Tía," I say. "Maybe Lou is right. Their parents will find other stuff for them to do."

She nods slowly. "It's just that I'm going to miss teaching them, too," she says quietly. "I hate to give it up."

We walk back to the house together.

One thing is for sure. Tía is not the giving-up type, just like Papi isn't.

The question is, what is she planning to do?

CHAPTER 20

IT MUST BE TRAUMATIZE A STUDENT DAY because I'm assigned Edna as a lab partner in Mr. Ellis's class. And, with only one day to go before the dance, she's especially tense. Only Wilson has it worse. His partner is Jason.

Edna brings her stuff over and slides into the seat beside me with a puss on her face, as if I smell like a dead fish. I think she's still sore about the toothpaste victory. Well, good. I put my free homework pass on the corner of my desk where both she and Mr. Ellis can see it when he collects our assignments.

Today we're working on geodes, which are basically rocks with a big surprise inside. Mr. Ellis brought us samples to look at. My favorite is the amethyst geode.

Outside, it's an ugly round rock, like any one you'd see in your yard. But when he held it open for us, amethyst crystals glittered inside like little purple ice chips. That's the beauty of geodes, according to Mr. Ellis. They're a surprise from nature.

A geode sort of reminds me of what Lolo used to say about people. That we all hold surprises. Like the quiet man at El Caribe who kept to himself at a booth for a whole year. Tía and the other waitresses used to make up stories about him—wondering if he was a fugitive on the run. It was Lolo who found out the truth with his bad jokes and some shared batidos de mamey. Turns out, the man's name was Jacinto, a botanist from Venezuela who missed everyone he had left back home. He liked plants more than people, he said.

Anyway, we're making our own eggshell geodes with Mr. Ellis today. Or at least starting them. They won't be ready until tomorrow.

"You get our supplies. I'll read the directions," Edna says, not even asking if maybe *I* want to call the shots this time.

But whatever. At least I can walk away from her for a couple of minutes.

I gather everything and come back slowly with the

tray that includes two raw eggs, a beaker of water, food coloring, glue, paintbrushes, thumbtacks, and a powder called alum.

Normally, I would think this lab would be fun, since it's almost like art. But it's hard to work with someone who's bothering you.

"Don't forget that you have to be at the dance half an hour early."

"I know."

"And we have two prices. Regular photos and the photos that you're going to edit. Don't mess that up."

"I won't."

"And you have to look professional—"

"Edna." I swear, she's zapping the life force out of me. "The lab." I put on my latex gloves and goggles.

She puts on her gear and reads the directions. "Step one is to empty the inside of the egg," she says. "Make a hole in the shell with one of the tacks."

She glances at me and smirks. "No offense, but hasn't anybody told you that you look ridiculous? How can you even work with goggles on top of your glasses?"

I look across the room at Hannah and Lena, who are happily working together. "Somehow I manage," I say. "How big a hole?"

"Small."

She starts to work at the shell, but she's trying to tap it in like hammer.

"Maybe wiggle the tack in, like a drill," I tell her. "It won't break that way."

"I'm giving the directions today," she snaps. "And I know what I'm doing. I have a 103 average in this class, for your information."

"Suit yourself, then," I say, secretly hoping her egg smashes to bits.

I press my tack in gently and then let the egg white and yolk drip out of my shell. It's sad to think this could have been a fluffy chick like the ones Lolo used to take us to see in Loxahatchee at the poultry swap.

"Mr. Ellis, should we be fooling with raw eggs? Salmonella is a risk, you know," Edna says. "It causes over 450 deaths in the US every year."

Mr. Ellis walks over to our table. "That's correct. But we're using approved sanitary handling precautions as described in the directions," he tells her.

Edna is still working on emptying her egg, but I'm done, so I move on to the next step, which is to cut the shell in half. She tries to catch up, and I guess she's not careful because that's when my evil wish comes true. The shell collapses into pieces, yolk dripping through her fingers.

She looks at me, murderous.

"You brought me a cracked egg, Merci," she says, flushed. She eyes Mr. Ellis's grade book.

"For the record," I say. "The egg was *not* cracked. I told you to drill it gently."

"Which I did!"

"There are more in the back," Mr. Ellis tells her. "It's not a problem."

"Get me another one," Edna orders.

I don't move.

Mr. Ellis looks at me, his expression hard to read. He's not one for allowing beefs in his class or any other "distractions." But am I supposed to get bossed around like this? My hands are shaking, and my eye starts to drift. Part of me wants to yell. But instead, all I can manage is one word.

"No."

"You're the supply person, Merci," Edna says.

"I *did* get the supplies," I say. "You can get a replacement. They're in the green basket."

Then I pretend to be fascinated by the next step in the directions.

Edna stalks off as I pierce the empty shell as gently as I can with the point of my scissors. I cut slowly so the whole thing doesn't shatter in my hand. Everything feels so fragile.

My stomach is fluttering with nerves as I read the next step: *Brush the inside of the shell and along the edges with white glue.*

"Aren't you going to wait for your partner to catch up?" Mr. Ellis asks.

Partner? Edna? Please. I glance at the clock. Time is running out. Still, I know he's big on working together.

"Fine," I say. "I'll wait for Her Highness to come back."

His eyebrows shoot up, but by then Edna is heading toward us.

"I'll leave you two to finish up," he says. "You can manage that, correct?"

We both nod.

This time, Edna wiggles the tack like I suggested, and I wait for her to wipe out the inside. When she's ready, we brush on the glue and dip the shells in a bit of alum powder.

"The last part is adding thirty drops of food coloring," Edna says.

I reach for the blue tube.

"This color will be nicer," Edna says, handing me the red.

"But I want blue," I tell her. "It's my favorite."

We face each other, seething, and hoping Mr. Ellis doesn't notice. I wish this period could be over so I won't have to work with her anymore. I have a good mind to quit as her photographer for the Heart Ball, too. Maybe *that* would teach her not to be such a brat.

"Where are you going?" Edna whispers when I get up.

"To boil more water," I say. "I want my own beaker."

"Sit down. The directions say we have *one* beaker of water. Can't you read?"

That does it.

"Yes, I can read," I say. "And I can also see that you're being impossible to work with, same as always."

She blinks a couple of times. It's like I've hit her. "I'm *not* getting a bad grade because of you," she hisses.

"When exactly do you get a bad grade, Edna? You said so yourself. You have an A-plus in here. A perfect grade for a perfect pain in the neck."

For a second it almost looks like she's going to cry, and I wonder what I've said that's so bad. But I don't wait for her to answer. I get another beaker and measure out the thirty drops of coloring until the water is the color of my best jeans. We each plunk our shells inside our beakers and push them down gently with our brushes.

Hannah and Lena are already putting their orange geodes-in-progress on the shelf when Edna and I bring our blue and red ones over. They've had such a good time; they don't even notice that Edna and I are staring hate darts at each other.

"Do you want me to come over right after school to get ready for the dance tomorrow?" Hannah asks me. "My mom wanted to know. She's going to call your mom about it. You know how she is."

"Oh, me too. It might be easier for me to ride home with you instead of going all the way home and back again," Lena says. She lives the farthest.

"Sure," I say, as my heartbeat slows down. "You can both come. We'll order pizza for dinner before we go."

Edna watches us like a girl trying to step into her turn at jump rope.

But she doesn't jump in, not even to be mean. Instead, she puts down her beaker and stalks off to gather her books and wait for the bell.

The next day, the whole school is buzzing about the Heart Ball. Edna gets a pass from Miss McDaniels excusing her from science so she can get down to the gym early for the preparations. Mr. Ellis doesn't like kids excused from his class, but I say good riddance. She's even bossier today than she was yesterday.

Anyway, the fun part is that our class's eggshells have

transformed into beautiful jewels, as if by magic. We *ooh* and *aah* as we fish them out of the solution with a mini strainer and lay them on paper towels to dry. Since Edna's not here, Mr. Ellis tells me to pull her geode and label it for her. I scoop it out of the red solution and lay it on a paper towel with her name on it. I have to admit, it's really pretty, almost like a tiny bowl of rubies. It's hard to think of something so beautiful coming from Edna. It's a surprise, a little wonder, like Lolo says, right in front of my eyes.

CHAPTER 21

HANNAH, LENA, AND I ARE locked in my bedroom getting ready for the Heart Ball with my box of Valentine's Day chocolates open on my bed. I've been nervous eating all afternoon, so we're down to cherry cordials and maple clusters, both of which I hate. Hannah has been following directions from a YouTube site on my laptop as she does my hair. A girl called Essence of Zoe demonstrates step-by-step how to make something called double buns. I'm not so sure about this. When I hear the word *buns*, I think bread or butts. What would any of that be doing on my head? But Hannah is sort of possessed. She's parted my hair down the middle and gathered each side of my curls into gigantic poufs.

"Ouch," I say as another hairpin scrapes my scalp. "You trying to draw blood?"

"Sorry, but your hair is thick. We need extra pins to keep it in place." She fishes around in the supplies that we borrowed from Tía when we got home. I still feel a little bad that I told Tía she couldn't help us get ready, although I *am* wearing the outfit she bought me at the Red Umbrella. Besides, she had a head full of hot rollers, waiting to get ready for her date later tonight.

"Are you sure about this?" I ask Hannah, reaching up to feel what's happening on my head.

She swats my hand away. "Hold still or you'll ruin it. This is the last part." She dabs glitter hair gel on a toothbrush and smooths down the edges around my face.

"That thing isn't used, is it?"

She ignores me and stands back to admire her work. "What do you think, Lena?" she asks.

Lena puts down the book she's been reading on Roli's bed. She doesn't have to worry about hair, of course. Her purple spikes are shellacked to perfection as always. "Nailed it!" she sings out dramatically.

I walk over to the mirror to see. Two perfectly symmetrical balls of hair are sitting on either side of my part. I swivel my head slowly to one side, afraid to make any sudden moves.

"Relax your head," Hannah says. "You're holding it a little funny."

"But it feels like I have water balloons attached to me."

Papi beeps the horn from the driveway to let us know it's time to go. He's vacuumed Mami's car and put in an air freshener for the occasion.

"We better hurry," Lena says. She's dressed in a flowing purple top and matching leggings. The better to move in, she told us, since she plans to try out what she calls "interpretive dance motion" that she's been studying on the Internet. "Ready?" she asks.

"Ready," I say, even though I'm not so sure. After this silly dance is all over, I'm going to make popcorn and watch *Iguanador Nation Rises* again, even though I've seen it. Maybe it will erase the memory of all this.

I glance over to Tía's house as we start to file out. I think of those high heels with bows and the sparkly dress I saw hanging on her closet door. I pull out my phone and text her.

Have fun.

Then I stuff one last chocolate into my mouth and switch off the light.

Papi drops us off near the propped-open gym doors. The dance committee and volunteers are still working. Mr. Vong, on overtime, already looks fed up.

To my surprise, Wilson is already here. The dance isn't for another hour, but he's helping Miss McDaniels blow up balloons. I almost don't recognize him. He must have gotten a haircut after school, and he's wearing a collared shirt, like the dance dress code requires for guys. He's got on nice kicks, too, instead of the brown or black loafers we always have to wear to school. They're Sk8-Hi Zips that come up on his ankles.

He's bent over to unpack the cartons of metallic balloon shells and ribbons. One box is already open. They have swirly words on them. *Be mine! Love is in the Air. Amor.*

"I didn't know you were coming," I say.

He looks up, startled. "Merci?" he says.

Oh geez. He's gawking at my head and then at my clothes. I pull at the waistband of my jeans nervously, already aching for my running shorts.

Miss McDaniels cuts the last of the ribbons and sees me, too.

"Oh, hello, Merci. Don't you look lovely!" She turns to him. "I'll leave you to inflate the rest of these, Wilson. Remember, no one handles the tank but you. No one uses the gas to get chipmunk voices, understood? If so, there will be a non-negotiable detention in your future."

"Yes, ma'am."

"Not to mention brain damage," I add.

Wilson's laugh withers under Miss McDaniels's sharp look. He quickly fits the first balloon on the nozzle and inflates it with a loud *pfffft*.

Michael and Jason come in hauling a big table between them that they set down near the doors.

"What are you two doing?" Edna's bossy voice is unmistakable. "Not there!"

"You said 'put the table by the doors,'" Jason tells her. "These are doors."

"The refreshments go near the *locker room* doors on the other side! Are you not following the floor layout I made for you?" She shakes her map in their direction, disgusted, and motions to the far end of the gym. "That way."

I can't help but stare at her as she stomps off. She looks tall in her platform sandals, and she's wearing makeup that makes her look older, too. Suddenly I want to know what happens to lipstick like hers when you kiss somebody. Does it smear all over the person's face?

Looking around, I have to admit that Edna has done a pretty good job in here. The gym has transformed. All the basketball hoops are folded up and the stands are pushed back. There are streamers and giant hearts stuck along the walls—the hearts Hannah and Edna were making in the lab.

Hannah walks over. "Your camera stuff is over there, Merci." She points at two black duffel bags propped up in the hall near the gym doors. Lena has already unzipped one and is unfolding the stand for the background.

The three of us set up the photo booth pretty quickly. It looks like Dr. Santos hasn't even used it. Is this what happens when rich people win stuff? Do they just keep it for show like those fancy satin-trimmed towels in Abuela's bathroom that we're forbidden from ever using? The hardware pipes are still inside the plastic bags, so I tear it all open and get busy. When I've got it set up, I test everything and take a few shots of Lena and Hannah to post samples.

"Check this out!" I upload the photo and put angel wings on Lena and Hannah.

"Oh, send it to me," Hannah says, grabbing for her phone.

Wilson stops making balloon bouquets and comes over to see what we're doing.

"Hey, I want a picture, too," he says in a cartoon chipmunk voice.

"Are you taking a break already?" Lena asks, laughing. "Don't let Edna see you."

I sniff the air. "Is that aftershave, Wilson?" I ask him.

"What? *No*," he says, still sounding like Alvin the

chipmunk. But it is. Roli wears the same kind. Axe.

"Stand over there," I say, "and make sure you can see yourself on the screen. Hold a pose."

He takes a wide stance and crosses his arms across his chest. The camera snaps and I download the picture. He comes to peer over my shoulder as I try to decide what to do to the shot.

"Make me Jake Rodrigo," he says.

"Sir," I say stiffly. "There is only one Jake Rodrigo." Instead, I click on the paintbrush icon and draw earbuds and wires snaking to a music player in his pocket. He looks cute, I have to admit it.

"You're a good artist," he says. "Now, do one of yourself."

"No way. I absolutely hate being in pictures."

Lena gives me a look. "Come on, Merci. It's fun."

"Yeah. Show off your beautiful buns!" Hannah says.

"Huh?" Wilson says.

"She means *these*," I say pointing at my head.

"Buns, buns, buns," Hannah says in a whispered cheer.

"One shot and then you all will leave me alone?" I ask.

"Deal," Lena says.

I show Wilson how to set up the timer and then I stand in the frame. I'm careful not to stare at the lens so that my eye doesn't stray.

I wait for the snap and then go look at the girl in the

photo. When I see the picture, I'm a little surprised. She's not really me somehow. She looks older and fancier than the real Merci.

I think about how to fix the shot. With a few adjustments, I draw Minnie Mouse's polka-dot dress and a bow on my head. I add big gloved hands, too. Then I post it on the gallery slideshow that's running on the laptop.

"Dead ringer, right?" I say. Better to make fun of myself before somebody else does.

Wilson is quiet for a second. "You look nice in that picture, Merci," he says.

Lena and Hannah exchange looks, and there's a weird silence.

"I mean, for a life-size rodent and everything," he adds quickly.

I stand there blinking as Wilson's cheeks start to flame. Did he say I look nice? Or did he say I look like a rodent? I can't decide.

"Funny," I say, and punch him a little harder than I should.

Just then, Edna's voice pierces the air again. She's marching toward Wilson, fire in her eyes.

"Where are the red balloons for the food table? It's in the plan! We have five minutes until the doors open, people, and there are no balloons at the table!"

For the first time ever, Wilson looks happy to see her. "Coming right up, Edna!" he says, still rubbing his arm. "I'll be back to help later," he says. "If you don't hit me." And then he's off, limping a little, the way he does when he's trying to move faster than usual.

I glance at the picture of me, the one before I turned into Minnie Mouse. I look a little like Tía did when she was about my age. I know because there's a photo of her and Lolo hanging in the hallway of Lolo and Abuela's house, right next to the photo of Mami and Papi at their wedding. She's fifteen, just three years older than me now, celebrating her quinceañera. She's wearing a blue dress with skinny straps, the one Abuela made special for that day. In the photo, Lolo holds Tía's hand to his lips as he asks her to dance. His eyes are shiny with tears, even though he's smiling.

I glance up and catch Wilson looking my way. He turns, but not before my stomach flutters a little. It must be the pound of chocolate I've eaten today.

I try to burp, just in case, and start getting ready for my customers.

CHAPTER 22

FOR THE REST OF THE night, I'm slammed. The IMA Paparazzi photo booth is so hot that the line snakes down the hall almost the whole night. People can get a plain selfie photo or sign up for an edited version by me. Almost everybody wants an edited one, even Edna, believe it or not. The list is four pages long and our money box is stuffed.

"Too bad I don't own an IMA Paparazzi. I'd make a fortune," I say as the line finally peters out. My buns have sagged to either side of my head, so I yank out the hairpins and let my hair fall loose and big, the way I like. I rub my scalp and sit down on the stool. Hannah and Wilson, who took picture orders, start packing up.

Wilson shakes his head. "We should have asked for a cut of these sales, too."

"Ruthless," I say. "I like it."

"I really do appreciate it, Merci," Hannah says. "You saved the day!" She checks her phone. "There's only ten minutes before the dance is over. You guys want a drink?" she asks. "There might be something left in the gym."

"I'm in," says Wilson.

"Breach of contract," I tell her. "You said I didn't have to go inside, remember?"

Hannah sighs. "OK. You put the stuff away, and we'll get the sodas."

They disappear through the gym doors.

I don't pack up right away. Instead, I check my phone. I have two messages.

One is from Mami:

> Having fun?

I don't reply. She'll have plenty of time to grill me later on the ride home.

The other one is earlier, from Tía. It's a picture of her in her bedroom.

> How do I look?

Her hair is piled high and she's wearing those high-heeled shoes with the bows. It's like she's not Tía anymore, like she's not the person I know at all. I should have said bye to her before I left for the dance, maybe thanked her for letting us use her hair things. But looking at the picture makes me feel queasy all over again.

I pocket my phone, suddenly parched and wondering what is taking so long.

I decide to peek inside the gym to see if I can spot Hannah or Wilson. I cup my hands near my eyes at the window to see better. Some of the streamers and hearts have come loose from the walls, and a few of the balloons that Wilson inflated are bobbing against the ceiling, searching for an escape.

Love. Be Mine. Amor.

The DJ is set up near the wrestling mats. He's dressed all in black and sports a huge pair of headphones that he has pressed to one side of his head as he fidgets with knobs and keys. Wilson has ditched his soda errand, lured by all the equipment.

Nobody's dancing, I notice, except a few boys who are flossing with Jason to be funny. Geez. Somebody should have told me that nobody really dances at a dance. They could have called this whole thing a hangout. Then I might have wanted to come.

Suddenly the gym door opens, nearly knocking me to the ground.

"Oh, sorry!" a boy says. It's Brent, the eighth-grade boy Edna likes. He's with a girl named Madison. They push past me and race toward the lobby doors that lead outside. I know there's a spot where older kids go when the chaperones aren't looking. Are they heading there?

Just before the door closes again, I poke my head inside to see if I can spot Hannah. She's not anywhere near the refreshments table, either. Maybe she got sidetracked like Wilson, or else maybe Edna has got her on some other forced-labor assignment. If I want a drink or something to eat, it looks like I'll have to get it myself.

I step inside the darkness. The air feels stifling in here, the way it does when we have a pep rally. *Make it quick*, I tell myself, ducking my head and trying to move like a ninja.

There's not much to choose from at the refreshments table, unfortunately. It's like vultures have been feeding. The only things left are a few broken crackers and those pepper cheese cubes that no one really likes. Still, I'm thirsty and my stomach rumbles. So, I tuck what I can inside a napkin, and then I stick my arm into the bin of melted ice to pull out the last ginger ale.

I'm starting to make my escape, undetected, when a loud voice booms across the room.

"Last dance of the night, Rams!" the DJ suddenly

announces. He bobs his head as a new song slides over the last one. The beat is loud enough that I feel it through my shoes. It's "Dale Fuerte," which dropped a couple of weeks ago and is already everybody's favorite. Girls sing it in the locker room all the time, trying to show off who knows all the words. A lot of the lyrics are in Spanish. It's a song about nice booties and other things that make Abuela complain about "modern-day morals" every time it plays on Tía's radio.

Looking around, it's a little weird to see kids who don't speak Spanish (except when they're in Señora Greene's class) making up gibberish and singing *dale, dale fuerte* in the right places. Even worse than listening to the white girls in homeroom say *Waddup*.

A few kids rush past me to the middle of the gym, though, excited. When they get there, they stare at one another for a second, trying to see who's going to make the first move. Nobody does. All that energy is rising and rising with nowhere to go, like one of the balloons trapped in the rafters.

But then a few girls start dancing in a group. Soon a few other kids get brave and join in until a lot of them are doing steps from the video that I wasn't supposed to watch. I see Michael and Rachel dancing. Lena is dancing with Darius, of all people, doing her spacey movements, a mix of what looks like hip-hop and belly dancing.

That's when I notice Wilson bobbing his head to the beat, too. My heart starts to race.

He dances?

Why does this surprise me?

I'm practically frozen in place, clutching sweaty cheese chunks to my chest. Everything gets all jumbled up inside me. Part of me also wants to move, maybe even dance, but I can't stop feeling ridiculous. It's my hair and makeup, these clothes. My eye is turning, and I'm sweating right down to my underwear.

Suddenly Wilson looks up and sees me from way across the room.

Gah! Is he going to ask me to dance? No. Please. I will die. I don't wait to find out. I toss my cheese cubes in the nearest trash can and do the only thing I can think of—run.

Luckily, the song is ending quickly, and all at once the lights come up. Everyone blinks into the glare, like burglars caught mid-heist. There's a loud groan as Miss McDaniels takes the squeaky microphone to bring us in for the crash landing.

"Thank you for coming, students. Please walk like ladies and gentlemen to the front exits, where you may line up for car loop pickup," she announces. "Manners, please. No pushing."

"Merci!" Wilson calls from somewhere behind me.

But I don't turn. I want to get out of here.

People are already crowding the doors like a mob, though, even as chaperones try to get us to make a line. It's no use with everyone giddy and pushing.

Finally, I squeeze through the doors and see the photo booth. That's where I should be, safely behind the camera, watching people, catching moments.

All the equipment is just where I left it, but I suddenly realize that a herd of kids is heading toward it. I left it there, out in the open, and now people start walking by too close. Shoulders are knocking into the stand, making it wobble each time.

"Hey, careful with that stuff!" I try to barrel through the bodies like a linebacker to reach the IMA Paparazzi before it's too late. But the kids are too jacked up on soda and music to listen. They're rushing toward the exits that lead to the parking lot.

"Stop!" I shout again as the stand gets jostled even more.

By now, Wilson has seen what's happening, and he's also trying to get to the photo booth. We're grabbing at people, trying to pull them away, when the worst finally happens. Somebody's shoulder catches the stand. It wobbles once, twice, three times, and then, as if in painful slow motion before our eyes, the brand-new IMA Paparazzi crashes to the ground like a felled tree.

Banged free from its grips, the LED light head spins away on the floor under everyone's feet.

"Get that!" I shout.

Wilson and I fall to our knees, trying to reach it as people step on our hands. Finally, I manage to snatch it from under somebody's platform shoe, and hug it to my chest. Wilson pulls me out of the crowd, and we huddle near the wall. My face is bathed in sweat. He's got a gray sneaker tread on the sleeve of his new shirt.

At first, I don't dare look at the screen. I won't let him, either.

"We have to," he says.

Wilson's eyes are saucers as he pulls it away to see. That's how I know that it's worse than bad. The LED light is dead, and the iPad screen is cracked into a thousand jigsaw pieces. Wilson blurts out a dirty word when he sees the mangled mess.

In a blind panic, I grab it from him and rush over to where I left the carrying cases. I shove the broken equipment inside and zip the case closed.

"Merci, what are you doing?" Wilson says. "You can't—"

"Quiet," I hiss.

Then I grab the stand, fold up the legs, and slide it into its bag. My heart pounds in my ears as I stare at the storage cases, praying that the broken light and iPad fix themselves by magic, pretending as hard as I can that I put everything away like I was supposed to, that the crowd didn't happen, that nothing got smashed, that Wilson isn't looking at me like I'm a criminal.

"You all done?" someone asks.

We turn to find Hannah. She's holding a can of soda in each hand and offers me one.

Beads of sweat have formed along my forehead, and my eye has tugged to its farthest reaches. *Tell her what happened*, a voice inside my head says. *Explain.*

But my mouth won't move.

"Are you OK, Merci?" Hannah asks.

Wilson's eyes dart from me to her, waiting.

"I'm just tired," I mumble. I hold my breath, praying that Wilson will keep his mouth shut. He does.

"You should go, then. I'll finish cleaning up," Hannah says.

"No," Wilson yelps. He gives me a pointed look. *Tell her*, his eyes seem to say.

I open my mouth to try again, but that's when I see

Edna and Miss McDaniels walking toward us. My stomach turns to lead all over again.

"I'll see you on Tuesday," I blurt out. And then, before Wilson can argue, I race toward the car loop, where Mami is already waiting.

"How was the dance?" she asks when I jump in. "Did you have fun?"

I don't look at her. "Not now, Mami," I say, slumping down.

"It's just a question, Merci." She sighs and gives me a fed-up look before pulling out.

Wilson steps through the school doors just as we drive away.

I lean my head back and shut my eyes on the world. The IMA Paparazzi is dead.

And now, so am I.

CHAPTER 23

WILSON HAS TEXTED ME TWICE, but I won't answer. He just needs to keep his mouth shut until I can think of what to do. The trouble is, there's no one who can help me. Roli's at school. And where is Tía in my hour of need? Still out dancing.

It's 3:09 a.m. I wish I had some Abre Camino right now: bath salts, floor cleaner, a candle—anything. But I don't, and every time I close my eyes, I imagine Edna screaming at me about what happened to her dad's equipment. It's all on disaster replay in my brain.

You did this on purpose! Who's going to pay for this? How could I have trusted you, Merci Suárez?

It was an accident, but even if I try to apologize now,

it won't change the fact that I hid the damage. Edna will tell on me, and Miss McDaniels will definitely call Mami and Papi.

And then I'm deader than dead.

This is worse than when I broke Abuela's favorite figurine on her coffee table and tried to stick the head back on with some of Papi's Gorilla Glue. Only this isn't something from the Dollar Store that I can pay for with my own money. I googled the price of fixing a broken IMA Paparazzi with eight different electronics shops as far away as Fort Lauderdale. Even if it's just the screen, it will cost me at least $300 to have it fixed. If I have to replace the whole thing, $2,000. That's what Papi gets paid for painting a whole house!

I'm still tossing and turning a little while later when I hear a car come up our shared driveway, the headlights dimmed to keep from shining in our bedrooms. Maybe it's an assassin here to slit our throats in our sleep if we've left a door unlocked, the way Abuela is always fearing. Even that grisly idea seems easier than having to tell Mami and Papi what I did.

I throw my legs over the side of my bed and tiptoe across the tile floor to the window to check. It's Tía getting back from her date with Simón. Thanks to the lights on Tía's porch, I can see their outlines inside the car.

I want to run out to Tía and tell her what happened, ask her what I should do.

But then I see that they're sitting close in a way that says *Stay away*. I know that if Roli were here, he'd throw a pillow at me and tell me to stop being nosy. He'd make me get back to bed. But he's not here, so I stay put, wishing I could run to Tía and tell her everything.

After a few minutes, though, Simón leans over and pulls her close. My heart starts to race as they kiss. It's not the peck on the cheeks he gives her when he and Vicente come for dinner and we're all standing around watching. This one is a big smacker right on the lips, and it lasts for a long time.

I can't look away.

Is it scary or nice or what? Does it feel squishy, like Edna described? Can you breathe when you kiss? Do you get dizzy from moving your head like that? Do your teeth bang into the other person's?

How are you supposed to know these things?

Tía opens the car door after what feels like forever. I step into the shadows and watch her from a little corner in the blinds. Simón waits for her to get inside. When he starts up the car, I lean back and watch him go as his headlights bathe my room in light.

I crawl back to bed in misery.

Tuerto, who's been licking his paws, pins me with his glowing nighttime glare and yowls. *Pathetic,* he seems to say as he slinks away. I drop back under the covers, ashamed, and try to sleep again.

CHAPTER 24

I PROP UP MY PHONE against my pillow as soon as the sun rises and dial Roli for a video chat. He doesn't pick up at first, but I keep hanging up and calling back. Finally, on the eighth try, he answers. He's in bed and looking pretty tough. Stubble, puffy eyes, hair sticking up. He only ever looks like that when he's on a science project deadline.

"What, Merci, *what*?" he groans.

"I need two thousand dollars right away. Either that or a hideout," I say without so much as a *hello*.

He frowns and rubs the sleep out of his eyes. "Slow down. Two thousand dollars? What are you talking about?" He checks the time on his nightstand clock and groans again.

So, I tell him what happened, blow by blow. When I'm

done, he takes a big breath and lets it out through puffed cheeks. Then he gives me the stupidest advice of all.

"Tell Mami and Papi."

I gape at him. "I see. You *want* me killed," I say.

"For waking me up at this hour, yes, a little. But, Merci, think about it. What choice do you have? They're going to hear about it as soon as you get back to school, if not sooner."

"And then what happens?" I say. "Nobody around here has that kind of extra money."

He leans back on his pillow and sighs. He knows I'm right.

"Which brings us to option three: running away to North Carolina," I say. "I've checked the bus schedule and—"

That's when I notice something that stops me in my tracks. I lean close to the screen. Right there in his earlobe is a glittery stud. I've got nothing against earrings. I have pierced ears, too. Dr. Ortiz, my pediatrician, did it in her office when I was six months old. But this is different. This is Roli. "What's in your ear?" I ask.

He grins and moves his head to the side to give me a better view. "Like it?"

This is way too flashy for him. He doesn't even like to wear T-shirts in bright colors. Now this?

"When did you do that?" I say.

He shrugs. "A couple of weeks ago. What do you think? A little like Jake Rodrigo, right?"

I roll my eyes, the heat rising in my cheeks again as I think about kissing my poster. "Please. You'd need six more in each lobe to even come close," I say. "Plus, green skin."

He snorts. "Whatever. Just be sure to pull those posters down by the time I come back for summer break. If you're alive, of course."

"The posters stay," I say. "And don't give me that look, either. I haven't forgotten your crush on Kim Possible. Her initials are still carved in the back of the closet, you know."

"Touché," he says, yawning.

"What am I going to do, Roli?" I say.

"You're in deep all right," he says.

We fall quiet, which happens sometimes when I call him these days. It's not like when he lived here in the same room and we could talk whenever we felt like it. I never had to think of what to say to him then or ask how he was. It all came naturally. But now that we're far apart, all those miles between us make us run out of things to say.

"You know what else is horrible? Tía and Simón went on a *date* last night," I blurt out. "I saw them kiss. A real face sucking. It was disgusting."

His eyebrows shoot up. "You creeping on people now?"

"It's not my fault people kiss in public! And now I have all these questions, like does someone else's spit have a taste?"

He closes his eyes and pinches the bridge of his nose. It's a habit he picked up from Mami.

"Listen, Merci," he says. "There's obviously more to talk about, but I can't do it without some serious coffee. I was out late last night."

"Don't you ever get sick of studying in the library?"

"Who says I was studying? For your information, I was at a party."

I stare at him. Is this my brother grinning at me? First an earring and now a social life? A party means he was out with other human beings. Who is this College Roli who's at parties? His hair is longer, I suddenly notice. His beard doesn't look scraggly anymore, either. And then there's his earring sparkling every time he moves his head. Would someone in this world call College Roli cute, I wonder. Oh God, is *he* kissing people, too? Just thinking about it makes me want to close my eyes.

So, I do.

"Hey." His voice is gentle. "Are you OK?"

"Yes." But really the world is just spinning. I'm sick

with all the trouble I'm in and sick with all the things that are different this year, too. Lolo and I don't talk about important stuff anymore. Tía is dating Simón. And now this stupid earring on my brother who does not wear earrings. Nobody is the way they're supposed to be.

I think back to Carolina Family Weekend when I drove up with Mami and Papi to see a free football game at Roli's school. Lolo and Abuela couldn't walk up and down all those hills, so they stayed home with Tía and the twins. It was hard to imagine Roli there, even though we were seeing it with our own eyes. I think Papi felt it, too. He kept looking around the stadium, staring at that huge marching band on the field in their funny feathers and shiny shoes. Mami tried to sound cheerful. She said she liked the shady paths and pretty old buildings on the campus, which was different from how she commuted to night school. She said Roli's roommate, Emory, seemed nice. Papi was quiet that day, though, even when he shook hands with Emory's dad, a big guy who wore a golf shirt and blazer. Emory invited us to dinner with their family that night, but Roli was quick to say no thanks, another time. He walked us to the barbecue joint where he works part-time instead, and we ate sandwiches and buttery corn on the cob from red plastic baskets.

"Do you like it?" I ask.

"Like what?"

"College. Living away." *Kissing, maybe?*

Roli thinks for a minute and shrugs. "Once you find your crew, it's OK."

I open my eyes and look at him square on.

"You have a *crew*?"

He shrugs again. "You have to find people who kind of get you or it's hard," he says. "That's not everybody around here."

"What do you mean?"

"You know what I mean. Think of Seaward on steroids."

"Oh."

There's another long silence, and then I motion to him. "Come close to the screen."

"Why?"

"Do it, please."

He looks over his shoulder to make sure he's alone. Then he leans in. "Well?"

His face is big now, and College Roli disappears at last. I can see Regular Roli again, the one with that tiny chip on his tooth and the little scar in his eyebrow from when he fell off the swing. He's still in there, maybe the way Lolo is Lolo on his good days. It's enough to help me swallow again.

After a few seconds, Roli puts his eyes right by the camera to look ridiculous. Then he gives me a super close-up of his nose.

"Ewww. Back away and get a tissue," I tell him. "I saw boogers."

He leans back, smiling.

There's a knock and Roli looks off-screen. "Who is it?"

There's a girl's voice in the background.

Roli wraps his sheet around his middle and hops out of bed. I'm left staring at his pillows. I turn up the sound, trying to listen in, but all I hear is mumbling. Who could she be? Is she in his crew? Is she who he's been kissing?

When he comes back, he doesn't sit down again.

"Who was that?" I ask.

"A friend. Listen, I'm going to get something to eat." He leans over his keyboard. "I'll talk to you in a couple of days. I still think you should come clean to Mami and Papi, Merci. But if you don't, at least don't do anything else stupid."

I nod, missing him already. *Don't go*, I want to say.

But before I can stop him, he hangs up and disappears.

CHAPTER 25

WHEN OUR REFRIGERATOR BROKE DOWN a couple of years ago, Papi bought us a new one on installments. He said sometimes you have to break a big problem into little parts. I've decided to apologize to Edna and pay her back a little at a time, the way we bought our refrigerator. If I can get Edna to agree first, I might not even have to tell Mami and Papi. All I need is a good deposit to flash under her nose.

I've had no sleep, and there are purple circles under my eyes. All of me feels slow and heavy as I bike over to the Red Umbrella that afternoon to see if there's any money waiting for me. Maybe one of their customers fell in love with the clothes I outgrew and bought them all. It's not that hard to imagine. Abuela sewed them, so they look like anything you can buy in a department store. Better, actually, some people might say. The shirts even had tags that said *Teresa Designs,* the labels left over from when Abuela ran a shop from the living room.

"Yes, you *do* have some earnings waiting for you," the salesclerk says when she checks the ledger. "Congratulations."

Then she opens the cash register and hands me a measly thirty-six dollars.

I stare at the bills. Normally, I'd be thrilled. It's more than enough for the bobblehead I've been saving for. But under the circumstances, it's useless.

"Is that it?" I ask.

She frowns and looks over the records again. "We sold two pairs of shorts, a dress, three blouses." She smiles primly. "I'd say you did very nicely."

"How about the St. Lucie Mets jersey?" I ask. "That must have brought in some big dollars."

She takes off her glasses and lets them dangle on her chain as she regards me. "I'm afraid it's still on the rack. Ketchup stains are a problem," she says. "We'll be marking it down."

I must look as desperate as I feel because she offers a pep talk.

"You still have several weeks for the rest," she tells me.

"Check in with us next week. Or maybe bring in more merchandise to sell." She smiles. "Maybe old toys or books. Anything with superheroes goes quickly."

I swallow hard. How much would my action figures of Jake Rodrigo go for? My posters?

"But, here, I see I have a voucher for Inés, too. Fifty-three dollars. Do you want to sign for it and save her the trip?" she asks. "Your accounts are linked."

My mind is whirling as I do mental math that Wilson would be proud of. What if I add my money and Tía's, plus the dollars I have in my dresser? Together that's about a hundred dollars. That wouldn't be a bad deposit, right? Maybe it would be enough to keep Edna quiet.

"Sure. I'll take it to her." I sign my name and put Tía's money in my pocket.

The saleslady walks me to the front of the store and watches as I unlock my bike.

"What a good-looking way to get around," she says. "Very stylish."

I straddle it and strap on my helmet. "Thanks," I say as I push off.

I stand up in the saddle and pedal toward home. I feel wearier than I ever have. Not even the breeze in my face perks me up.

Am I stealing from Tía?

No, I tell myself firmly. I'm borrowing during an emergency. We've lent Tía plenty of money over the years. For the twins' school supplies. For a new set of tires for her car. She'd understand. I'll give it all back to her as soon as I can. Besides, I'm old enough to fix this myself. And she's so busy with Simón now, she probably won't even notice.

But still something gnaws at me as I get closer to home. I lean into my handlebars and steer fast around the corner, skidding in a sandy patch so hard that my bike slides out from under me, and I crash to the sidewalk. I sit there, stunned. The pedal has dug into my shin, and the pink flesh quickly fills with blood that runs down my leg. My ears buzz the way they always do when I start to cry. I get up and dust off, light-headed and mad at myself for crying—for everything.

I force myself back on my bike and try to ride off as if nothing has happened. *It's just a scrape*, I tell myself. But I'm hurt, even if I'm not going to tell anyone. And no matter how hard I push now, my legs still feel like Papi's weights. It's as if Tía's money has become an anchor and I can't get away.

CHAPTER 26

MAMI STANDS BESIDE LOLO AT his kitchen sink on Sunday.

"Let's see if we can raise your right leg for ten seconds this time," she tells him.

Lolo stares ahead blankly and doesn't move his leg at all. His recent cold must have really knocked a lot out of him. Mami smiles back at him, though, and taps his right leg. "This one, viejo. Just a few inches. You can do it. Pretend you're winding up for a pitch."

Abuela and I are at the kitchen table waiting for them to finish up. Abuela wants to pick up chicken legs that are on sale at Walmart for President's Day weekend, and Mami is going to get antacid for me. She's sure my stomachache and moping are because I ate almost a whole pound of chocolates. "I *told* your father all that sugar was a bad idea," she said earlier.

Anyway, I'm grateful they'll be gone for a while, even if it means keeping an eye on Lolo and the twins.

"How much longer are you going to be, Ana?" Abuela asks. "Lolo has been a little sick, you know. I don't think it's a good idea to work him so hard."

Mami looks over her shoulder. "He just had a little cough, barely more than a scratchy throat. That's not a reason to stop moving. Anyway, this is the last exercise."

For the past few months, Lolo has been working with Mami, just like she works with her own patients at the rehab center. She says that physical therapy can really help Lolo keep up his skills and his spirits. Walking the twins to school with Abuela is good for him, she says, but he could use a lot more exercise.

"But isn't the problem up here?" Abuela asks. She taps the side of her head.

"The brain is connected to the rest of your body, Teresa," Mami tells her. "We have to keep you both strong. Otherwise, it will get harder to care for him here at home."

"Por favor, Ana," Abuela mutters. "Don't start."

I don't really blame her for getting grouchy when people talk about Lolo getting worse. Who wants to imagine him getting weaker or thinking about how we'll have to help him even more as time goes on? Abuela already sits on the toilet while he showers and bosses him around about holding on to the grab bar that Papi screwed into the tiles. She even tells him where to wash—and she checks in case he forgets. Dios mío! How embarrassing! I don't even do that to the twins.

Mami lets it go and turns back to Lolo, who finally lifts his leg for the last exercises.

"Primer strike!" he says in Spanish, as if he's just pitched. His voice sounds thinner today, like there are spiderwebs inside his throat.

"Good job," she whispers to him.

Just then, Papi pokes his head in the kitchen window. "Gente, we need to move the cars in the driveway. You've blocked me in again. Simón and I have half an hour to get to Broward, and I need to keep this customer happy." He looks at me and frowns. "Why is your phone off? I tried to call from the van."

I've kept my phone off all weekend to avoid Wilson, just in case.

"I forgot to charge the battery," I mumble. "Sorry."

"We're leaving right now," Mami tells him. "Where's Inés? I thought her shift would be over by now. She was going to help look after Lolo while we're gone."

Papi gives her a look. "Pouring some coffee for Simón at the bakery." He looks at the sky and shakes his head. "I'll be lucky if they remember a to-go cup for me, too."

Mami smiles. "Leave them alone. It's cute. Merci, hand me my keys."

She settles Lolo down in a kitchen chair and walks over to the ancient CD player perched on Abuela's windowsill. Mami ends every session with songs Lolo has always loved. She says music makes the longest-lasting memories in our brains even though nobody really knows why.

She must be right because as she gathers her things, Lolo starts humming along. It's a warble-sounding love song in Spanish that I don't recognize.

But Abuela does. "It's Beny Moré!" she says.

She hums the last few notes along with him, too. Then she puts her hand over his. "We used to dance to that old bolero en La Habana, viejo," she says softly. "¿Te acuerdas?"

Lolo's whole face smiles. Then he serenades her in his tiny voice. He knows the whole verse, every single word.

When he finishes, Abuela kisses him on the head. "Save the last dance for me," she says. "I'll be back soon."

She slips her purse onto her arm and whispers to me, "Let him take a nap."

Mami kisses me, too, as she goes past. "I left the video game set up for all of you in the living room," she says. "Have them do at least fifteen minutes."

I nod at her.

Just Dance is one of the twins' favorite ways to play with Lolo these days. Tía bought it for them—a dance game, of course. Lolo sits in a chair alongside them as a neon moose and a panda dance to Daddy Yankee songs. The twins copy their moves exactly, just like Tía can when she's playing. When it's time, Lolo moves his arms in a chopping motion like the video animals and sings the only part he knows. The three of them find the *"poom poom"* line hilarious.

And me? I usually watch from the sofa.

I look over at Lolo, still singing with his eyes closed. Last year, I might have waited for a private time with him, just like this. I could have told him all that happened at the dance, and he would have hugged me and told me what to do now. But *that* Lolo is gone.

Focus on his abilities.

I watch Mami and Abuela pull out of the driveway and wave. I leave Lolo in the kitchen chair, humming, and shut myself in the bathroom. I power up my phone for the first time since Friday night. And just as I knew would happen, the text messages start pinging at me like bullets. The first one is from Lena yesterday:

> Wanna go to the movies? Call me.

But then, there are six from Hannah, one after another:

> Merci, call me when you get this.

> Merci, I have to talk to you. Important!!!

> Merci, it's about the photo booth. Call me. Something really weird happened.

> Hey. The photo equipment got wrecked!!! Edna is really mad!!! When you put it away it was fine, right???

> Merci? Where are you?

> Merci!!!! Answer me!!!

I shut down my phone again. I could pretend that I don't know anything. Wouldn't that be easier? But when I close my eyes, I see Wilson's face as I shoved the broken equipment out of view. He saw what happened, so what if he decides to tell?

Outside in the kitchen, Lolo is still singing to the music. I stare at myself in the mirror, every part of me feeling all wrong.

Tía shows up later that afternoon and makes Lolo his lunch. The twins are hunting lizards outside, and I'm working on my lab to get my mind off the trouble that's coming. I've been trying to pretend nothing is wrong, but every time I look at her, my stomach closes into a fist. It's like I'm trapped with all my troubles. I think of her and Simón kissing, and, even worse, I think about the money that's hidden in my dresser, tucked inside a pair of my socks. I managed to avoid Tía most of yesterday because she worked a long shift. But there's no getting around her today.

"What are you cooking there, preciosa?" Lolo says.

It's the third time he's asked me in the last hour, and it's starting to bug me. I look up from the coffee grounds that I've been mixing with flour and sludge from the pot, just the way the directions on the lab worksheet say. Can't he see? The gray paste looks lumpy and foul, like something Tuerto coughs up behind the couch.

"It's not food, viejo," Tía says gently.

"It's the dough I need to make a fossil for Mr. Ellis," I say again. I turn the screen on my tablet and point to the picture of the baby dinosaur bones preserved in a rock. "See?"

He squints at the screen. "A fossil, eh?"

"Yep. Old bones basically."

"Old bones like mine," he says, repeating the joke he made a few minutes ago.

I heave a sigh.

"Viejo, your con leche is getting cold," Tía tells him softly.

She circles another ad in the business classified section as Lolo settles back with his cup of coffee. Maybe she's going to look for that new job after all. Strangely, though, it's for rental space. She catches me looking and asks, "What do you need next?"

"Rolling pin, please," I say. "What are you looking for?"

"Me?" She brings me the old wine bottle that Abuela keeps on her windowsill. "I'm just curious about all these empty shops around here," she says vaguely. Then she sits down again, pulling her knees up to watch me work. Her toenails are still polished bright red, I notice.

"You don't have to watch," I tell her. "You're making me nervous."

She purses her lips and turns back to her ads. "Sorry."

I mold three patties and try to flatten the first with the bottle the way Abuela makes empanadas. Outside, the boys are squealing, chasing some poor creature. The only sound in here, though, is the squeak of the table as it wobbles with each of my strokes.

Without a word, Tía folds a napkin in a tight square

and tucks it under the short leg to steady the table for me.

"Thanks," I say, and get back to work.

We're all silent for a while, and soon Lolo is snoring softly.

"You've been so quiet today," Tía tells me after another little while.

I don't lift my eyes. "I'm just busy doing homework," I say. "As you can see."

She nods thoughtfully, her eyes flitting to Lolo, whose chin has bobbed down to his chest.

"So, how was the dance? You looked so pretty, but you haven't told me a thing about it. I was gone when you came back."

"I know that." My voice is sharp again in that way that surprises me. It seems to bounce off the kitchen walls sounding ugly. "How was your date? You haven't told me anything, either." I ask like it's an accusation.

She taps her nails against the side of her cup, thinking. "It was very nice, thank you. Simón is an excellent dancer. Who knew?" She presses her coffee mug to her lips and smiles as she takes a long sip.

I don't answer. What is she remembering exactly? Her long smooch in the driveway?

I pound the fern clipping from Lolo's garden into the first patty. Then I peel back the leaf slowly to reveal a perfect imprint.

Tía leans across the table and takes the bottle from me.

"May I try the next one?" she says.

I give her the bottle.

She rolls out a disk, flat and thin, in just four hard strokes. Then she reaches for my hand. She places mine next to hers and pushes down. When we lift our palms away, the handprints left behind look like the plaster ones she has of the twins' feet when they were first born. My hand is almost the same size as hers now, I notice. My first finger curves the same way, too, just like hers and Papi's.

The whole thing makes me want to cry.

I glance at Lolo, who's asleep in his chair.

"Are you going to marry Simón?" I ask her so softly that I'm not sure I've spoken aloud. My chin is quivering as I hear all the other questions still inside me. *Are you going to move away? Take the twins? Leave us? Do you love him more than me?*

She puts her hand on mine.

"That's a very big leap," she says. "Niña, we just had a first date. We went dancing. Dancing isn't love. It's more like a conversation."

"You did more than dance," I say.

She gives me a long look. "I don't know if I'll marry Simón or anyone again," she says. "I have the boys to think about. And Lolo. And most important, maybe it's time to think of myself, too, and things that I might want to do on my own. But I don't *have* to decide about Simón just yet. And he doesn't have to decide about me. We like each other. We have fun together. He's a good man. That's enough for now."

She picks up our hand fossil and lays it on the sunny counter to dry. Then she turns to me and leans her bottom against the sink. "Now, do you mind if I ask *you* something personal?"

I give her a careful look.

"What is it that has you so upset? I've never seen you like this." She looks at me evenly, but I can't say a word about the anchor pulling me down. A voice inside my ears is shouting at me. *Thief! Liar!*

"I'm here," she says after the long silence that I don't break. "You let me know if you want to figure things out."

CHAPTER 27

THE YARD IS PALE GRAY and quiet as I walk to Tía's house
the next morning. The birds haven't started singing yet, so it
feels like the world is frozen and silent, waiting to wake up.

She's already gone to work, and the twins are asleep in
Roli's bed. I pull open her mailbox and toss out the dead
lizard the boys put inside to scare the mail carrier. Then I
put an envelope inside. There's a message written on the
back.

I meant to give this to you.
It's from the Red Umbrella.
Sorry.

And I am.

I'm just about to turn back for home when I notice

Lolo standing in his yard. His back is to me. Was he there when I walked by the first time?

He's still in his pajamas, and the kitchen door is wide open behind him. I don't see Abuela through the window. She's usually an early riser, but their whole house still looks dark. Something isn't right.

So, I walk over to him slowly.

"Lolo, what are you doing up so early?" I whisper.

He turns to me slowly. "I had to use the bathroom," he says.

That's when I see that there's a big wet spot on the front of his pajama pants and another one on the ground near Abuela's flower garden. A strong smell of ammonia rises from him, a stinging odor stronger than even Tuerto's cat box.

Color rises to my cheeks. I know what's happened.

I look around to see if any of the neighbors are out, if anyone else is on the street. Should I wake up Abuela? Maybe not. She'd die if she thought someone had seen him this way, peeing in public. She'd yell, make a fuss.

"This is outside, Lolo," I tell him. "The toilet is inside, not here, OK?"

"I needed the bathroom," he says again.

I take him by the hand, the way Abuela sometimes does when he doesn't use his walker. "Come with me."

We make our way back inside, and I put my finger to my lips to signal quiet as we creep across the kitchen to their back mudroom, where Abuela has the washer and dryer that we all share. Every plank under the linoleum creaks as if the house itself wants to wake her and tell on us.

Luckily, there's a pair of clean pajamas already folded on the dryer.

I hold them out to him. "Take off your wet clothes and put these on before Abuela wakes up," I whisper.

But Lolo looks at me and can't seem to decide where to begin. *Please, please,* I think. *Don't let this be one of his hard days.* "Lolo, start with the buttons."

"Sí, claro," he says, but he doesn't reach for them.

My fingers tremble in frustration as I unbutton his top, wishing I hadn't seen him in the yard, wishing I wasn't the one doing this. I peel off his pajama shirt, keeping my eyes on the wallpaper. I don't want to see his old body. Not the white hairs on his skinny chest, and not the way his brown skin hangs loosely like chocolate frosting on a too-warm cake.

I work as quickly as I can to untie his waistband. I look away again as he steadies himself against the dryer and steps out of his soaked pants. The smell makes me gag. Holding my breath, I crouch down and hold open the legs on the fresh pajamas.

"Step in," I say, guiding his foot.

When we're done, I dump his wet clothes into the washer and turn on the machine. Then I walk him back to the kitchen table.

The scent of urine feels stuck on me. I scrub my hands with Palmolive at the sink, trying to kill it. When I'm done, I sit down and look at him for a long time.

"I'm in trouble at school, Lolo," I say. "I don't know what to do."

"Ay, preciosa," he says. But he doesn't ask me what I mean or why I'm in the yard so early. He doesn't say I've been quiet, that I don't seem like myself. And that's how I know that today Lolo will be a ghost. He won't be the Lolo who can help anymore. I'm on my own.

I get him a bag of Cuban crackers and butter a few for him. He smacks his lips and takes a big bite, smiling as the crumbs tumble down his chest.

I wait with him as he eats until I finally hear the squeak of Abuela's bed.

"¿Leopoldo?" she calls from back in their room. I can hear her nerves in the tremble of her voice, still hoarse from sleep. She uses his whole name when she's worried. "¿Por dónde estás, Leopoldo?"

"He's here, Abuela," I call to her. "He's fine."

I stand up, not wanting to be here when she comes out. I don't want to tell the story of this morning.

"Stay inside, OK?" I whisper to him. Then I set the lock from the inside and close the door quietly behind me.

I don't go home. Instead, I take my bike out for a ride. I start on our loop around Las Casitas, practicing how to ride with my eyes closed on the long part of the path, peeking just a little on the turns the way I finally learned to do. Though I'm not supposed to, I leave Las Casitas without telling anyone and pedal my beautiful machine through our neighborhood, still quiet in the morning. I ride for as long as I can, past the condos and along the canal, where I stop to see a young gator, no bigger than a yardstick, sunning itself on the opposite bank.

I don't come back until my legs are burning, but at least I know what I have to do for sure. I've been thinking all weekend, and now, at last, I think I have a plan. I lean my bike against our shed and wait until Mami and Papi leave for work.

Then I send a text to the only person I can think of who can help me with what I have to do:

> Meet me at the park at 10. Don't
> tell anyone. It's an emergency.

CHAPTER 28

SIMÓN GETS OUT OF HIS old Toyota, his face wrung with worry. He rushes over to where I said I'd be waiting.

"Merci, are you all right?" He looks me over to make sure I'm OK and tosses a vicious glance at the older kids in the park, who've been hanging out, gawking at my bike since I got here. "What's wrong?"

I'm sitting on the bench with my helmet in my lap. I've gone over my plan a million times, and I know this is the best way.

I look at him sheepishly, remembering how I've been hating on him. Now he's the person I have to ask for help. He's Papi's number one, I remind myself, the guy he trusts to do the hard jobs. I try to forget about Tía in his car, how he leaned over to kiss her.

"I'm fine," I say. "I called you because you're the only adult I trust who has a car. I really need your help."

His face twists in confusion. "You're not making sense. Your father has the van. Your mom has a car, and so does Inés."

I swallow hard. "None of them can know," I say. "I need you to drive me downtown this morning. It's too far for me to ride to the stores over there. Otherwise, I would have gone by myself."

His mouth drops open and he crosses his arms over his chest. "You got me away from work to take you *shopping*?"

I get to my feet and take my bike by the handlebars, tears already building. There's no use dragging this out, so I swallow the lump in my throat and just say it.

"Not shopping, Simón." I start walking my bike toward his car. "Selling. I'll explain everything in the car. Now, can you help me load this thing into your back seat? I need to bring it to the bike shop downtown and see what they'll pay for it secondhand."

CHAPTER 29

HANNAH IS WAITING NEAR MY locker when I get to school on Tuesday. Wilson is there, too, just a few lockers over. He gives me a worried look and pretends to fiddle with his lock.

"There you are! Didn't you get my texts?" Hannah asks.

I work my lock as fast as I can.

"I'm sorry," I say. "I wasn't feeling good. My phone was off." All true. Every word.

"Well, I've been trying to reach you all weekend!" Hannah's pulling on her hair and talking fast, like she's scared. "There's an emergency and we're both in big trouble."

I open my locker and stare inside at the mess.

"Edna's camera equipment is *broken*," she continues. "The IMA Paparazzi got smashed to bits. Nothing works! She claims she found it that way in the case. And now we're getting blamed even though we didn't do it. Can you believe her?"

It feels good to hear Hannah on my side for a change, even if she doesn't know the whole story. But then I see Wilson out of the corner of my eye, and he ruins everything. He slams his locker closed and stares at me dead-on.

"I just can't imagine how that stuff got wrecked, though. You didn't see anything, did you?" she says. Then she lowers her voice. "Maybe Jason did it. It's just like him to be sneaky like that."

My neck feels prickly and my tongue gets fat. Jason deserves to be in trouble every once in a while. Think of all the other times he gets away with being awful.

Wilson starts coughing.

"Anyway, my mom is going to flip if Miss McDaniels calls home to tell her we broke the equipment. And I—"

"Hannah."

"—don't want to get grounded for no reason and—"

"Hannah, *stop*," I say, louder. My eyes dart to Wilson, who nods at me.

She stands there blinking for a second. "What?"

"It was an accident. I saw it happen," I tell her. "The stand got knocked over at the dance when everybody was charging for the door."

She looks at me, relieved for a moment. But a second later, I swear I can see the gears of her mind turning and fitting things into place. "But how did it get back in the case?"

I stare down at my shoes. "I put it there after I realized it was broken. I don't know . . . it was a panic move."

Hannah stays very still. "You didn't say anything," she says slowly. "You didn't answer my texts." Her cheeks are getting blotchy, the way they always do when she's flustered. "I texted you all weekend long, Merci, worrying about this."

"I'm know," I say. "I'm sorry."

But she looks like I've punched her. "Sorry? I can't believe you! I stood up for you! I told Edna we didn't know anything. She's so mad!"

"Edna is always mad, isn't she?" I say.

"Not at me, she's not. And this time she's got every right to be!" Hannah says.

I give her a dark look. Now Hannah's taking Edna's side again. It's bad enough that I lost my bike—my favorite thing in the world—to that girl. "Who cares about Edna?" I mutter. "I hate her."

It's strange to see Hannah's face when I say it. She never fights with anyone. She's always the peacemaker. But right now, she looks like she wants my head on a pike.

"That doesn't mean you can break her stuff and lie about it! Hiding broken equipment makes us look like big fat liars, Merci! I want you to tell Edna that I didn't know."

"I'm going to fix it, OK? I have a plan. Now, stop bossing me," I snap. "You think I didn't worry about this all weekend? You could have put the stuff away, too, you know. You just left it for me so you could suck up to Edna."

Our voices are loud now, and everyone near us in the hall has turned to see what's going on.

"I don't suck up to anybody, Merci Suárez." She hitches her backpack on one shoulder and glares at me through teary eyes. "All I know is you better fix this or else."

"Or else what?"

Her eyes are pooled with tears. "Or else . . . we're not friends anymore."

Someone says, "Oooh," as Hannah storms off.

"There's nothing to see here," I shout. Then I slam my locker, daring Wilson with a glare to say a single word.

I head to homeroom by myself. The morning announcements come on just as I take my seat, fuming.

"Good morning, Rams! This is Lena Cahill and Darius

Ulmer with the morning announcements. Today we are celebrating National Do a Grouch a Favor Day . . ."

Oh, shut up, I think. Then I put my head down and wait for the bell to ring.

I've been keeping my eyes peeled for Edna, hoping I can give her my hush money before she tells Miss McDaniels. Unfortunately, I run out of time. I'm in English, third period, when an office monitor comes in. A few seconds later, Mr. Blume drops the note on my desk and another one on Hannah's. I already know it's from Miss McDaniels. Four words. *See me after class.*

Can handwriting shout? I think so because it looks like Miss McDaniels pressed really hard on her pen as she wrote to me. There's a little tear in the paper to prove it.

Hannah doesn't wait for me when the bell rings. She has refused to look at me all hour long, and already I've heard people asking questions and whispering about our fight. She bolts out the door on her own, still furious.

I pack up as slowly as I can and decide to take the long way to the office. I walk right by the Ram Depot, where Wilson is shelving our new merchandise in between bites of his sandwich and chips. I stand at the customer window, half expecting him to give me the same lecture Hannah did, but he just looks at me.

"I have to go see Miss McDaniels," I tell him.

He nods. "I heard. Good luck, comrade." It's how soldiers of the Iguanador Nation send each other into battle.

I go through the courtyard, where Lena sees me and runs to catch up. I keep walking.

"Merci. Stop."

"Why? You going to yell at me, too?" My eyes are filling up again. I hate that people are talking about me and saying who knows what. Rumors will fly around in no time, like last year when everyone was saying Missy Phillips ran away from home because she can't stand her stepmom, but really she just had the flu.

"I don't hate you," Lena says. She digs in her pocket and hands me a pretty purple crystal. "Here. You need this."

She hands me a rock.

"What's this for?" I ask.

"It's lepidolite," she says. "The stone of transition and tranquility. Maybe it will help."

Hannah is still an iceberg as she sits on the bench with me, waiting for our Meeting of Doom. We sit beside each other like two strangers on a bus. Usually, we look out for each other, but now it's like we're enemies. I've never felt so lonely in my life.

After nearly forever, Miss McDaniels finally opens the door to the conference room and signals us in. Dr. Newman usually runs discipline meetings, but I guess he's out of the building today, because it's just Miss McDaniels. Not that this works in our favor. I've seen her in action. Let's just say that the government should hire her to crack spies.

She motions us to sit and slides over a box of tissues in preparation. Then she folds her hands on the desktop. "In the interest of time, I will dispense with formalities. I imagine you girls know why you are here."

Hannah becomes a waterworks right away. All she can manage is a nod. I can see I'm going to have to do the talking.

"Yes, miss, I think so," I say.

"And why is that?"

"Because of the damaged IMA Paparazzi, miss."

"Correct. Dr. Santos came to me today with information about his disturbing discovery. It seems that the equipment he generously loaned us for the dance was not returned to him in the same condition it was given. Do either of you know anything about that?"

I stay quiet for a second, but Hannah glares and nudges me hard with her foot.

"It wasn't our fault, miss," I begin. "It was crowded in

the hall when you dismissed everyone. Nobody had the manners you told them to have, you know, like being ladies and gentlemen and all that. We may need a refresher on that sort of thing around here."

She frowns. "The point please, Merci."

I swallow hard. "Somebody knocked it over by accident."

"I see," she says. "Is this true, Hannah?"

Hannah's whole face looks puffy. "I—I—I don't know how the camera got broken. I wasn't there when it happened."

Miss McDaniels looks completely unconvinced. "Really?"

Hannah starts gulping for air.

"She's telling the truth, miss," I say. "Hannah wasn't there. She told me to pack up and went to get us drinks."

Hannah gives Miss McDaniels a teary nod and reaches for another tissue to blow her nose.

"So, if I am understanding correctly, a crowd of students pushed you, Merci, out of the way at the photo booth and knocked the equipment over?"

I hesitate. "Well . . ."

"No? This is not how it got damaged?"

"Not exactly, miss. I had gone to the gym, too. I went to see where Hannah was."

"The equipment was left unattended, then. By both of you." It's not a question.

"Just for a few minutes, miss. Hannah went to get us drinks, and she was taking so long. I was going to put things away when I came back. But then you dismissed people, and it got rowdy in the hall. That's when someone knocked it over by accident."

"And then what happened?"

I stay so still that I can hear the hum of the air conditioner. My eye feels as if it has turned straight to the back of my head.

"Well?"

"I grabbed it off the floor and zipped it back in the storage case."

Miss McDaniels stares at me for a long time. "I see. Were you aware of the damage?"

There's another long silence. If I lie and say no, maybe she'll go easier on me. But then, what if she asks Wilson and he cracks?

"Yes, miss."

"And did you report the accident to any of the chaperones in charge?"

"No, miss."

"Did you tell Hannah what happened?"

I shake my head.

"Did Hannah help you put away the damaged equipment?"

"No, miss. She didn't know it happened."

"I see."

She turns to Hannah, who's pulling on her hair again. "You may go now. Stop at the restroom and wash your face before you return to class. A comb might help as well."

Hannah's watery eyes dart to me, but then she gets up and leaves the room.

After the door closes, Miss McDaniels studies her pen for a minute and then sighs. "Accidents happen," she says.

I look at her hopefully. Maybe she'll understand for once. "Yes, miss. They do. And this was a big one."

"But what does *not* happen here at Seaward Pines Academy is *covering up* accidents and pretending we know nothing about them, particularly when it involves damage to property. That is a poor moral decision that is utterly beneath our student conduct code. I will not have it."

All hope shrivels.

"I am shocked and saddened. Merci, I consider you one of our most responsible and honest students. It's one of the reasons I made you co-manager of the Ram Depot."

I bite the insides of my cheeks. *I'm sick of being*

responsible, I want to yell at her. *Sometimes it's too hard.*

She takes off her glasses and lowers her voice. "What remains now is the more important matter of correcting this mistake."

"I've already thought of that, miss." I reach into my pocket and pull out all the money I have in the world. The thirty-six dollars from the Red Umbrella and the money I got for selling my bike.

She looks at me as if I've put live snakes on her desk. "What in the world is this?" she asks.

"It's almost three hundred dollars to use as a deposit, miss. I'll pay Edna's dad back a little at a time. Every penny—"

"Put that away at once! Money is neither the problem nor the solution here." She motions impatiently toward my backpack and waits as I zip it inside.

When I'm done, she leans over her desk. "You are very fortunate, Merci. Dr. Santos has an insurance policy that will pay for most of the repair. Our school funds will cover any part that is left over. You will not be required to pay money personally."

Relief starts to flood through me. "You mean, I don't owe anything?"

She looks at me irritably. "Quite the contrary. You owe Dr. Santos *and* his daughter Edna a huge apology for your dishonesty, which I'll expect in writing tomorrow. And you owe our entire school community a debt for embarrassing us in this way—a debt that you will pay with substantial additional community service hours. I will be calling your parents this afternoon to advise them of these events and the resulting consequences."

Blood drains into my shoes. First of all, this means that I sold my bike for nothing. My whole plan was to tell Mami and Papi that my bike got stolen. That way, they'd be mad, but at least I'd have the money to pay Edna. Now they'll have two things to be furious about: the broken equipment *and* selling my bike behind their backs.

"Do you have to tell them, miss?" I say. "Can't I solve this here at school with you? You're always reminding us to be responsible."

She pauses to consider things. "I will allow you to tell them what has happened yourself, Merci, but then I'll make the call home tomorrow afternoon to confirm. Please let them know that your disciplinary hours will start this Saturday."

I grab my backpack and rush to the door.

"And where are you going in such a hurry?" she asks.

My heart is racing as I turn to her. I have to get my bike back before the end of school or Mami and Papi will find out what I've done with it. It will be bad enough to tell them about the rest. No need to add selling my bike, if I can help it. "Back to class, miss," I say. "I don't want to fall behind."

She narrows her eyes at me, so I know she smells a rat.

"You'll be working our school's information booth at the Street Painting Festival. Setup is at nine o'clock sharp."

"I'll be there." I swing open the door and race down the hall.

Miss McDaniels's voice follows me. "WALK!"

CHAPTER 30

I SLIP INTO THE GIRLS' room on the way back from the meeting and text Simón.

> We have to run another errand today. Important! Can you pick me up from school?

If I get my bike before Miss McDaniels calls tomorrow, Mami and Papi will only have to be mad at me for lying about the broken equipment. It will be one less thing to be grounded for, which right now I'm estimating at life plus five years.

I wait for what feels like forever for a reply and nada. Three different kids come in to use the bathroom while I'm in my stall, but there's no response. Finally, I have no choice but to go to class. If I don't, the rumors will add in that I have the runs.

I try to message him again between classes, but Simón still doesn't reply.

By the end of the day, I've heard nothing, and I'm starting to get mad. Is his phone out of charge? Is he ignoring me? Is he somewhere smooching with Tía?

I take as long as possible at my locker that afternoon, hoping that Simón might text me back before Mami picks me up, but when the halls start to clear after school, there's still no word.

Wilson is at his locker, though, waiting. He comes over to where I'm standing. "So, what happened with Stopwatch?" he asks, looking around for her, just in case. "Do you have detention until the twelfth grade?"

I shake my head. "I have to pay back the damage in even more community service. She's calling my parents tomorrow."

"Ouch," he says.

I check my phone again. Nothing.

He stands there, quietly, like something is on his mind. "What?" I ask.

"Here." He shoves a paper lunch bag at me.

"I'm not hungry, but thanks."

"It's not a sandwich. It's a present for Fat Tuesday."

"Fat what?"

He shakes his head. "Nobody knows about anything good around here. Fat Tuesday, woadie. Shrove Tuesday?" He sees my blank expression. "Party time before Lent."

"Oh," I say. Our family is technically Catholic, but we hardly ever go to church unless it's for a wedding or baptism. Abuela says God can hear her praying from her recliner just fine.

Anyway, when I open the bag, I find a green and orange Ferociraptor bobblehead. It's Felecia, the greatest fanged threat to the Iguanador Nation universe. She's my favorite one.

"They came today in our new shipment," he says. "I know you've been wanting one. She's dressed up for Mardi Gras, see?" A strand of purple and green beads is draped over her shoulders like a necklace.

"Thanks," I say. "She's gorgeous. But you better let me pay for her now. I can't add inventory theft to my rap sheet."

I dig in my pocket for my money, pulling out a crisp ten from my roll. Wilson's eyes grow large when he sees the wad I'm holding. "You win the lottery or something? Where did you get all that money?" His face turns bright red. "Anyway, it's a present."

I stand there for a second, blinking. The Ferociraptor

is *a gift*? A bubble rises up through my chest, the first happy feeling I've had all day. Somehow it makes me want to punch him.

I shove the money back out of sight. "It's mostly from something I have to buy back this afternoon—*if* I can get down to Florida Avenue. You think I can Uber out of here?"

"Not without a note. But what's there?"

I give Wilson the whole ugly bike story, complete with Simón's current MIA status. "So, you see, if I can't find him, I'm toast."

"Do you mean Jack the Bike Man?" he asks. "It's got a big mural out front?"

I think back. "Yeah. I think that's the one."

"I know them. They adapted my bike a while back." He nods thoughtfully. "I might have an idea. My mom and I drive by there on the way home. Why don't you tell your mom that you're coming to my house today? We can pick up your bike, and she'll never know." Then he shrugs. "We're having pancakes and king cake for dinner, if you want to stay."

I stare at him. "You'll be an accomplice."

"I'm aware."

I've never gone to a boy's house after school. I've never

eaten dinner at a boy's house. I've never tricked someone's mother on purpose, either.

"OK," I tell him.

He texts his mom as we hurry to the glass doors. Mami is waiting at the curb.

"Good on my end," he says when he gets a reply. "Your move."

"I'll be right back, then," I tell him, pushing open the door. "You're a lifesaver. I won't forget this!"

He grins and goes back to get the rest of his things from his locker while I go ask Mami.

I swear, I could kiss Wilson's whole smiling face.

Mrs. Bellevue looks at me in the rearview mirror of her SUV as she pulls away from the curb. She's a redhead with freckles across her nose like Wilson, except she's a white lady, so her skin is much lighter than his. I don't know if Wilson has a lot of friends who come over from Seaward. People like him well enough at school, but he's not one of the A-listers who everyone wants to know, like Michael. A-listers get a lot of attention all the time, but I think that would be scary. You'd always have to worry about what everyone thinks. Plus, one false move and—*whamo!*— you're kicked to the curb. Look what happened to Edna.

Maybe Wilson is more like me. I'm in the middle, like maybe an L-M-N-O-P-list kid.

Anyway, maybe Mrs. Bellevue thinks things are looking up for Wilson in the friends department. Or maybe she's one of those moms who thinks everyone is a potential love match. I mean, she made a point of getting out of the car to meet Mami. She told her that we'd be supervised. Supervised doing what? Eating Fat Tuesday pancakes? God.

"I've heard a lot about you, Merci," she says as we drive along.

Really? He's talking to his mom about me? Interesting. I glance at Wilson, but he just sinks in his seat. "Mom," he mutters, and looks out the window.

After we've driven a few blocks, Wilson gives me a nudge and winks. Then he leans toward his mom's seat.

"We wanted to ride bikes after we finish our homework," he tells her casually. "Merci left her bike at Mr. Jack's for a tune-up. Can we pick it up on the way? We can throw it in back and save her mom the trip."

Smooth. Makes me realize that Wilson is a whole lot sneakier than I thought.

Mrs. Bellevue says it's no trouble at all, and then chatters on about Wilson's first bike, which Mr. Jack adapted for him with special extra wheels until Wilson got the hang of balancing. It was easier, she said, here in Florida where the ground is so flat. I wonder how long he had those wheels, or if he still has them.

My knee bounces nervously. *Focus*, I tell myself. I'm going to get my bike back. I don't have to tell Mami and Papi all that I did. I have a new Ferociraptor from Wilson.

The world is good.

We ride along toward downtown talking about Rotz's and Felecia's origin stories and which one of those villains is the bigger threat to Jake Rodrigo. I'm arguing for Felecia so hard that I don't even notice when Mrs. Bellevue pulls into the lot that faces the big turquoise mural of a bicycle. The doors to the bay are wide open, just like they were yesterday.

"Here we are," she says, grabbing her purse and keys. "I'm crossing the street to the bakery. Meet me back here when you're done."

"Come on," I tell Wilson. And then we go inside.

The place is wall-to-wall bikes, from shiny red tricycles to racers you might see in the Tour de France. I take a deep whiff of new rubber tires.

"Hello?" Wilson calls out.

"Be right with you." The guy at the counter doesn't look up. He's busy filling out paperwork for two tourists who are renting bikes. It's not the same person who was here yesterday. This one has tattoos and ear gauges.

I'm too impatient to wait. "This way." I point Wilson toward the section for used bikes.

"What does it look like?" Wilson asks. He runs his finger along the seat of a sleek mountain bike.

"Blue and gorgeous. A Schwinn."

The bikes are arranged by size, so I start looking at the twenty-six-inch models, like mine. I walk the whole row twice, but I don't see it. I look it again, and then I go through all the aisles of used merchandise for sale. Wilson calls my name every time he spots a blue bike, but none has that perfect basket and water bottle holder, the great headlamp and bell.

My stomach is starting to feel jumpy when I meet Wilson back at the counter. "No sign of it," I say. "Maybe they haven't put it on display yet."

The tourists finally finish getting fitted for their helmets and pedal out the open bay.

"Hi, Will," the clerk says, and does some sort of handshake with him.

Will? No one calls him that at school.

"Haven't seen you in a while," he says. "What brings you down here, man?"

"My friend," Wilson says, jutting his thumb at me. "Merci needs to buy her bike back."

I step forward. "That's right," I say. "I sold you guys my bike yesterday, but I've changed my mind, and I'd like to buy it back." I pull out my money and lay it on the counter. "You can count the money. It's all there."

The guy looks at the stack of bills and tugs at his earlobe, thinking. "And what bike was that?"

I tell him.

"Yeah, I remember that one." He types something into the computer and clicks around staring at the screen. "One second," he says. He picks up the phone and makes a call. "Jack? The Schwinn twenty-six-inch blue we had on the floor? The original owner is here. Wants to buy it back." He listens for a moment, nodding. "Yeah. That's what I thought. I'll tell her."

He hangs up the phone and leans over the counter. "Bummer news, guys. I can't help you. We sold that bike this morning."

CHAPTER 31

I'M IN A FOG AS we head back to Wilson's car.

One of our vocabulary words in English last month was *inconsolable*, which means being so sad that nothing in the whole wide world can make you feel better. It's spelled exactly the same in Spanish and English, too. Right now, in both languages, that's how I feel. Inconsolable. *Een-cohn-so-láh-blay.*

The clerk took my number. He said that since I was "Will's friend," he'd call the couple to see if they might want to bring it back. He said it was the best he could do, but he sure didn't look hopeful.

We have no choice but to tell Wilson's mom that my bike wasn't ready yet, but she can sense something is wrong. The whole ride to Wilson's house, I'm quiet, imagining some stranger pedaling around West Palm Beach on my wheels.

"Don't be too sad." She looks worried, like maybe the day is ruined or maybe I won't want to stay for supper after all. "Fat Tuesday is a day to be happy and eat pancakes! You can borrow my bike for today, if you like."

I try to smile. Me on a mom bike. I've hit a new low. "Thanks, Mrs. Bellevue," I mutter.

Wilson takes pity. He gives me one of his earbuds so we can block out the world and listen to some music for the rest of the ride home. But it doesn't help. My bike belongs to some stranger now. The only thing I can do is tell Mami and Papi that it was stolen, just like I planned, and pray Miss McDaniels doesn't mention the stack of money I brought to school. It's risky at best.

The trees are old around Wilson's neighborhood. The roofs are flat, like ours. His is the last townhouse in the row, the one with the plaster pelican on the stoop.

I slip off my shoes at the door and look around while his mom cuts us some pieces of king cake for a snack. It's bright pink and green and covered in colored sugar. The idea, she says, is to have one last food frenzy before Lent, which starts tomorrow. "Watch for the plastic Jesus," she says as we take our cake out to the patio. "If you get him, you have to bake the cake next year."

Chomping on El Señor must be universal. I mean, Tía always brings home a Mexican rosca de reyes from the bakery on Three Kings' Day in January. Abuela is always worried that someone's going to choke or bust a molar on the little ceramic Jesus that's baked inside.

I have to admit the cake is pretty good. But I'm not really into it today. All I can do is stare miserably at the lizards that are running up and down the areca palms out back.

"Maybe you can save up and buy a new bike that you'll like even better," Wilson says. "You've already got a lot of cash. I can call Mr. Jack and see if he'll help."

"There isn't one I like better. Plus, how would I explain to my parents about the new bike?" My voice is a little more bitter than he deserves. I know he's just trying to help.

Wilson looks lost for what to say, so we sit there in awkward silence for a while. Finally, he balls up his napkin. "Let's watch *Temple of the Ferociraptors*," he says. It's the fourth movie in the Iguanador Nation franchise.

"You have it?"

"Of course. Who knows when you'll be able to watch TV again?"

I give him a steely look. "You have a point."

So, we cut ourselves more cake and climb the stairs to his room. It's shockingly neat compared to how Roli and I used to keep ours. He's got a basketball hoop hanging over his closet and a poster of two players from the New Orleans Pelicans. There's also a decent collection of Iguanador Nation figurines, though not quite as good as mine.

Wilson unstraps his foot brace and disappears into the bathroom to change out of his uniform. I suddenly wish I had a change of clothes, too, a way to shed School Merci. It's not like when I'm at Lena's or Hannah's where I can borrow something to wear. All I can do is unclip my neckerchief and slide into his beanbag chair in front of the screen to wait.

He comes back a few minutes later wearing shorts and an Iguanador Nation T-shirt.

Something about seeing him this way makes him look completely different, like at the dance. He grins at me and starts the movie. Then he drags another beanbag chair next to mine.

It's great, of course, and it does help me forget about my bike for a little while. Turns out, we both have the same favorite part, too. It's where Jake Rodrigo, who has a genetic link to Rotz's mother, goes mano a mano with

Rotz and the other Ferociraptors on the cliffs of the planet Zyphin. One slip and our hero will go careening into the blackness of space forever. I hold my breath every time.

We're sitting close, our legs touching. Then, at that exact spot when Jake Rodrigo is being held over the chasm, Wilson takes my hand and squeezes it in excitement.

What. Is. Happening?

I don't look at our hands. All I feel is a buzzing in my ears, and it's not because Jake Rodrigo stabs Rotz through the neck and breaks free. Then Wilson lets go of my hand.

"That is so sick," he says, standing up.

The movie? My hand?

"I'll get us some Cokes," he says. "Wait here."

He-ah.

I nod, speechless, and watch as he takes the steps, two at a time.

Did Wilson Bellevue just hold my hand? I reach for my phone, thinking I might text Lena and Hannah. But then I remember Hannah's still mad at me.

So, I lean back and take another bite of king cake. And wouldn't you know it? I find baby Jesus.

Blueberry pancakes for dinner is a great idea, especially as a last meal before I have to face the music. I'm stress-eating my sixth one when my phone vibrates. It's Papi.

> I will be there to pick you up in ten minutes.
> And who's this Wilson?

I keep my phone under the kitchen table to hide my screen as I type back:

> I'll be outside.

Third degree, here I come.

"My dad is on the way." I pocket my phone and bring my plate to the sink, where Mrs. Bellevue has started on the dishes. Then I find my shoes near the door. "Thanks for having me," I tell her on my way out.

"Any time, Merci," she says. "And bring your bike another day after it's repaired."

My stomach clenches all over again. Life as a liar is turning out to be kind of tense. "I will."

She motions to Wilson with her chin. "And why are you standing there, sweet boy? Walk her out, please."

Wilson slips on a pair of sneakers that are near the door, and we walk to the curb to wait. It's dark and quiet out here, just the two of us. Bugs dance in the streetlight that's shining over the parking spaces. We watch them darting crazily.

"So, what are you going to do now, Merci?" he asks me. "You going to tell them what happened?"

I peer down the street, wishing I knew the answer. One

lie makes a bigger lie that makes a bigger one after that.

"I'm not sure." But if I don't, Stopwatch will.

Headlights appear at the entrance to his neighborhood. I already know it's Papi. His van comes up the street slowly, the squeaks sounding all the way here. "Don't worry about my dad," I whisper.

"Why would I worry?"

"You'll see. Thanks for the movie, though," I tell him. "And for Felecia, too. I really like her."

He stares at his sneakers. "OK."

Papi pulls up to us just then, the van clattering as he throws it into park. Sure enough, he eyes Wilson as if the kid is prey.

"Hello," Papi says. His voice sounds low, like a bear's growl.

Wilson half raises his hand. "Hi, sir."

"See you tomorrow, Wilson," I say.

He's still watching from the curb when we turn for home.

Is half a lie as bad as a whole lie? *Just say it.*

The entire ride home, I try to decide whether to lie about my bike or tell Papi the truth about both my bike and the IMA Paparazzi. I hold Felecia in my lap trying to gather courage, but a clock is ticking down in my head as we get closer to our house.

So, I let Papi talk. He asks a million questions about Wilson first, of course. I keep it simple and explain he's the kid I run the school store with. "The numbers guy," I say.

"Oh yeah? Just that?"

"Yes, Papi. Just that," I say, even though I don't really know.

"Good, because you're too young for any of that other stuff."

I look out the window. *Basura*, I think. Liking people, holding hands, wanting to kiss someone. If I'm too young for it all, why is it happening anyway?

After that, Papi tells me about his fussy customer today over in Royal Palm who made him paint a bedroom in a calming color for her cats. I'm barely listening until he gets to the part about Simón.

"And I had no help. Of all days, Simón had to get down to Miami for the lawyer . . ." He shakes his head.

So that's why Simón didn't answer.

We're at our corner, and Papi signals to make the turn. My palms are soaked. I'm almost out of time, even though he's a slow driver.

"Papi, I have to tell you something. It's sort of bad."

He looks over at me and almost takes out a mailbox as he slams on the brakes. Buckets and brushes go flying in the back. "Is it that Wilson kid? I knew it. Did he disrespect you? You tell me everything and I'll—"

"What? No! Wilson is great."

"He's *great?*" His eyes get wide.

"I mean, he's fine. Papi, it's not about Wilson."

"Then, what?"

Up ahead, Las Casitas is in view. It's past sunset, so the lights are on in each of our houses. *Just lie. Plenty of kids do it. If they skip a class. If they sneak out at night during a sleepover. What's the big deal?*

"It's about my bike."

He sucks his teeth and lets out a breath. "Oye chica, don't scare me like that. Your mother already talked to me about your bike."

He starts driving toward our driveway, the van's chassis heaving noisily as he pulls up to our house.

I stay very still. How would *she* already know that I sold it?

Papi puts the van into park and shuts off the engine. "She said to go hard on you, y tiene razón. How could you be so irresponsible?"

"I can explain," I said.

"Not this time. We've told you over and over again to put your bike away in the shed and not leave it outside for everyone to see. Some malvado is going to steal it, and then don't come crying to me, little girl, because it's going to be gone for good if that happens. Now, put your bike away and lock the shed like you're supposed to," he continues. "You're not allowed to ride it for a week, oíste? After that, if you leave it out again, I'm going to take it for a long while. You understand?"

He motions at the shed with his chin, and when I follow his gaze, I see it. There, like some sort of wheeled mirage, is my bike.

CHAPTER 32

I RUN MY FINGERS ALONG the basket and seat. I even ring the bell once to be sure I'm not hallucinating. Then I drag my bike into the shed and lock the padlock.

It's mine all right. But how did it get here? Abre Camino?

I'm walking across the driveway to go inside when a single sharp whistle makes me turn. It's the signal Papi's team uses to get one another's attention on the soccer field. I squint in the direction of the sound, and I see that it's Vicente. He's on Tía's stoop, signaling at me, so I jog over.

"Where have you been?" he says. "She's had me on lookout for you all afternoon." Then he holds open Tía's door. "And she's mad as a wasp."

The kitchen smells like boiled rice still drying in the

pot. Baked chicken legs are cooling on the counter. Tía puts down the knife she's using to chop salad and turns to me as soon as I come in.

"Gracias, Vicente," she says, keeping her eyes trained on me. "Can you see about getting the boys to wash their hands? And send your brother in here, too, por favor." When he leaves, she narrows her eyes and pulls out a chair for me. "You. Sit."

I do what she says. The sounds of *Super Mario Odyssey* cut off, and I hear the twins running down the back hall with Vicente. Then Simón comes into the kitchen. He exchanges an uncomfortable glance with Tía and puts his hands in his pocket.

"I'm sorry, Merci," he says.

"Simón told me everything," Tía says.

It's ice water down my back. Then, before I even have a chance to say a word, she starts whisper-yelling at me.

"Were there little birds flying up in that head of yours yesterday, muchachita? What were you thinking? Selling the bike your parents sacrificed to get you! Thank God, it was still there when we got there this morning!"

My mouth drops open. "*You* guys brought my bike home?"

Tía rolls her eyes to the ceiling. "Of course, we did. You think that thing just appeared in your driveway by magic? Not even Abre Camino can do that! We drove to that shop as soon as Simón got the courage to tell me what you two did. And not a moment too fast! When we got there, two customers were already drooling over it!"

My eyes flit to Simón. He's leaning against the sink, looking like the traitor he is.

"It nearly cost the eye off my face to get your bike back," Tía continues. She swats the dishrag she's holding against the sink in frustration. "I had to take a big loan from the tip jar at work, and Simón and Vicente put in the rest from their rent money. Do you know how many extra hours we have to work for that kind of cash? Do you?"

I wince at her words, thinking of her swollen feet, but I put on my hardest expression anyway.

"What else could I do, Tía? I sold it so I wouldn't have to ask Mami and Papi for money. I'm not a baby. I know they don't have any to spare."

"Well, did you think about Simón, then? How could you put him in such a position? You think your papi would appreciate that he helped you do this behind your papi's back? There could be big trouble for Simón!"

I glance uneasily at Simón. Just thinking about Papi's temper can be scary for me. When he's angry, Papi's words rumble and his face gets dark red. What if Simón lost his job because of me?

She looks at me for a long time and sighs. "Merci, sometimes we need help solving a problem. Why didn't you come to me first? That's what hurts most of all."

Silence fills the kitchen as my heart pounds.

"You're too busy these days," I say quietly. "And that hurts, too."

She looks at me for a long time. "I'm not too busy for you," she finally says. "Not ever."

All my feelings are so confused. *Thank you* and *I love you* and *I'm sorry*—all of them harden in my chest, and words just can't get out.

Tía walks over to me and puts her arms around me. I'm stiff with fear, but as she pulls me closer, I smell her hair, that shampoo she lets me use whenever I want. It's the scent of home, and relief floods through me. "I wanted to fix things myself," I say. *Because Lolo can't. Because you're too tired. Because maybe you're in love. Because soon I'll be thirteen.* Then I hide my face in her neck so Simón can't see me cry.

"Calm yourself," she whispers. "And don't you dare wipe your nose on my shirt."

I let out a laughing snort. Simón wets a paper towel and hands it to me.

When I'm done, I dig in my pocket and pull out my money, all of it. "Here," I say. "Take it."

"What's this?" Tía asks cautiously.

"It's the money I got for my bike yesterday, plus a little more from my drawer." I close her fingers around it. "Miss McDaniels said Dr. Santos has insurance. I'll have to do service hours, but at least we don't have to pay for the repairs to the equipment. All I have to do is tell Mami and Papi about what happened at the dance." I pause and look at her. "We don't have to get Simón in trouble, do we?"

Tía lets out a long breath and glances at Simón warily.

Just then the twins and Vicente come back from the bathroom. Axel and Tomás wave their wet hands in the air, smelling of Dial soap.

"The ugly giant!" Tomás screams. "Get her!"

"Shhhh!" Tía says, shielding me. "That's enough of that awful game. Now, sit in your chairs. Dinner's getting cold."

She tucks the money in her pocket and looks over to me. "Why don't you eat here with us? There's room."

I glance around at Tía's kitchen. She has always eaten with the twins at folding tables in front of the TV. Either that, or at our house or Abuela and Lolo's. Tonight, though, the table is set and there are also two extra plates out. Will this be how they'll eat from now on? With Simón and Vicente?

"I already ate, and I'm supposed to be putting my bike away," I say. "Besides, I have to tell them about the broken equipment and my community service punishment. Miss McDaniels said I could tell them myself first, before she calls tomorrow."

I shut the screen door behind me and start down the path that leads past Abuela and Lolo's house.

"¡Merci, espérate!"

I stop and wait for Simón to jog over to me.

"I want to explain."

"Why did you tell her?" I asked. "You promised."

"I made you a promise not to tell, but keeping it was going to hurt you. I couldn't let that happen to a friend."

I look at him. Maybe he's been a better friend to me than I have been to him.

"It's OK," I say. "It wasn't my best idea. I'm not going to mention the bike to Papi, though, since we have it back."

We shake our soccer handshake, and then, for the first time, Simón pulls me in for a quick hug before heading back to Tía's.

When I get to our door, I stop and watch my parents for a second through the window. Papi stands behind Mami at the sink, kissing her cheek and whispering something in her ear. I don't turn away like I usually do. Instead, I take a deep breath and step inside, making a racket as I go, light-headed from all these kinds of love.

CHAPTER 33

"GOOD MORNING, RAMS. THIS IS Lena Cahill flying solo here today. It's National Random Acts of Kindness Day. Darius Ulmer has been given the day off. You're very welcome, Darius."

I turn around while everyone is listening to the announcements and drop my apology letter on Edna's desk.

She stares at the note without picking it up. She knows exactly what it is, of course. Everyone is aware that Miss McDaniels makes you write formal apologies when you mess up.

Besides, Mami called Dr. Santos last night after I told her and Papi about the IMA Paparazzi damage.

"¡Qué pena nos has hecho pasar!" Mami said as she searched for the Santos's number in the parent directory. I broke the news right after they finished their dinner. When I got to the part about zipping up the broken stuff in the bag, I thought Mami was going to faint. If there's one thing she and Papi hate, it's being "embarrassed," especially about school stuff. They already think any slipup will get my scholarship cut or even get me tossed out of precious Seaward Pines.

"I wasn't thinking straight," I told her.

"I can see that!" she snapped.

"Well, maybe if you didn't make me so worried about getting kicked out all the time, I wouldn't have hidden it."

"Don't you dare blame this on anyone but yourself!" she shouted.

"Ana," Papi said.

"What! We sacrifice everything for our kids! They should be grateful we worry!"

For once it was Papi who had to calm us both down.

Anyway, later that night I heard her tell Dr. Santos how sorry she was, how they had raised me better, how she couldn't believe I would do such a thing. It made me wonder if Dr. Santos is ever sorry about how Edna acts Does he even know she's a beast? Does he care?

I turn back around and stifle a yawn as Lena finishes

ticking through all the news of the day. Then, as she's wrapping up, she drops what feels like an atomic bomb on me.

"Heart Ball photo files from last weekend's dance will be placed in students' e-folders starting tomorrow, so be on the lookout!"

"What?" I blurt out.

I feel eyes turn to me, and I suddenly understand how Darius must feel every day, pinned like a bug under everyone's stares. I swivel in my seat and look right at Edna.

"Who decided that deadline without telling me?" I whisper.

Edna gives me a smug look. "Moi. And what's so crazy about it? The photos uploaded automatically as you took them. Getting them back fast is the very least you can do to make things up to me, considering all the trouble you caused."

"But there are two hundred pictures to edit! How am I supposed to do all of that in one night? I'll never be able to get through them all."

"Time management."

"I manage time just fine," I say.

"Should I ask Miss McDaniels to help us settle this?"

"Edna, be reasonable. I agreed to take the pictures. I did

not agree to become a one-hour photo center all by myself."

"And I did not agree to have my equipment smashed to bits, did I? But here we are."

I stare at her and then at Hannah, who is in the next seat. I know Hannah hears the whole thing, but she doesn't stand up for me this time. She doesn't try to smooth anything over. In fact, she turns her head and looks the other way, like I'm invisible. Suddenly I wonder if Hannah and I are ever going to be friends again.

"I'll tell you what," Edna says. "Just so that you know that I'm a fair person, Merci, I'll make you an offer that you don't really deserve. Since it's National Random Acts of Kindness Day and all, I'll give you until Monday to finish the pictures."

"Thank you," I say through gritted teeth, and then I turn back around.

The hard part of warring with your friends is the icy feeling inside you, plus the fact that then other people are expected to take sides. Lena is miserable. She's been struggling to stay neutral because she's friends with both me and Hannah. But it's not easy, especially when all three of us have to pretend nothing is wrong during class.

I barely pay attention to Mr. Ellis droning on about divergent boundaries and other earthquake stuff. It figures that this is the day he assigns Hannah, Lena, and me to the same group, something we've begged for all year. Normally this would be cause for celebration. But today, it's exactly the worst thing. Hannah is still mad that I didn't tell her the truth. Now she's holding a grudge. All period long she has been answering me with just a single word—and only when she absolutely has to. Lena keeps looking from Hannah to me, trying to fill in the silences, but it's useless. Finally, she gives up, and we just work next to one another quietly while all the other groups around us have fun.

The assignment is to build a 3-D fault model of the earth's crust out of poster board so that we can figure out the effects of an earthquake on land features. We've colored each layer in a different shade and then labeled the railroad tracks, the river, and the rest of the land features. When we're done, I cut and fold the flaps, and Lena tapes it all together. She puts the finished model on the table.

We stare at it miserably.

"Well?" Lena says at last. "Who wants to start?"

Hannah and I stay quiet.

Lena sighs and picks up the model. "I have an idea. Something a little more creative." She turns to Hannah. "Why don't you be the earthquake?"

"And how am I supposed to do *that*?" Hannah says.

"Well, hold the model in your hand and think of something that makes you mad. You pretend your feelings are crashing into each other like plates. And then . . ." Lena makes a motion like her head is exploding. "You let it out."

"That's dumb," Hannah says.

"Just try it," Lena says. "For me. Channel your sense of rage. Let it all go." She glances at Mr. Ellis across the room and leans in to whisper. "We're being graded on this, remember?"

Hannah snatches up the model and glares at me. "Fine. I have just the thing to focus on."

For a second nothing happens, but then she starts to frown.

Hannah hates fights, so her face looks completely changed, angry as she is. It's like watching the sweetest kitten morph into a rabid, fanged beast.

"*Purrrshhhhh*," she says with her eyes closed, her hands moving our model around like a strike-slip fault. Judging from how she's wringing it, I'd say I'm lucky to be alive. She's still smashing the model to bits when Mr. Ellis comes over to see what we're doing. He's got his grade book open as he watches Hannah the Earthquake.

"Destroy, destroy, destroy!" she says in a demon voice.

"I'd say the Drama Club could use you, Hannah," he says brightly.

She startles and opens her eyes again. I've dared to giggle, so she scowls at me, and I stop.

He looks from one of us to the next, taking it all in. "I've noticed a pretty glum group here. It's a bit of a surprise."

No response.

"Well, let's focus on our task, then. What do you scientists predict would really happen in this catastrophic scenario?"

I don't even bother trying to answer. I'll take the zero. Hannah's too angry to even pretend we're a group.

"Everyone would be really upset," Lena offers quietly. "The ground under their feet would be moving in a way they hadn't expected. Everything they thought was safe forever would be crumbling. They wouldn't know how to make it better or what to do next. They'd want things like they were before."

I stay quiet, but when I look over, I see that Lena's eyes are misty behind her stylish glasses. Hannah must notice, too, because she starts chewing on a hangnail. Mr. Ellis looks at each of us and then closes his grade book.

"I meant scientifically. As in, what might happen to the railroad and river," he says, "which I suspect each of you would answer correctly if you were concentrating properly. That is clearly not happening." He turns to Lena.

"You're probably right about people in trouble, though. It's very disorienting. Maybe you three can step out in the hall and discuss it a little more."

And with that shocking offer, he leaves us.

Lena stands up and pushes in her stool. She motions to us and, reluctantly, Hannah and I follow her out into the hall.

At first, no one says anything. We just stand there, feeling toxic.

"I don't want to be in the middle anymore," Lena says. "It's hard to be a friend to both of you right now. Not even the lepidolite is working." She pulls out a hunk from each pocket and shows us a little pendant hanging from the chain around her neck, too.

"Well, that's her fault," Hannah says, pointing. "She did not act like a friend at all. Maybe she should look the word up in the dictionary."

"How long are you going to hold a grudge?" I say. "Especially since nothing really bad happened to you. I saved you, didn't I?"

"*One*, that's not the point. And *two*, you didn't *save* me because it wasn't my fault."

I roll my eyes. "Did your new bestie, *Edna*, tell you to say that?"

"Shut up," Hannah says.

Lena holds up her hands like a referee. "Stop fighting." She looks at me through her big glasses. "You should have told Hannah what happened, Merci. It was wrong to hide that stuff and then avoid her all weekend like a coward."

Then she turns to Hannah. "And where's your heart, Hannah? People do strange things when they get scared. Remember last year when you ate the note that I passed to you so Mrs. Robertson wouldn't see it? You had blue ink on your teeth all day."

Hannah opens her mouth to argue, but then we all laugh a little, remembering how hard she tried to get the ink off her gums.

It feels like the tiniest break in the clouds.

"Can't you two just apologize and move on?" Lena says.

I stay quiet, thinking. "I'm sorry I hid the damage from you," I tell Hannah. "I know I should have said something. If it makes you feel better, I have extra community service for the rest of the year. Plus, my parents took my bike away for a while."

Hannah stares at her hands. "That sounds pretty bad," she says. "I'm sorry I yelled at you. I guess I would have been scared, too."

Lena slings her arms around both our shoulders. "So, we're good?"

I hold my breath, waiting. When you fall and hurt yourself, it takes a few days for the scrape to heal or the bruise to disappear. Maybe it's the same with friend fights.

Slowly, Hannah puts in her fist and we all follow. We bump a closed-hand "potato" and pull back with wiggly-finger "french fries."

Then we go back inside to finish our work, forgiven if still a little tender.

That night, I get started on the dance photos to get them done by Monday.

When I open the file, I wince. Edna's is first up since she was the last one to get her picture taken, right before all the disasters. Most kids came by with a group of their friends to have their picture taken, but not her. She came alone. Maybe she'd already figured out that Brent likes Madison.

Anyway, I enlarge her with a pinch. And then, because it feels good, I draw horns on her. Then I add fangs and a mustache, and I blacken a tooth, too.

When I hear Papi in the hall, I undo my edits and revert to the original. If they ever found out I'd tried to shame somebody with one of my pictures, I'd lose my phone forever. Not to mention that messing with photos can land you in even hotter water than I'm already in at

Seaward. Last semester, Samantha Allen set up a page called Big Butts and took pictures of people's bottoms. She fuzzed out the faces, but we could all still tell whose butt was in question, and some people got their feelings hurt. Miss McDaniels got wind of it in no time via her Internet spies, and Samantha got put on probation. Thanks to her, the entire seventh grade got hauled in for an assembly on "responsible social media behavior." Anyway, a few kids still Snap pictures of people chewing during lunch. They send it around with the hashtag #ChewMuch? It makes me feel grateful that I eat my lunch in peace with Wilson at the store.

I come back to Edna's original shot and close my eyes, thinking. I draw a crown on her head and give her a cape. Then I scribble in the words *Dancing Queen* in a plaque that I sketch over her head. I shrug, hoping she'll like it. It's the best I can think of for now.

CHAPTER 34

IF IT WEREN'T FOR BEING trapped in a booth all day with two teachers, I might actually say the Street Painting Festival is fun. All the streets get closed to traffic around Lake Worth Road and Lucerne Avenue so that artists from all over the world can make their work right on the asphalt. What's especially cool this year is that Lena's dad is one of them. Our school sponsored him so he could paint a fluorescent Tokay gecko from the Philippines, where he's from. Lena has been there a few times to see her cousins. She says the real ones make a sound at night like a squeeze toy. *To-kay, to-kay.*

Of course, I won't be wandering much to see the art. I'm on Miss McDaniels's chain, after all, helping with the

Seaward Pines information booth to work off my crimes.

As far as I can tell, our job is to snag families and tell them how great Seaward Pines Academy is, especially if we notice that they've visited the Poxel School's booth, which is right across the square from ours. Even here they're fancier than we are. They've got lounge chairs and a film that's airing on computer screens.

The weather has started to warm up again, so I'm grateful Miss McDaniels said I could wear my school T-shirt and knee-length shorts instead of our usual polyester getups. It would be murder sweating in my full uniform all day.

Not that she would let hot weather stop us. Miss McDaniels brought a fancy bladeless fan and has it pointed right at our table. That plus the bowl of candies and other giveaways should bring a steady stream of people. We've got pretty good stuff, too. Flash drives and phone cases with our school crest, even a few fancy metal water bottles with a ram head on the side, which we're supposed to save for people who sign up for a school tour. All this must have cost a bundle. I know because I'm always after Papi to order us some marketing merchandise for Sol Painting. The most he's ever agreed to is pencils, the cheapest and most boring thing.

"Here, Merci." Mr. Ellis holds out a shrink-wrapped

package of our school brochure. "The table awaits."

I tear open the brochures. For the first time since I've been at this school, Roli isn't gracing the cover. It looks like Mr. Ellis is his replacement. There's a big picture of him wearing goggles and holding up a test tube for one of his chemistry kids, Destiny Adolphe, whose family is from Haiti. It's picture-speak for "brown people welcome," even though, let's face it, Seaward Pines is pretty slim on the "brown people" part, especially when it comes to the teachers. Mr. Ellis is the only Black man in the Science Department. He tries to fill in the obvious space with posters all over his room of scientists we should know, like George Washington Carver, Mae Carol Jemison, and Neil deGrasse Tyson. But it's not the same as having more teachers like him or Miss Calderon to teach us. I wonder if it's lonely for them. I mean, even for us students, there are at least a few other kids in each grade who are brown or from different places.

"Nice shot of you, Mr. Ellis," I tell him. "You have a future as a supermodel. Maybe I'll hire you as our spokesperson for Citrus Chompers."

He looks down from the stool where he's hanging our banner and grins. "Have your people talk to my people," he deadpans.

"All right. I think that does it," Miss McDaniels says, surveying our table. "Best faces forward."

I look out as people start to trickle in and paste on my best school-loving smile.

Around noon, Lena texts me that she and Hannah are over by her dad's assigned space.

> Come see it if you can.

Miss McDaniels is busy talking with a dad who has signed up for a tour. He claims his daughter, a girl named Hiya, is "the number one in her class." Hiya looks like she wants to crawl into a hole as he goes on and on about her. We have a lot of Hiya types around Seaward, girls who know how to crush school and never get anything less than As. Not me, of course. On some test days, I feel like a mouse about to be dumped in Miss Kirkpatrick's snake tank.

My stomach makes a loud gurgle. There's ice cream across the way, and the smell from the food trucks wafts on the breeze. Burgers, fish tacos, fried everything.

Miss McDaniels shows no sign of ending her conversation with Hiya's dad, so I go to the second-in-command.

"Mr. Ellis, can I get some food? I want to check out Mr. Cahill's painting, too."

He looks up at me. He's been bored, scrolling through his phone. He glances over at Miss McDaniels and sees she's busy. "Be back in twenty minutes." He hands me a five-dollar bill. "Bring me back a fresh lemonade, please. Extra sugar, if you can."

I find Hannah and Lena at Mr. Cahill's assigned spot, drinking sodas by the curb. Unfortunately, Edna is with them, too, which I wasn't expecting.

I take a deep breath. I know Hannah isn't mine. Nobody belongs to anybody else. But things are still just getting back to normal with Hannah and me. Does Edna now have to be part of the deal? I hope not. When Edna is around, I can't completely relax. I always feel like I have to be ready for one of her zingers.

"Merci!" Hannah says.

"You've been released!" Lena says, running over.

"Temporarily. I have only twenty minutes to eat. Plus, I have to get Mr. Ellis a lemonade."

Edna treats me to a smug look and takes a long sip of hers.

We all walk over to where Mr. Cahill is working. His long braid snakes down the back of his soaked T-shirt. His feet and hands are covered with rainbow streaks of oil pastel chalk. He looks sort of like a painting himself.

"Wasn't he drawing a lizard?" I whisper to Lena. I've seen plenty in my yard, and none of them look like these detached shapes. Even when I squint, I don't see it.

"It's abstract," she tells me. "He's not trying to make it look real. He's trying to make you put it together in your own way."

I'm confused, but the colors are nice, anyway. And abstract things must be important because Dr. Newman had our school pay $5,000 for him to work here. There was an article in the paper about it and everything.

I pull out my camera and come in for a close-up of Lena watching her dad.

That's when Edna opens her mouth. "No offense . . ."

Warning, warning, warning, I think. *Activate the force shield!*

". . . but I've never understood why you'd work so hard on something that's going to disappear anyway."

I lower my camera to see what Mr. Cahill is going to say. I hate to admit how much I want to know the answer, too. Mr. Cahill's painting won't last; none of the art here will. When the streets open again on Sunday night, cars will drive right over their work, and the pastels will start to fade like colorful ghosts until they're just a memory. That's what happened to my favorite painting last year. It was the one that looked exactly like a big hole in the ground.

In fact, it was so realistic that people kept sidestepping it for days after. Though, once the hard rains fell, it washed away for good.

Mr. Cahill looks up at her and smiles, just the same way Lena does. He stretches his back and winces. "Everything vanishes eventually," he says. "Civilizations, species, people. That doesn't mean they don't have value while they exist. People will enjoy this work while it's here. Live in the moment. That's the whole point."

"Speaking of moments." I push up my glasses and check my phone. I only have fifteen minutes left to get back. "Are any of you hungry?"

"Starved," says Hannah.

"I saw cheesy tater tots that way," Lena says.

We walk along the shady part of the street, until we get to the food trucks. Hannah and I ask for a large order to share and then wander under a tree to eat. Edna insists on sizing up the truck's cleanliness first, which the guy inside doesn't seem to appreciate, especially when she demands to see his Health Department certificate.

"You want the cheesy tots or not, kid?" he asks.

In the end, she tosses him a dirty look and agrees to share an order with Lena.

I'm digging into our tots with relish when I spot two kids playing Frisbee, which is one of my favorite games.

I'm surprised when I see that it's Wilson and Darius. They're having a toss on the main lawn, where people sit on blankets and chairs to hear the bands. Wilson is doing pretty well, except for the tosses that go too wide or over his head.

"What are you looking at?" Hannah asks.

Was I staring?

"Nothing." I concentrate hard on the tots. My stomach did that strange flip again as I watched, so I sniff the tots, wondering for a second if Edna's right, and the food's gone bad in this heat. "Do these taste all right to you?"

But Hannah has spotted the boys.

"Oh," she says, grinning.

"Oh, what?" I say.

She snorts a little and takes a dainty bite of her snack as we watch Wilson make his next throw. "Do you think he's cute?" she whispers, giggling.

"Wilson?"

I could say yes. I could tell her about holding his hand. But then Edna and Lena arrive, and it's too late. So, I toss a tater tot at her instead. "Don't be gross."

"What's gross?" Edna says. "Is there a fly in the food?"

"Wilson," Hannah says, motioning with her chin.

Edna rolls her eyes when she sees them. "Oh. Well, obviously," she says.

270

I can feel my cheeks burn. That's *not* what I meant at all. There's nothing gross about Wilson. But somehow, I can't find words to say so. In fact, I can tell by how she's looking at me that Edna's diabolical wheels are turning. Her eyes grow wide and her mouth flaps open: "Mon dieu! You don't like him, do you?"

Just then, the Frisbee flies too high and far. It sails over Wilson's head, out of his reach, and lands just a few yards away from us. I try to duck behind the tree trunk, so he won't see me, but I'm not quick enough. He's already jogging toward us. He stops when he sees the four of us watching him. Farther back, Darius stuffs his hands in his pockets, looking unsure.

"Hi," Wilson says.

Hannah looks embarrassed. She stuffs a bunch of tots in her mouth, cheese oozing from the sides. Lena shifts from one foot to the other. She raises her hand to say hi.

"Aren't you going to say hi to Wilson, Merci?" Edna says in singsong voice. She gives me a wicked smile like we're sharing a joke.

But I stand there, mute. What are the rules here? Outside of school and with other people around, it feels dangerous to be ourselves. Even a *hello* or *where y'at* can mean teasing and trouble. So, it's squash or be squashed.

"No," I say, like it's the stupidest idea in the world.

271

Then, rolling my eyes, I turn my back on him.

Now I'm nauseous, for sure. I don't dare look at Lena, who hates it when people are mean. I glance over my shoulder to see that Wilson has picked up the Frisbee and walked slowly back to Darius, not running the way he was just a second before.

Even though I've hardly eaten, I can't get out of here fast enough. I push the rest of the tots toward Hannah. "I've got to go," I say. "I'm out of time."

Then, ashamed, I go buy Mr. Ellis's lemonade.

That night I'm trapped in my room with the twins as I work hard to finish up the photographs. Tía's out "running an errand" with Simón, but I don't know whether I believe her. They've been out a lot on so-called errands. It's probably weirdo adult code for "we're sneaking off somewhere to hold hands and kiss."

Meanwhile, Tomás is jumping on Roli's bed, trying to see if he can rip one of the stars off the ceiling. Axel is swinging a plastic bat at his feet as Tomás hops. He calls it his machete and says it's to chop off feet. What can I say? The future looks dim for this kid.

"If you bust the slats, Roli's going to be mad," I tell them without looking up from the computer.

But Tomás and Axel keep at it.

"What are you drawing? Show me." Tomás stops, out of breath. Axel whacks him in the ankles. "Ow!" he screeches.

Before things get worse, I turn the screen and show them the picture I'm working on.

"Who's that?" Tomás asks.

"Nobody," I say. "A kid from school." Which is a lie that makes my face burn because it's Wilson. It's my friend until maybe today when I was a jerk for no good reason.

"Let me turn you into a wolf," I tell Tomás.

I grab my phone and snap a picture of him as he mugs for me. With a few strokes, I give him ears, a long snout, and sharp teeth. He bursts into giggles, and then Axel wants me to do the same for him.

Soon they're back at it, the springs on Roli's bed sounding like a trampoline.

"We're in the circus," Axel yells, changing the game on a whim.

I watch for a second, thinking about how it was a whole lot easier to be six. I got picked to erase the whiteboard at the end of the day. I was line leader once a month. A boy named Jorge drew a line down the middle of our table, so we'd know which was our side.

It's different now. I think about lots of things, like how Wilson's hand was warm.

"Wait," I tell them. Then I close my computer and climb up on the mattress to join hands with them in their game. "Ladies and gentlemen," I call out. "The Amazing Suárez Family Flyers!"

CHAPTER 35

IT'S ALMOST THE END OF the day when Dr. Newman gets on the loudspeaker to announce the names of the kids who made the High Honor Society. First semester ended a few weeks ago, and the results are finally in.

I tune his voice out and concentrate on the worksheet that Hannah and I are still writing answers on. We're partners in Mr. Ellis's class today, and things are going much better than when we were fighting and studying earthquakes. I wish I could say the same for Lena. She's at the next table with Edna, who has been fussy all hour about one thing or another. Not even the fact that I finished all the Heart Ball photos on time perked her up. At least I'm not her partner today. The only thing worse would have been to be partnered with Wilson, who is—thank goodness—absent.

I look down at my worksheet again and fill in my definitions. Then I notice Mr. Ellis giving me a stern look because I'm not listening to the announcements the way I'm supposed to. So, I put down my pencil and try to look like I care.

But really, what's the point? My name isn't going to be read, even though I got three As this time, which is an all-time record for me. I got one in PE, of course, but also an A in social studies and one right here in Mr. Ellis's class, of all places. I have Bs in the rest.

To get on Dr. Newman's list, though, you have to get *all* As for the whole semester. For all that trouble, you go to a special breakfast with him and your parents. You also earn a fancy brass pin that you're supposed to wear on your blazer. I know because Roli had so many that he looked like a five-star general.

Dr. Newman drones on about how proud he is of "these fine students who represent the best of Seaward," and yada, yada, yada.

Then he reads the names slowly and clearly. One thing snags my attention when he's done. Edna Santos's name is not on that list. He must have missed it or else I didn't hear it. She's *always* on the list, same as Jason Aldrich, who literally pats himself on the back as soon as his name is called. More than once he's reminded us that it makes sense since his last name is Old English for "wise ruler."

I look over at Edna carefully, expecting her to lodge a complaint about this mistake. But she keeps her head down, eyes on her worksheet. Even from here, though, I can see that her cheeks are blotchy. She doesn't say a word for the rest of the hour.

After school, I head to the main office. Per Mami, I'm supposed to get a new community service assignment from Miss McDaniels every single Monday afternoon until the end of the year. They've become co-conspirators in my suffering now.

I take the long way there, hoping Miss McDaniels might forget about the arrangement and leave early today. But, no, she's still in the office. I let myself in and stand near the potted palm, trying to make myself very small as teachers file in at the end of the day to check their mailboxes. I inch behind the branches for some camouflage and narrow my eyes so that I can only see Miss McDaniels through my lashes. *Think invisible*, I tell myself as I watch her close shop.

She locks up the TV studio door and tidies up her desk one last time. Then she puts on her oversize sunglasses and reaches for her car keys.

"Merci," she says suddenly, her back to me. "Do you plan on sleeping inside that planter this evening?"

I startle and open my eyes. "Oh, hello, miss," I say. "I was just . . . admiring the shiny leaves. You're doing a fine job watering this little guy."

Unimpressed, she holds out a community service assignment slip in my direction. "I believe you are looking for this."

I sigh and shuffle over to her desk. The pass reads:

REPORT TO MR. VONG

TOMORROW AFTERNOON, 3:45 P.M.

Mr. Vong! Why him of all people? Our custodian generally seems to hate kids. Not that I can really blame him. We're always scuffing the floor he's just buffed or leaving fingerprints on the glass doors or throwing up in the least convenient places, like the carpet in the library. It's Mr. Vong who has to come in with his bucket of sawdust, while we step into the hall with our shirts pulled over our noses to avoid the stench.

"Custodial services, miss? I can barely keep my own room clean! You can ask my mom. She's found apple cores in my room from the third grade."

"Perhaps Mr. Vong can offer you some pointers in that area, then," she says. "Besides, you won't be cleaning as that would be a violation of our students' rights code, section A, paragraph six."

"Then, what's the job?"

"I've assigned you to the One World Week celebration committee. You'll help Mr. Vong with the flags first. You know it takes quite a bit of time to hang them all."

I try not to roll my eyes because that would fall in the Impertinent Behavior category of Miss McDaniels's list of pet peeves. One World Week is Seaward's cultural celebration event. It lasts five days. We fly world flags in the gym and cover the office doors with signs that say welcome in lots of languages *¡Bienvenidos! Swagat! Velkommen! Khosh Amadid!* Some classes have a food fair. We have assemblies, too, which are probably the best part. I liked the bagpipe players last year who wore cool kilts and sounded like a traffic jam. The year before that, we saw a Chinese opera with actors in wooden masks. I don't know who we're having this year. It's always a surprise.

But here's the thing. One World Week is also very weird. First of all, it's really the only time you hear anybody speak anything but English outside of the language labs— even if they really do speak another language at home. It's also the week when some of us have to brace ourselves for a lot of bonkers lunchtime questions about our families, such as "Are your parents going to make you marry someone you don't know?" and this one from Jason, which made Hannah, whose mom is Korean, kick him hard last year: "Do your people eat dogs?"

Anyway, Mr. Vong is the one who hangs the flags in the gym every year. Helping him is going to be as boring as watching paint dry—and I've done *that* plenty of times for Papi, so I know exactly what it's like. Mr. Vong works at sloth speed.

Miss McDaniels holds the door open. "If there's nothing else . . ."

"No, miss."

I watch as she hurries for the parking lot. After she's gone, I start down the hall, dribbling a crunched-up piece of copy paper like a soccer ball.

I take a shot at the girls' bathroom door and hit the sign dead-on.

"The crowd roars!" I say, and duck inside to pee before I have to go find Mami in the car loop.

When I step inside, though, I find out that I'm not alone. We've got a weeper, ladies and gentlemen. She's in the last stall, sobbing.

At Seaward, somebody is always getting their feelings trampled, one way or another. Your earrings are cheap.

Your house is small. You missed the ball in gym. You failed a big test. You have zits. You're ugly. You're just all wrong.

I know it's none of my beeswax, but I peek under the stall to see who it is. We're all required to wear the same loafers and red knee socks, so you'd think I wouldn't be able to tell. But when I look, I know exactly who's crying. It's the backpack on the ground that gives her away. It's fancy red leather and monogrammed. It's the one that slams into me carelessly at our lockers almost every day.

Edna Santos, the Queen of Mean herself.

I stay very still, like I'm trapped in a closet with a black widow, wondering how to back out of the door.

But just as I turn to go, I hear her gulp for air. What if she's sick or something? It's after school, and there are no teachers around to help. So, against my better judgment, I creep closer to the door and listen.

"Are you OK in there?" I ask.

No answer.

"Edna, I know it's you. What's wrong?"

I hear some shuffling and then I see her bloodshot eyeball pressed near the space between the door and the stall's frame.

"Go away, Merci Suárez," she says.

"Suit yourself," I say, and step into my own stall at the other end of the row. I don't get started on my business, though. Suddenly I don't really feel like peeing with Edna listening to me. Knowing her, she'll tell me I'm peeing wrong, or too loud, or whatever. Not that she'd hear me since she's sniffling even harder now.

So, I try again. "What's the matter?" When she doesn't answer, I make a hypothesis that would make Mr. Ellis proud. "Are you sore about the silly High Honor Society?"

Her voice is angry through the partitions. "What do you know about whether it's silly or not? You've never been on the list!"

I grit my teeth. "I've also never locked myself in a bathroom stall to cry over getting perfect grades. So . . ."

There's a long silence, and I think maybe I've finally shut her up. But a few seconds later, she's crying again, this time really hard. How can being smart make somebody feel this bad? One list shouldn't ruin your whole day, should it? But I can see that it has.

Then I remember how Tía helps the twins regroup after lousy days at school. At night she lies in bed with them, and they list aloud all the things they're good at. "Tomorrow will be better," she always tells them, even if she's not sure it's true.

I've had to make a Merci Is Good At list plenty of times myself, sometimes on account of Edna's mouth, in fact. I've done it enough times that I practically have mine memorized, which is the point, according to Tía. "You have to know who you are," she says, "because sometimes other people try to tell you who that is."

Listening to Edna, I remember that "I try to be kind to people" is one of the things I'm good at.

"Come on, Edna," I say softly. "You know you're one of the smartest girls in the whole school."

After a while, I hear her unlatch the door. Slowly, I do the same and step out to look at her head-on. Her face is red and swollen; her nose is dripping. She's the picture of misery. I wish I didn't care, but I'm so surprised by her sadness that I stand there gaping. Our truce has been hard to keep this year. Sometimes I think it would be easier to just write her off, to hate her forever and let that stand. But she looks pathetic, and I did promise Hannah and Lena that I'd try.

"The list isn't everything." I yank down an old Heart Ball flyer from the stall door and hand it to her. "You planned a huge dance that made tons of money. Who else in the seventh grade could do that?"

I hitch up my backpack, my bladder still full, and leave her washing her face at the sink.

CHAPTER 36

WILSON DOESN'T SAY ANYTHING ABOUT the Street Painting Festival last Saturday, and so neither do I, which is A-OK with me. We're back at the Ram Depot, running our sales numbers now and thinking up new business plans to present to Miss McDaniels. We've already crossed off a few ideas from our list, like selling tickets to a movie night. I wanted one of the earlier sagas in the Iguanandor Nation franchise to tie in with what we sell at the store. But Wilson found out that we'd need to buy a movie license. "Too much coin," I told him when he showed me the cost.

"But I think it's time to go epic," Wilson insists. "This place was a money pit before you and me. Now we've got customers in here every day *and* we're turning a profit."

"What's epic, though?" I ask.

We both get quiet to think some more. I glance into the cafeteria, watching kids eat their lunch in the same setup as always. Nobody is assigned seats, and yet everyone gravitates to the same territory every day. How does that happen? It would be nice to shuffle the deck every once in a while. I mean, why do only certain people get the good tables all the time? The bouncy seats on the field trip bus? The best spot on the bleachers? The most popular friends?

Slowly an idea starts to form.

"How about if we move into real estate?" I say.

Wilson looks up from his calculator. "Real estate? What are you even talking about, Merci?" he says.

"Well, look at those prime spots near the windows. Why don't we use those as a way to get customers? We can give away a ticket with each sale from the Ram Depot and do a drawing every week. The winner gets to host their friends at whatever table they choose."

He looks at Jason and the other boys at their table and chews on his pencil. "They'll kill us."

"Why? They don't own that table. Plus, they have as good a chance as anybody else—if they're customers. I mean, I think they do. You're the statistics guy."

"What about the kids who can't afford to buy a lot of stuff?"

I dig my hand into the endless box of pencils. "We'll point them very quietly here. Anybody can afford a quarter—and a sale is a sale. Think of it this way, we can be like social Robin Hoods—taking from the haves and giving to the have-nots."

His face brightens slowly into a grin, all those freckles like stars on his nose and cheeks. "You know, Merci, you might be a pain, but you're also kind of a genius," he says. "I'll bet you can convince Stopwatch to go along with it, too."

I feel the color rising to my cheeks as we sit side by side on the floor, contemplating. I should never have been a jerk to him. Here's the truth. It feels good to eat lunch and share pie every day in here with him, and I like tossing around business ideas and arguing about the finer points of Jake Rodrigo movies. It's not like anybody else wants to do that with me, not even Lena and Hannah. I wonder if he likes it, too, or if that's just dorky me.

"Thanks," I say.

I stare into my hands, thinking back again to Saturday. "Hey," I say. "I'm sorry I was such a butt at the Street Painting Festival. With the Frisbee and all that."

He keeps his eyes on the calculator, and I wonder if he's even heard me. Then he taps 53045 and turns the calculator upside down. "Did you know you can spell on this thing?" ShOES.

I did know, thanks to Roli. So, I type in 8075 for *slob*. We figure out *giggle* (376616) and *egg* (663), too. The only word I really wish I could type, though, is *sorry*.

A knock at the store window startles us.

Jason and a few of his goon friends stand there, money in hand, leering at us. It only takes a flash of his ugly grin to realize that Wilson and I have been sitting a little too close to each other. I brace myself and sure enough, Jason starts in.

"*Eww.* What are you two doing in there?" He elbows the kid on his left like it's all a big joke.

"Working," I snap. "What else?" I show him our idea notebook to prove it.

Wilson is bright red as he scrambles to his feet. "What do you want?" he asks.

But I don't hear the answer. My mind is circling back to *eww*. Does he mean that *I'm eww*? Or that Wilson is *eww*, the way Edna said? Or does he mean that the idea of both of us together is *eww* like liver and onions?

Jason points out a Ferociraptor from our new display and plunks down his twenty-dollar bill like it's nothing. Wilson puts the toy on the counter and gives him his change. He turns to me when they're gone, and I can see that his shoulders have hunched up near his ears.

"Too bad it's not like in the movie where he'd be

shredded to death before he got back to his table," Wilson says.

I try to laugh, but my eyelid droops, and I feel the drift. "Who cares about him?" I say. "He's a jerk."

That's what I'm supposed to feel when I shrug things off. Except I don't.

I care. We both do. And I hate myself for it.

Suddenly, the store feels too small for us, like we're in a fishbowl where everyone can see us.

"Where are you going?" Wilson asks as I grab my things and head for the door.

"To see if Miss McDaniels will sign off on our idea," I say.

I walk from the cafeteria until I'm out of view and near the main office. But I don't go to see Miss McDaniels. Instead, I duck inside the girls' bathroom for my turn to hide for a while.

CHAPTER 37

I USED TO SCARE OTHER moms to death on the playground with my climbing. They'd point at me and yell for Mami to save me from the top of the slide, where I'd followed the big kids. But Mami knew I didn't need saving. I could get to the top of the rock wall when I was still in diapers. My favorite place to think was the highest branch of the bottlebrush tree in our yard, when Abuela wasn't looking, of course.

Too bad Mr. Vong doesn't know this about me.

"I don't like to brag, Mr. Vong, but if you let me up on the scaffolding with you, I could cut your work time by maybe half."

I look up at him hopefully but don't add what I'm

really thinking. *And then we would not have to hang flags for weeks on end.*

He frowns at me like I am already on his last nerve. "You will not climb up here. You will organize the flags by alphabet and do what I say."

We're in the gym after school. The flags are in two big bins in the corner. Inside are pieces of neatly folded fabric in plastic bags with the country's name on white stickers. I've never heard of some of these places. Nauru? Benin? Palau?

"How many flags are in here, anyway?" I ask, dejected.

"One ninety-three," he says.

My heart sinks. Mr. Vong averages hanging only three or four of these a day. "It's going to take us forever," I mutter.

His excellent bat hearing goes into full effect. "People are proud of their flags. They give their lives for them. We will not rush."

No, clearly, we will not. His walkie-talkie crackles as he finishes the first knot. It has taken ten whole minutes.

"Afghanistan is first," he says. "Hand it here."

One down. One hundred and ninety-two to go.

Mami texts me that she's running late with a patient, so I sit at the car loop curb to wait. I'm there only a few minutes when my phone buzzes.

Roli. He's wearing his visor and work shirt from Snout

BBQ, so I guess he's on break. I can practically smell the hickory sauce.

"Oh good," he says. "I see Mami and Papi didn't murder you after all."

"Funny," I tell him. "That might have been less painful. I have community service for the rest of the year."

"Doing what?"

"Whatever Stopwatch says. Like hanging world flags with Mr. Vong."

He shoulders shake as he laughs. "Oh man," he says when he finally catches his breath again.

"Hang on." I move to a shady spot near the building and sit down where no one can hear me.

"Hey, can I ask you something?" I say.

"I'm not giving you two thousand dollars or harboring you as a fugitive," he says.

"Just listen." I take a deep breath. "Am I . . . *eww*?"

"What?"

"You know: *eww*. Am I gross as a girl? You have to tell me the truth."

He leans back against the cinder-block wall behind him. "Brothers can't really weigh in on this stuff, Merci. It's super weird."

"Can't you try?" I hope my voice is steady around the lump that's stretching my throat. "Please."

He stays quiet for a minute, looking straight at me. "Who said that to you?"

"Nobody. I'm just asking."

He waits with that annoyed expression he puts on whenever I try to lie to him.

"OK. Jason Aldrich," I say.

He heaves a heavy sigh and shakes his head. "I'd say that to somebody that's thirteen—who is not related to you in any way and who has a brain and good taste and a sense of humor—you are definitely not yuck."

"Eww."

"Right—*eww.* Whatever. You're not that."

"How do you know?"

"Merci!"

"How?" I ask.

"Because thirteen can suck, OK?" He stands up. "Look, my break is almost over. Do yourself a favor and block out that kid Jason. He probably wishes you were his girlfriend or something."

"Ugh!" It's like he's splashed me with acid. "Why would you say such a thing? GOD!"

"Because . . . thirteen," he says. "Gotta go." And then I'm by myself again.

CHAPTER 38

"WHERE ARE YOU GOING?" I ASK.

It's after school when I find Tía about to climb into Simón's car. Again.

She stops when she hears my voice and looks over the roof of his Toyota. I'm standing near the laundry line, and I guess she didn't see me. She's got her sunglasses perched on her nose and a newspaper folded under her arm.

"Oh, hi, Merci. We're just going to run an errand."

"Oh." I make a face. She's not telling the truth. I can tell by the way she chews her lip.

She's been disappearing a lot lately and coming home at dinner with no real explanation. Even now that she's not teaching dance, she still seems to be busy all the time.

How much kissing can you do? And today I'm stuck hanging laundry—which is *her* job—when I should be helping Wilson with ads for our tickets for the table raffle idea. Miss McDaniels loved it. We start next week.

"Don't worry," Tía says. "The boys are watching TV at Abuela's."

I don't answer her. I just shake out the next towel and pin it to the line.

Tía pauses. "Merci, don't be like that."

I pin Tomás's T-shirt next.

She shuts the car door and walks over to me. She nudges the basket with her foot. "Thanks for doing this."

I glance back at Simón. "Mami said you missed the twins," I say. "You could be here with them now."

"I do miss them." She looks back over her shoulder at Simón and then lowers her voice. "It's not what you're thinking, you know. About me and Simón."

My cheeks blush. It's none of my concern, as Mami would point out. I shouldn't get into Tía's business. And for a second, I think that's what she's going to tell me.

But Tía takes the clothes from me and drops them back into the basket at my feet.

"Come with us. I want to show you something," she says. "We're taking a ride for a few minutes," she yells to Mami.

A little while later, Simón pulls his car into a strip mall

that we pass on the way to the supermarket. It's the one on Haverhill with Tinto Service Station selling GOMAS DE MICHELIN: $70 on one end and the shuttered drive-thru bank on the other. We maneuver around an abandoned grocery cart in the empty parking lot and pull into a spot near a vacant storefront. It has a faded red awning and three tiny bullet holes in the plate-glass window.

"What are we doing here, Tía?" I ask her.

She pulls out a key from her purse and turns the lock. The door takes three hard shoves to unstick. "Follow me, please," she says.

I step over the threshold and go inside. The air-conditioning has obviously been off for a while because the smell of mold in the carpet is overpowering, and the air feels stuffy. My allergies kick in right away. I feel a tickle at the back of my throat.

Simón goes somewhere in the back, and the lights come on a few seconds later. I just stand there in cautious silence, like Jake Rodrigo when he's landed on a new planet that might be hostile. We're in a large room. I can see that there are two smaller rooms in back, along with what looks like a bathroom behind an old beaded curtain.

"This place is kind of spooky," I say. "What is it? And why do you have the key?"

"Nada de spooky," Tía says, flashing me a smile. "It's

an old nail salon that went out of business a few years ago. But as of yesterday, it's my new dance studio and after-school center." She moves her hand along an imaginary marquee in the air. "Welcome to the Suárez School of Latin Dance."

"The what?" A dance school? My hands go sweaty in the heat.

"Yes. And in time, I want to make it even more. I can add homework help if kids need it and healthy snacks until their parents come home from work. There's plenty of room for activities for adults during the day, too." She turns to me, her voice clearly excited. "I couldn't leave all those kids without anything to do. And I've always wanted a business of my own. It's time to do something else besides waiting tables. And now I can even bring the boys with me after school."

I look at her, dumbfounded. So, this is what they've really been sneaking away to do?

"Does anybody else know yet?" I ask her.

"You're the first," she says. "Which makes sense. I'm going to need a good assistant manager in training to help me run things. Are you in?"

"Who's the manager?"

"Remember Aurelia?"

"Tía," I say.

"She'll be fine."

I walk around, checking things out slowly. It's hard to picture Tía anywhere but at the bakery. But maybe that's not fair. She was imagining something else for herself instead, something we didn't see.

Simón knocks on the wall. "We'll need drywall repair in a couple of spots."

"And two coats of paint," I say. "Walls, ceiling, trim."

"Mirrors over here," Tía adds. "And a new floor."

I look around, thinking. "It's going to take a lot of work," I say.

"I know," Tía says. "But do you think we can do it?"

I look from Simón to Tía. I hear the word that drives almost everything about our family, from how we eat to how we sent Roli to school and how we take care of Lolo.

We.

Around here, it usually means free labor, lots of it. But I know it also means family.

And so, I say, "Yeah, I think we can."

CHAPTER 39

HANNAH AND LENA WENT TO the movies this afternoon, but since Mami said I couldn't go, Edna went with them instead.

I'm so mad.

We were in the middle of yanking up carpeting so Simón and Vicente could install the new floor next week. I was sweaty right down to my underwear thanks to the busted fan on the air conditioner.

"But why?" I said. "It's Saturday. This isn't fair!"

"Merci, for goodness' sakes. Look around!" She had drywall dust in her eyelashes from the morning work on Tía's studio. "¡Tienes obligaciones! We all do. There are only three weeks left before this place opens, and we have to finish up. Now, hand me that hammer."

I did, but as soon as Mami pulled back the pad, an air battalion of palmetto bugs swarmed us from a nest underneath.

"*Argh!*" Mami screamed. I had to duck to save myself from the hammer she tossed across the room in her panic.

The roaches glided through the air until Papi came running in with a can of Raid to fog the whole place. Afterward, all that was left were heaps of shiny brown carcasses as far as we could see. Guess who had to sweep those up, too? I can still hear them crunching under my shoes.

Now all I can think about is how my friends—and Edna—are having fun while I'm bored at home eating dinner at Lolo and Abuela's with the twins. I'm on babysitting duty while my family works on the dance studio until they drop. I check my phone. The movie started an hour ago. I'll bet they're at the best part, too, sitting in the last row, like always, with a double tub of buttered popcorn and a box of Milk Duds to share.

"Why are you picking at your food, niña? Masitas de pollo are your favorite. Are you getting sick?" Abuela puts down the tissue paper flowers that she's making for the studio and places her hand on my forehead. "The stomach flu is going around, you know."

"It's not the flu. Sweeping up roaches can kill anybody's

appetite," I say. But the truth is that the roach fiasco and missing the movies are only part of the reason for my bad mood.

Lolo has been even quieter than usual today. He didn't even say "Hi, preciosa" when I came in, and when I sat close to him on the couch and whispered about what Mami had done to me, he didn't say much, except "figúrate" under his breath. I had to be satisfied with resting my head on his chest and brooding on my own.

I miss his voice.

Abuela looks over at Tomás. "Mi cielito, stop wiggling that tooth at the table. It's not polite."

"And also, it's gross," I say.

"But it's almost out." Tomás thrusts his remaining baby incisor out with his tongue until it's practically horizontal. "I want Ratoncito Pérez to come. He said he'd be back when I lost another tooth."

"He only comes for children who eat their dinners," Abuela warns.

Tomás's eyes widen. "Is that true?" he asks.

I shake my head when Abuela turns back to her work and make a mental note to keep track of that tooth. With all that Tía has on her mind, she might forget.

"Vamos, viejo, you, too," Abuela tells Lolo gently. "Your

food is getting cold, and you hate it that way, remember?"

Probably not, I think.

Lolo's plate is still more than half full, which isn't like him. He loves fried chicken chunks even more than I do, especially when Abuela puts soft onions on top of his rice like tonight. He smiles and stares at the silverware for a few seconds before finally picking up his knife. He tries to spoon rice on the blade.

"Lolo," I say, alarmed. "The *fork*."

Abuela puts her hand on mine.

Was my voice too loud again? Maybe. It happens that way sometimes when I have to repeat myself.

"Merci, I think we've all been working too hard," she says. "My eyes are getting tired, at least. Why don't you put these paper flowers back in my sewing room for me? I'll work on them again tomorrow. You and the boys can watch TV," she says.

Tomás and Axel race away from the table without a look back. I start to scrape what's left of my dinner into the garbage can. For once, Abuela doesn't even fuss at me about wasting food when there are people all over the world muriéndose de hambre.

"I'll get those," she tells me. "Go on."

I gather the flowers like a bouquet to my chest and

walk them to her sewing room carefully. The twins have turned on the TV themselves in the next room. Zany cartoon *boings* sound through the house.

When I go back to join them, I glance into the kitchen. Abuela is still sitting next to Lolo at the table, and our plates are still uncleared. She holds a spoonful of onion rice near his mouth, and he opens wide when she tells him. All I think of are the hungry chicks that nest in our ferns—helpless, with mouths wide open to the sky.

I turn away. I can't help it. It scares me to see.

CHAPTER 40

TUERTO HAS A BAD HABIT of stealing my socks from the basket of clean laundry. He's done it as long as we've had him. He pounces on them when they're balled up in pairs and wrestles them like they're his sworn enemies. Sometimes, like today, it takes a while to get them unhooked from his claws.

I forgive him, even if he does make pulls that ruin them. He's not the easiest cat to love sometimes, but he's ours.

We got him a long time ago or, really, he got us. Tuerto just appeared one day in the yard and set himself down in the sunshine, tail twitching, already a full-grown cat.

"Don't name it," Roli told me. "It's feral." He meant Tuerto was wild and wouldn't like people. And he was right. Tuerto wouldn't ever get close enough to pet. He'd just stand at our screen door, watching us and running away the moment we invited him in.

All that changed when Tuerto got hurt. He came into the yard injured one day, limping and bloody in the face. Mami guessed he had been in a bad fight, probably with the mama raccoon that she'd seen raiding our trash a few nights before.

Mami wrapped him in a thick towel and sped to the vet. The sad part is that Tuerto lost his eye that day. But the happy part is that he also became ours.

After he came back from the animal hospital, things changed. We kept him on the patio in a crate that we borrowed from our neighbor until his bandages could come off the next week. We named him Tuerto, and he stopped hissing and even let me scratch his ears once in a while in the yard after that. And a few months later, when the socket was healed to a slash, I opened the door one hot day, and he finally came inching in.

Lolo watched me serve him tuna from Abuela's pantry. He told me that Tuerto had wanted to be ours all along. "He just didn't know how to trust us," Lolo said.

We haven't talked much since I found her in the bathroom, but I run into Edna in Miss McDaniels's office on Monday afternoon. She's plastering the door with welcome phrases in different languages. They're preprinted in all kinds of fonts on sticky plastic.

Anyway, I'm here to get my community service marching orders for the coming week as usual, hoping she'll release me from flag duty with Mr. Vong. Miss McDaniels is on the phone, though, so she motions me to have a seat on the bench to wait for her. I heave a sigh and drop my backpack like an anchor at my feet, hoping to give her a clue. She should know that Edna and I are like a blow dryer and bathwater. Putting us together can produce deadly results.

Edna turns to me and skewers me with a doubtful look. Then she says the weirdest thing.

"So, I hear you have a dance studio."

I blink, caught completely off guard. Edna isn't one for small talk with me, or anybody else for that matter. "Who told you that?"

"Hannah." She rolls her eyes and glues on *Bienvenue* in a big curly script. "So, when did *that* happen?"

I didn't say it was a secret when I told Hannah and Lena about Tía's plan and how we're all fixing up the studio these days, but I wish I had. Plus, now I know that they were talking about me at the movies, which makes my gut flutter. Saying what, I wonder? I get mad at Mami all over again, but I don't want to give Edna the satisfaction of seeing me sweat.

"Just recently," I tell her vaguely. "We're still getting ready for our grand opening."

"You said you *hated dancing*," Edna reminds me. "I'm quoting you here."

"One hundred percent," I tell her. "But it's my aunt's place." I try to shrug like it's no big deal, but my shoulders still ache from pulling up carpet. "I mean, your dad's a podiatrist. Are you going to tell me you love feet?"

She turns away to choose her next sticker.

I sit on the bench staring straight ahead and wondering exactly what Edna thinks about our studio. Tía isn't like those ballet teachers with the turned-out duck feet and French words like Edna knows. And Tía probably won't have fancy students who perform at the Kravis Center, either. Ours is a homemade place. We don't even have a shiny brochure. Nobody around here is going to think that's legit, especially not Edna.

Bored, I pick at a knot of wood in the bench. But after a few minutes of silence, Edna pipes up again.

"¿Enseña merengue?" she asks me quietly.

My eyes dart to hers. Edna and I barely speak to each other unless we have to, and *never* in Spanish even though it's one of the few things that we have in common. (The

306

others are that we are human and female.) Her family is from the Dominican Republic, and mine is from Cuba.

I look over my shoulder to see if anybody else is in the office, listening. Mr. Vong and I have been working on hanging up all the flags for One World Week, but none of those pretty banners really protect you from stares when people think you don't belong here.

"Yes. Y otros bailes también," I say.

Just then Miss McDaniels hangs up the phone and comes to the counter.

"Merci," she says. "I apologize for the delay. What can I do for you?"

I step forward. "It's Monday, miss, so I need my community service assignment."

"You'll be with Mr. Vong again, of course," she says. "The job is not done." Edna stares down at her shoes as Miss McDaniels hands me my pass. She doesn't look as smug as she usually does when I'm suffering.

"Thank you." I stuff the sheet in my book bag and walk out the door. I don't get far when I hear Edna's voice behind me.

"I like merengue," she says.

I stop in my tracks and turn around in the hall.

"What?" she says in a huff. "It's true."

I head to the car loop, thinking about Edna the whole

way. She was in little pieces when I saw her last, but now it's like she's put herself back together in a slightly different way that I don't recognize. I think I've seen the tiniest bit of friendliness, but I'm not really sure. It reminds me of Tuerto at our front door all those years ago, hissing, and unsure if he really wanted to come in.

CHAPTER 41

"**WHAT ARE YOU SWATTING AT** now?" Wilson asks me. We're in the Ram Depot, happily watching Jason sulk over his PB&J at the unsteady table near the salad bar. Diandra Allen, from the Chess Club, is eating with her friends by the windows for a change today. She was our first winner of the drawing.

"Sorry. I thought I saw something buzz by." I shudder a little. I just haven't been the same since the palmettos.

Anyway, I keep rummaging in my backpack for the sample flyer I've brought to show him. At times like this, I wish I were a neat freak. Headbands, dirty gym shorts, chewed pencils, and crumpled papers come tumbling out. Finally, I just shake it all onto the floor by our feet.

"There it is," I say when I spot it. "It's not done, but what do you think?"

Wilson reads aloud:

PUT SOME TINGLE IN YOUR TANGO AND MOJO IN YOUR MAMBO!

THE SUÁREZ SCHOOL OF LATIN DANCE

ENROLLING STUDENTS NOW

CLASSES START APRIL 3

REASONABLE RATES!

INÉS SUÁREZ, DIRECTOR

"'Mojo in your mambo'?" he says, as he reads it again. "I thought mambo was a snake."

"That's a mamba," I say. "Don't make fun."

"I'm *not* making fun," he says.

"Who's making fun?" Lena is at the window with her bag lunch. She's eating in here with us today instead of in the courtyard where she likes to read.

"Not me," Wilson says.

She opens the half door and lets herself in.

"Good, you're here, too," I say. "I need a favor." I hand Lena the flyer and point to the spot where I've left space for a photo. "I need pictures of people dancing. It's for ads and the website and stuff."

"And?" Wilson says.

"And I was hoping you guys could come over to do a photo shoot."

Lena breaks into a huge grin. "Cool," she says. I'd feel hopeful except that her tastes aren't like anyone else's around here. With Lena, *cool* and *strange* are sometimes hard to tell apart. I mean, when I told her about the studio, she suggested that Tía teach us how to dance with eggs.

"Once, Dad and I saw a company that tossed them to each other as they swung on trapezes," she told me. "It was very cool."

Wilson wrinkles his nose. "Modeling? I don't know."

"It's photography," Lena says. "And maybe Darius can come, too," she says.

"*Darius,*" I say. "You realize I need people who don't look terrified."

"He's calmer every day," she says.

"Come on, Wilson, please?" I beg him. "It's for flyers like this one. I need people who look good on camera."

Wilson grins. "You saying I'm good-looking?"

Wait. *Is* that what I'm saying?

I put my mouth into overdrive to throw him off the trail. "Nobody really has to dance. We'll just pose you so you look like you know what you're doing."

When he doesn't answer, I lean in and lure him with the very last thing I can think of. I slide my uneaten pie in his direction.

"I'll let you have my dessert for an entire month."

He hesitates. "I'm not wearing funny shoes," he says.

Lena claps. "Oh, good! I'll bring the eggs!"

Mr. Ellis is starting a new unit, so we all know it's going to be a DBBD—death by boredom day. Even though I do my note-taking on an iPad, my eyes get tired when I write this much. I always end up with a headache.

I'm just about done when Edna and Hannah come over to my table. Everyone else is already packing up since it's the end of the day, but Edna's here to bug me, I guess. I rub my temple. A visit with Edna is only going to make my head feel more like it's squeezed in a tight vise.

"Hi, Merci," Hannah says. She looks a little skittish, like something is on her mind—or else she has to go to the bathroom. Is she going to back out of coming to the photo shoot? Maybe she's decided to go to Edna's house after school instead. "We were wondering—"

Edna cuts her off. "I'll get to the point. You haven't officially asked, but I'm willing to do you a solid and offer up my services. When should I report?"

"Report for what?"

"The photo shoot," Edna says impatiently. "I'm extremely photogenic, as you probably know."

Of all the people I want to photograph, Edna is at the bottom of my list. But just as I'm about to tell her so, I remember her face on all the Heart Ball flyers. Annoying but effective.

Maybe I should reconsider. Edna will be easy to pose since she can follow directions. And she did say that she likes to dance merengue. She can make that fierce look, too, that says, *I will knife you in your sleep.* A face like that is practically made for some of those dramatic dances I've seen Tía studying on YouTube. Plus, there's the brag factor. Let's face it. She'll want to show everyone her pictures. That means more eyes and more website clicks and maybe some customers.

So, I tiptoe out on the ledge. "OK," I say slowly. "We're meeting tomorrow afternoon at four thirty."

She opens her mouth to argue but pauses, confused. "OK?" she asks.

I rub my temples harder. "Yes."

"Well, then, you're welcome," she tells me, and then turns to Hannah. "I'll arrange our ride."

That afternoon, I head over to Abuela and Lolo's. Tía sent me over to find that old picture of them dancing from when they were young. She loves the idea of using my pictures in her lobby, but she wants the biggest one to be the old photograph that Abuela has in her bedroom. A young Abuela is in a flowery dress, and Lolo is wearing a bow tie around his skinny neck. They're all smiles, in midspin. Tía wants to enlarge it, she says, to poster size and put it in the lobby where everyone can see it.

But when I reach their screen door, I don't go in. There's music coming from the CD player, and Lolo and Abuela are inside *dancing*—or at least standing very close and swaying.

I think of all the times I've seen them dancing. Tía Inés's wedding when I was five. At parties, too, back when Lolo was sure-footed and he'd let me stand on his shiny shoes as he moved. With Abuela at the baptism for Doña Rosa's granddaughter. People watched and clapped when they were through that time.

Lolo barely moves. He's fading like one of those colorful street paintings Mr. Cahill works on. "Everything vanishes," he told us at the festival. "Live in the moment," he said. "That's the whole point."

I swallow hard just thinking about the fact that it's true about people, too. They vanish, sometimes a little at a time. One day, Lolo won't know how to move his legs anymore. One day soon, he won't be able to dance.

One day, which feels like it is right here at every turn.

Abuela whispers in his ear as he struggles to move his heavy feet. What is she telling him, and does he still understand? What do they say to each other when his mind is fading like this?

I hear rustling behind me, and I turn. It's Mami, still in her scrubs. At first, I'm sure she's going to scold me for spying again.

But this time, she puts her fingers up to her lips and hugs me tight. We sit on the stoop together, watching for as long as the music lasts.

CHAPTER 42

"BIENVENIDOS TO THE SUÁREZ SCHOOL of Latin Dance!"

Aurelia puts away her nail file as people start to traipse in on Thursday afternoon. She's perched behind a repainted desk near the entrance. She's wearing a flowered blouse that's a little too tight around her bosom and fake pearls at her thick neck. "Sign in, por favor," she tells Wilson and Darius. They rode here together. Lena steps in right behind them.

"These are just my friends, Aurelia, not real clients," I tell her. "Do they have to sign in?"

She looks at me over her glasses. "As the front desk manager, I have to follow the rules," she says primly. "Last name first, please."

Just then, Tía spots us from the back room.

"Hello, everyone!" she calls out from the folding table she's set up near the back. She's arranged for snacks before we start taking pictures.

Stela is already here, since she walked across the street after school. She's watching my friends with worried eyes as she munches on another cookie, and of course the twins are here, sock-skating back and forth.

The bells jangle as Hannah and Edna step in last. Instantly, the twins squeal and go running at Hannah full speed.

"Incoming," I call out.

"They're harmless," Lena tells Edna, who turns away, horrified. "Mostly."

Hannah gathers them up in a hug and swings them around the way they love to say hello.

That's when I notice that Edna has come in lugging two black storage cases that I recognize only too well. It's the IMA Paparazzi equipment that we broke at the dance.

She walks over to me and holds the bags out like an offering. I stare at her, blinking and afraid to reach for them.

"You'll get better pictures with this," she says simply.

Then she sets them down and heads to where the others are already putting their things away in the cubbies that Simón installed only yesterday.

Vicente steps out from the door in the back just then. Everyone turns. He's not in work clothes or his soccer shorts. Instead, he's wearing black pants and a red T-shirt. His longish hair is gathered in a neat bun.

"I thought we might need another male dancer to mix things up," Tía says, motioning him forward. "Everyone, this is Vicente."

He raises his hand to us, still shy about his English. Wilson and Darius look relieved to see another boy older than six. Hannah wiggles her fingers at him. But Edna looks like she's become a victim of the full-body-bind curse from Harry Potter. Her face is bright pink, and she can barely say hello.

After everyone is finished snacking, it's time to get started. I unzip the IMA Paparazzi bag slowly and see the new iPad inside. I pull open the background and put the stand together carefully, too.

"This way, please," Tía says as she leads everyone else back to the dressing rooms. A few minutes later, they all come back wearing matching red T-shirts like Vicente's and the black pants I asked them to bring. The girls have roses in their hair, too. Abuela sent them over. I know they're paper, but they look so real. Hannah's even has special glitter bling, just the way she likes.

"Light test," I tell them. I pose them against the backdrop and shoot a few pictures to see if we're getting glare.

That's when Tía comes to look over my shoulder. She purses her lips, thinking.

"What's wrong?" I ask. "This thing takes great pictures."

"I'm not a photographer," she says, "but nobody looks alive. See?"

I already know she's right. Darius and Lena have fake smiles. Edna, still in shock over Vicente I guess, reminds me of the cheap wax dummies at Ripley's Believe It or Not! up in Saint Augustine. None of these pictures will be any good.

"Hmmm," Tía says. "I have an idea. How about if we loosen up these robots a little?" She calls out to everyone, "New plan, friends. In a circle, please."

I stand by the camera, waiting.

"Merci?" Tía says. "Will you join us?"

"But I'm taking the pictures," I say.

"You need to loosen up like the rest of us, amorcito." She wiggles her finger at me and then turns back to the group. "We're going to stretch a little first and then do a few simple steps, nothing fancy, I promise. Tomás, Axel, why don't you lead us off with your favorite warm-ups."

The twins are only too happy to be in charge, especially

if they can show off for Hannah. Tomás warms up his face, he says, by puffing his cheeks and doing gross tricks with his loose tooth. Axel shows us how to swing our arms in a big circle in both directions like windmills.

Then it's everyone else's turn. Lena makes us wave like grass on a plain. Edna does something she calls jetés, which are little side jumps in ballet. Wilson shows us his foot alphabet to warm up the ankles. When it's my turn, I ask Vicente to help me demonstrate Frankenstein kicks from soccer, so you don't tear your hamstrings.

Then Tía fetches a few of Papi's old T-shirts and rags from the back room. "Now we're going to clean the floor together," she tells us.

Floor cleaning? My eyes dart nervously to Edna. "But the floor is brand-new," I point out.

She ignores me and drops a shirt on the ground. She puts one foot on the shirt and pushes it to one side. "Slide-together. Slide-together. Slide-together. Now you try."

She arranges us in a line and drops a T-shirt beside each of us. "I want you to slide sideways until you get across the room."

We start moving with our shirts. I get tangled once or twice but keep at it. As we go, Tía walks around and makes us hold our elbows up, a little like chicken wings.

When we finally reach the other side of the room, she applauds. "And *that* is the merengue," she says.

"From the Dominican Republic," Edna calls out importantly.

"Very true," Tía says. "Let's try it with music!"

Tía pairs us like mismatched socks: Hannah and Tomás, who is only up to her belly button and wants to show her his tooth. Axel and Stela, who immediately try to bend back each other's wrists to see who's stronger. Wilson stands with Lena, comparing who's taller. Edna is still wide-eyed and staring at Vicente, who's probably wondering if she's hypnotized.

Tía calls Darius, who is blushing deeply, to be her demonstration partner.

"The leader puts their hands here." Tía shows us by placing Darius's hands on her waist. "Hold your arms up in frame, like this, from the shoulders," she says. "No wilting limbs."

I stand behind my camera as she turns on the music. Suddenly, it's as if a mood lifts and we're at a party. I snap photos as fast as I can, clicking as she makes them switch partners again and again, girls with another boy, girls with girls, boys with boys. Everyone is laughing and talking.

When Tía stops the music, she turns to me, eyes flashing.

"Come with me." She grabs me by one hand and Wilson by the other.

"What?" I blurt out. "I don't dance." But Tía ignores me.

"Wilson, why don't we start with you in the lead? Then, when you feel like it, you can switch."

His ears are glowing. "But doesn't the boy always lead?" he asks.

"Dancing is like a conversation," Tía says. "It's a give-and-take. There's no reason it can't be a back-and-forth of who leads if we want to be more modern."

"Wait. Modern? Do you want to use my eggs?" Lena says.

"Eggs?" Tía says.

"I'll explain later," I whisper.

Tía turns back to Wilson and me and arranges our arms in a frame. I'm dying inside as she places his hand on my back and makes us clasp our other hands high. His hand is sweaty, or is that mine?

"Look at one another, please."

Wilson blows up his cheeks like a puffer fish.

I'm praying for my eye to stay straight for once. I concentrate as hard as I can on Wilson's face. Freckles. Brown eyes with a little yellow. Tía stands close enough that I smell her Abre Camino body spray. "You're working together, OK? Just like in your store at school. But now the job is to make your four legs look like two," she says.

Worry flashes across Wilson's face at the word *legs*. I feel his hand wilt a little as his eyes flit down to his own feet. Tía lifts his chin.

"Eyes up and shoulders back. You will help each other move. Otherwise, it will be like trying to push a refrigerator across the room." She tosses a single shirt on the ground for us to step on. "One foot here, please."

"But, Tía," I begin.

"Here, please."

We place our feet where she says.

Tía stands at the sound system, and a new song starts. The tempo is so fast, it's almost funny. My face is flaming red.

"Ready?" Tía calls out.

"Ay, ay, ay," Wilson mutters.

The beat is steady—*pun-pun-pun-pun*. Tía claps it for a few bars. Wilson closes his eyes for a second, like when he's doing a math calculation. He nods his head to the beat until he's got it. And then he says, "Ready?" I feel him push slightly against my back.

My heart is pounding as I push my foot against the T-shirt exactly the way he does.

Slide-together. Slide-together. Slide-together.

Think sports, I tell myself.

"Wonderful!" Tía calls out. "Eyes on each other's faces, please. Smaller steps, Merci, so we don't move like speed skaters."

Wilson looks like he's in agony. "You're crushing my fingers," he whispers.

"Sorry."

"We have to turn," Wilson tells me as we're moving.

"Why?"

"Because we're going to dance out the door and into traffic," he says.

We switch leads without missing too many of our steps. Then Tía motions everyone else to join in.

I don't know exactly when she starts taking pictures because I'm concentrating so hard on keeping my steps right. But I eventually notice her standing where I'm supposed to be. She snaps pictures until the music finally stops.

We're out of breath and sweaty, but everyone is having a good time.

Wilson drops my hand just as the bells on the door jangle and his mom steps inside. She's here to pick him up. Outside in the parking lot, Mrs. Kim is locking up her car to come get Hannah and Edna. Lena's dad stands outside, studying the empty wall of the buildings that face the street.

"Oh! We lost track of time!" Tía says. "But thank you all so much for helping us with the photos today. I hope I'll see you again."

As everyone gathers their things and says their goodbyes, Edna walks over and helps me break down the photo stand.

"Thanks for letting me borrow this," I say. "I think we got some great pictures."

She leans in. "Send me the ones of me with Vicente."

Then she hoists the bags to her shoulder and heads out to Mrs. Kim's car, where Hannah is waiting.

After they're all gone, I look over the shots with Vicente, who's helping us pack up. They're beautiful pictures, if you ask me. We'll have a hard time picking which ones to use.

"What are you doing with that one?" Vicente asks.

It's the shot that Edna told me to send her.

"Sorry. Edna wanted it. Is that OK with you?"

He shrugs. "That's one strange kid," he says. "She doesn't talk much, does she?"

"It depends," I say carefully.

"At least she can dance." He heads to the back room.

I press send, but there's another picture that I study for a long while after that. Tía took this one, I guess. It's me and Wilson, both of us smiling wide, not really thinking about anyone's eyes on us at all.

"Nice one, right?" she says, peeking suddenly over my shoulder. "He's a good dancer, don't you think?"

I shrug. "I guess."

"Admit it: dancing isn't so bad if you have a good teacher." She wiggles her eyebrows at me. "And a partner you like."

"Don't," I say.

She throws up her hands and goes to the back to shut off the lights.

When she's gone, I download the shot to my favorites folder and then help her lock up for the night.

CHAPTER 43

"THIS IS EXCITING," I TELL Mami. We're sitting at Abuela's table, cutting out page five from a stack of newspapers we collected. There's an article about Tía's dance studio in today's *La Guía*. That's the Spanish paper Abuela reads for all the stuff the *Palm Beach Post* doesn't cover. The reporter came last week to interview Tía and take some pictures. They also used two of our shots. One is Edna posed with Vicente, as if they're doing the tango. There's a photo credit for me, with my name in tiny letters running underneath: Mercedes Suárez. The other shot was taken by Tía. It's the one of Wilson and me.

I cut out the article carefully, making sure my name doesn't get snipped. I want to frame one and take copies to school to show my friends.

When I get to our lockers, I hand Edna and Wilson each a copy of the article.

"Check it out. We've made the big time."

Wilson breaks into a huge grin. In the photo, he's standing tall, his hand clasped with mine.

Edna purses her lips. "No offense, but my right side usually photographs better."

Hannah and Lena crowd around to look. "Let me see!" Hannah says.

"Be careful not to smudge it," Edna tells her. Then she turns to me. "Do you have more copies for me? Or is there a link? I'll need it for my portfolio."

"You have a portfolio?" I ask. "Of what?"

"My accomplishments," she says. "My parents say it will help me get into college."

"Hello. You're in seventh grade," Wilson points out.

"Meaning?" she says.

That's when Jason horns in out of nowhere. He sticks his head over Lena's shoulder to see what's happening.

"What's so interesting over here?" He snatches the article from my hand, nearly ripping it, and snorts. "Dude! Is that *you*?" he asks Wilson.

Wilson doesn't say anything, but Jason squints and looks closer. "It *is* you! Dancing like a princess and holding hands with Merci. Oooh!"

I feel my fists ball up.

"Give it back," I say, but he ignores me.

"They're not holding hands," Hannah snaps. "They're modeling as dancers." She crosses her arms and gives him a satisfied look as if she's been helpful. I swear, sometimes she's like a baby crawling into rush-hour traffic.

Sure enough, Jason zeroes in. "Modeling, too!" He rolls his eyes at Wilson and shakes his head. "At the Suár-ess Eh-schoool of Lah-teeen Dahnze." He says it thick and slow with an accent that is supposed to sound Mexican, I think.

Before I can say a word, Edna steps right up to him. She puts on her angriest face and grabs the article back. "Knock that phony accent out of your mouth and get lost," she snaps.

"Or else?" Jason says.

"Or else you'll be telling Miss McDaniels how you lost your teeth," Edna says.

He makes a rude gesture with his finger.

Without warning, Edna shoves him as hard as she can. His head bounces against the lockers, making them rattle.

I stand there, stunned, as Jason reaches for his scalp and comes back with bloody fingers.

Everyone has started crowding around as he scrambles to his feet. It's like clash of the Ferociraptors. Which man-eater will win?

That's when we hear a sharp whistle and high-heeled clicks coming in our direction. Miss McDaniels's lips are drawn to a tight line and her eyes are steel points.

"What *on earth* is going on here, seventh-graders?" There's almost never a fistfight at school, something she always brags about to parents who want to know about safety at Seaward Pines. She looks around at all of us, but the entire hall stays silent. So, she lowers her voice to a deadly quiet that makes the hair on my neck rise. "I expect an answer."

Hannah shrinks into me in horror.

"She pushed me for no reason!" Jason blurts out. "And now I'm bleeding." He shows her his fingers.

Miss McDaniels arches her brow and slides her eyes to Edna. "Miss Santos?" she says in disbelief. "Did you lay hands on someone?"

"He had it coming." Edna's voice is sassy, even though her eyes are puddled with angry tears.

"Follow me. Both of you," Miss McDaniels orders. "As for the rest you, get to class this very minute. You're all tardy and unexcused."

CHAPTER 44

JASON AND EDNA ARE GONE all morning. They're not in gym or math. They're not at lunch, either. And when Hannah sneak-texts Edna from the girls' locker room, she gets no reply, which never happens. The last time they were seen alive was by Lena in the office during announcements, when they were waiting on opposite sides of the bench for their parents to be called. It's like now they've been teleported somewhere far away.

"You don't think they expelled her, do you?" I ask.

Wilson takes a bite of his sandwich. "Prolly. I mean, we're talking Miss McDaniels." He gives me a knowing look.

"But it's not fair," I say. "Doesn't that bother you?"

Wilson shrugs.

"Maybe we should tell Miss McDaniels what really happened," I say. "It's not like Edna lost her temper for no reason the way Jason said. The liar."

Wilson frowns at me. "No, thank you. I don't need Jason on me for anything else. He's enough of a pest as it is. Besides, Edna can take care of herself. Remember, she's not exactly the sweetest specimen."

I glance at the picture of all of us in the newspaper clipping. He's right about Edna, which makes everything even harder to sort out. Why are people so complicated? Bad guys should always just be bad guys, and good guys should always be good guys. That way, you'd be able to like them or hate them all the way through.

"But Jason started it all, and she stood up for us this time," I say. "Don't we owe her? I mean, we saw what happened. We're witnesses." It still burns me up that Jason teased us—and that I couldn't find my own words to shut him up myself.

He takes a swig of milk. "Do you know what happens to witnesses, Merci? They end up dead or in a witness protection program."

"Don't be so dramatic."

"I'm being realistic," he says firmly. "Snitching will make everything worse. Believe me. Stay out of it."

I don't respond, but the whole time, I'm in a battle with myself over what I want to say. I'm thinking of my truce with Edna this year and how hard it has been to honor it. But I'm also thinking of something bigger that has nothing to do with Edna at all. I must be staring off into space for a while, because Wilson nudges me with his foot.

"Snap out of it," he tells me.

So, I turn to him slowly. "Can I ask you something?"

"Listening . . ."

"Did you have fun dancing with me?" I push the newspaper toward him. "It looks like you were having a good time in this picture."

When he doesn't say anything, I think maybe I imagined that it was actually cool to dance with him. Maybe the whole thing is as made up as Jake Rodrigo. I feel like a giant hole is opening up in my stomach.

But then he says, "Did *you* have fun?"

Heat creeps up my neck. "I mean, not like World Cup soccer pleasure, but . . . yeah, I think I did."

He lets out a breath, his cheeks bright red. "I had fun, too," he admits. "Except the hand crushing. That hurt, actually. I have bruises."

My throat closes a little with excitement, so I have to wait until I think my voice can sound regular enough. "If we both had fun, why does Jason get to stomp on that? And why does he get to lie about Edna now?"

He stares at his hands and doesn't answer me.

I grab my things and head for the door.

"You can stay here, if you want," I say. "But I'm going to Miss McDaniels."

"Not feeling well?" Mr. Ellis is in the main office, filling out paperwork for our end-of-the-year field trip to the Museum of Discovery and Science in Fort Lauderdale.

"I'm fine. Just waiting to see Miss McDaniels."

Just then, the conference room door swings open and Miss McDaniels comes through. She has a writing pad clutched to her chest.

"Hello, miss," I say.

She turns to me and I wave weakly. The look on her face when she sees me is like someone has dumped a year's worth of student folders on her desk. She checks her watch and walks over to where I'm waiting.

"Merci," she says. "Is this important?"

"Are Edna and Jason expelled?" I ask.

She gives me a severe look. "It would be completely inappropriate for me to discuss other students' disciplinary issues with you. Now, is there something else you want to talk about? Because if not, you need to head back to class at once. The bell is about to ring."

She walks back to her desk, but I'm on her heels like a puppy.

"I wasn't just being nosy, miss."

"You most certainly were."

"OK, miss, maybe a tiny bit. But I was just wondering because I saw what happened with Edna and Jason today, and I have some intel you might find interesting."

She looks at me over her glasses. "Intel."

"Yes, miss. I'm here to make a witness statement." I look around her desk. "Where's the Bible to swear on?"

"This is not a court. I do not require Bibles," she says.

So, I pull a chair close to her desk. "OK. Then get your tape recorder."

"Merci!"

"All right, pen and paper are fine if you want to go old school."

I wait for her to flip to a clean page in her pad.

"Be quick," she says. "What information do you wish to share?"

I hand over the newspaper clipping.

"This is my family's new dance studio. The fight with Edna and Jason all started because a few people came over to help us take pictures so we could run ads. Some of those pictures are these." I point at my photo credit in *La Guía*. "I took that one. See?"

I wait as she scans the piece over her glasses. Mr. Ellis catches my eye and looks away. He's pretending not to listen, but he can't fool me.

"Impressive," Miss McDaniels says. "Congratulations. But I don't see how it impacts this morning's unfortunate events."

"Jason Aldrich saw the pictures, and then he got really rude, miss." I pause, wondering how much to say. From the corner of my eye, I see Mr. Ellis still at the boxes. "He made fun of Wilson for modeling and dancing, for one thing. And then he said 'the Suar-ESS Eh-school of Lah-teen Dahn-z' in a pretend accent, like he was making fun of us—and I don't have an accent, miss. Only Abuela and Lolo have one in our family, and also—who cares? But anyway, when Jason said *that*, Edna told him to shut up."

I don't add what I'm thinking, which is that I was glad.

She narrows her eyes at me and flips back through her pages until she finds the right spot. "Actually, I have sworn statements that she told him he was going to 'lose his teeth.'"

"Well, OK, miss, but what she *meant* was for him to be quiet because he was being rotten. Don't you see?" My chest feels tighter as my thoughts get jumbled. Mr. Ellis is still there, and I glance at him. He isn't pretending to look at his mail anymore. Instead, he's watching me like he's doing one of his observations, and it's up to me to show him that I know how to think.

So, I take a deep breath the way Lena always says I should. "If Wilson wants to dance, nobody should make fun of him. And also Jason needs to pass the basketball in gym the right way and stop saying *eww*."

"Excuse me?" she says.

"And he shouldn't copy people's accents like he did today. I don't like it." My eyes go to the word strips that decorate the office door. I'm thinking about all the little pieces of these countries that are inside all of us here at school, parts of us that we try to hide or forget sometimes to get by. "It's not very funny, miss, or welcoming."

I come to a full stop when I realize that I'm sweating and that my hands are trembling a little. I swallow hard and force myself not to cry the way Hannah does when she's upset. Maybe Miss McDaniels will say I'm too sensitive. Or maybe she'll say I should ignore Jason, the way Mami does, which always makes me so mad because *how can you ignore someone in your face like Jason, when there are lots of Jasons and only one of you?* So, I say the next part slowly to see if she can really understand. "It's like getting paper cuts all the time, miss. They don't look like much, but they hurt, especially if you get a lot of them, day after day."

Mr. Ellis comes around the counter without being invited and sits beside me, with his hand on my shoulder. "That's a lot to put up with," he says. "And you shouldn't have to."

Miss McDaniels has stopped writing. Her hands are folded on her desk, and she stays silent for several long minutes.

"I'm very disappointed to hear about this, Merci," she says.

For once, I don't look away. "Jason isn't telling you the truth, miss. He was being horrible. Edna didn't shove him for no reason. She pushed him because she was sticking up for me and Wilson. Doesn't that count for something?"

Just then the warning bell rings, and she stands up to let me know my time is done. "You're going to be late. Mr. Ellis, perhaps you can walk Merci to class." She turns to me. "Thank you for your statement," she says. "Dr. Newman and I will take the matter from here."

"Yes, miss." I try to take the clipping from her desk, but she puts her hand on mine.

"I'll keep that, if you don't mind," she says.

CHAPTER 45

IT'S ALMOST DINNERTIME, BUT I'M at the studio where Tía and Simón are putting the finishing touches on the decorations for opening day this weekend.

She listens as I explain all that happened because of the dancing pictures.

"But did I do the right thing?" I ask. "Do you think everything is going to be worse for Wilson because I went to Miss McDaniels?"

Tía steps off the stool and puts down the garlands of paper flowers that Abuela made for the doorway. "I think it depends on what you mean by *worse*."

She crosses to the cooler and gets us two Jupiñas before sitting on the floor with me, our backs resting against the new mirrors. Her mascara is smudged around her eyes, and she smells a little like dirty socks. The air conditioner still isn't working so great.

"You told the truth," she says. "That takes guts—and so does doing what makes you happy. It's better to be who you really are, but it's not always easy, Merci."

She twists open the bottle tops, and we clink in a toast.

Just then, Tomás peeks his head in. He's with Simón, who's behind him and wearing a big grin.

"We have an announcement!"

Simón digs in his chest pocket and produces Tomás's tooth.

"Ratonthito Péreth ith going to come for it," Tomás lisps through the big space in front of his mouth. "Ith's my turn." He looks at Tía. "I want to go home now, Mamá." The whine in his voice tells me he's been here long enough.

"Just a little while longer," Tía says. "I have to finish up here first, cielito."

"I'm done fixing the bathroom sink," Simón says. "I can drive them home. I have to pick up Vicente from there, anyway."

Tía looks at him with moony love eyes. When Tomás runs off to tell Axel they're leaving, Simón puts the tooth back in his pocket and whispers to me.

"You going to be the mouse tonight, or you want me

to do it?" he asks. He doesn't say what I know. That he stays late sometimes, long after the twins are asleep, so he and Tía can be alone.

"Be my guest," I tell him. "It's a buck, though."

He winks at Tía and gives my head a squeeze on the way out.

Then Tía and I get back to work.

I have not ever texted Edna in the two years I've known her. That's what I'm thinking as I stare at the phone on my nightstand. Finally, I pick it up:

It's Merci. Are you OK?

That's not all I want to say, though, so I tap out a few more words that feel even harder to write:

Thanks for sticking up for us, btw.

And I add the link to the article in *La Guía*.

I wait a long time for a reply from Edna, staring at the rolling ellipsis that appears and disappears until finally there are words:

You're welcome.

We're in PE the next day. Mr. Patchett is starting our flag football unit outside, which I love since the weather isn't too hot yet. He makes us sit on the bleachers for attendance, though. They're damp with dew this early in the morning and sitting here wets our shorts. Edna scowls at him, her hands tucked under her bottom to keep herself dry. She'll have detention today. Hannah told me. So will Jason, who did not need a stitch in his scalp after all. And of course, they had to trade apology letters in homeroom, the way Miss McDaniels always insists.

Anyway, Mr. Patchett asks us to count off, one-two, and line up for passing drills. Michael is our center. He crouches low and peeks under his thick legs at Wilson, who's going to throw the first round of passes before it's Lena's turn.

For once, Jason doesn't run his mouth, not even to laugh at the kids who drop a pass or seem scared of the ball, not even when someone gets bonked in the head. I don't know if that will last or if he'll just get mean again next week. But for now, it feels like a relief.

I get into the rhythm of the drills.

"Hut!"

Snap.

Throw.

Wilson is doing great, I think, though the passes are short. People aren't running far enough away. I know he can throw better, if only he had the chance.

When it's my turn, I run as far as I can across the wet grass, pumping my legs hard like I would in a soccer game. I turn to look at him, ready to receive. He pauses for a second and grins before twisting back. A wobbly spiral sails through the air and lands right in my arms, just like I knew it would.

I hold the ball high over my head and let out a hoot.

Even from here, I can feel his smile.

CHAPTER 46

WE'RE ALL DRESSED UP FOR opening day on Saturday. My whole family is here, plus Lena and Hannah, who offered to help. Aurelia, dressed in a bright pink suit with lipstick to match, is sitting behind her desk, arranging and rearranging the pencil cup and sign-up sheets. Music pipes through the speakers that Papi hooked up late last night. "Dale Fuerte" is playing, and Abuela keeps muttering complaints about indecencia, but at least Lolo looks excited. He's wearing his best button-down shirt and shiny shoes, and Abuela has combed his hair back with that gel that makes his curls sit flat.

Tía looks the best of all. She's wearing her new pair

of yoga pants and a bright red T-shirt with our logo, a flamenco dancer. Her hair is in a pretty bun, too. You'd never be able to tell that she hasn't slept in weeks.

Our main job today, according to Tía, is to greet people at the door and steer them to Aurelia, who will sign them up for the mailing list.

I have to admit, everything is beautiful in here. The new floors, the sparkling mirrors, the curtains, the framed pictures in the lobby. Even the bathroom got new toilets and sinks, and they smell of the incense sticks Señora Magdalena sent to wish us luck. You'd never know this was a roach motel just a few weeks ago.

Tía adjusts the refreshments table again and peers out the window. The balloons we tied to orange cones in the parking lot are bobbing in the *whoosh* from a passing car.

"What if no one comes?" she whispers.

I check my phone. We've been open for seven minutes. "Ánimo, Tía. Everyone is on their way."

But is that true? If it's not, this whole day is going to feel like if nobody showed up to your birthday party. When Tía's not looking, I light another Abre Camino incense stick, just in case.

Finally, though, people do start to arrive. Stela is the first to get here.

"Bienvenidos!" Tía throws open her arms for a hug.

Right behind Stela are the boys from Tía's old class, and some new boys I don't know.

"¡Que rico huele!" Stela says, making a beeline for the treats. She pauses to make her selection.

"There are drinks in the cooler, too," Lena says. Hannah lines a few bottles on the table to show her.

Soon other people come, new faces we've never seen before. There's a lady pushing a stroller, who needs to kill time while she's having her tires changed at Tinto's. A boy and his parents who were curious about the balloons. A few others say they saw our flyer at the laundromat or the library. Tía talks with them all and points them in Aurelia's direction.

Finally, she flickers the ceiling lights.

"It's time for the demonstration," she announces. "Por favor, que vengan los niños."

I'm just finding my way to the chairs she's lined along one side of the studio when the bells on the doors jangle again.

This time, I stare in shock. Miss McDaniels steps inside.

Hannah, Lena, and I exchange looks. "What is she doing here?" I say.

Lena smiles and heads for the door with Hannah. "Let's find out!"

But I feel stuck to my chair. It's only when Mami gives

me a warning look that I unglue my feet and walk over with her and Papi to say hello.

"What a surprise!" Mami says.

Miss McDaniels starts to extend her hand, but Mami has already come in for a polite hug and kiss, which is how we say hello. So, Miss McDaniels kisses each of her cheeks, too.

"Mr. and Mrs. Suárez, so nice to see you," she says. "I had a chance to read about your family's new dance school. We were very proud to see Merci's photography featured as well." She motions to the article from *La Guía* that we have framed near the door. "I decided to stop by, since I'm doing some school errands today."

I don't believe a word of it. I can still picture her at the Heart Ball making sure kids are far enough apart. "You dance, miss?" I blurt out.

Mami gives me a little pinch near my elbow.

"Not very well, I'm afraid," she says. Then she breaks into a smile because she spots Abuela and Lolo sitting near the pastries. Lolo was always her favorite presenter on Grands' Day, back when he still attended. She moves toward the empty seats near them. "And how are you, señor and señora? It's been a long time."

Abuela hugs Miss McDaniels, too, but Lolo only

smiles. I can see he doesn't recognize her at all. "It's Miss McDaniels," I whisper to him. "From school."

"Yes," he says, but there is nothing behind it.

Miss McDaniels glances at me and then sits beside Lolo anyway. "Why don't you girls keep us company while we watch the lesson?"

So that's what we do. Tía demonstrates how kids do the warm-ups. Then she lines them up in pairs to show how to dance the merengue. Miss McDaniels's legs are crossed, I notice, but she still moves her foot in time to the music. And when it's time to applaud, she and Lolo clap the longest every time.

Tía tells us the history of merengue, which was banned for a while because of all that booty swishing. Then she also tells people about why she wanted to open the center in our neighborhood, and why it matters to give kids a place to learn fun things after school. She tells them about adding homework help in a few months. She has Mami stand up and explain that we'd like to add a movement class for older adults during the day. Finally, she introduces Aurelia and all the rest of us in the Suárez family, and we each have to stand and wave, even Lolo.

"Now, who would like to try the cha-cha next?" Tía asks.

Hannah and Lena partner up and run to her.

My eyes dart to Miss McDaniels, wondering what she's thinking. When she sees me watching her, she says, "Don't you want to dance, too?"

"I'm fine here," I tell her. "I'm not very good at it."

"I see," she says, but her eyes flit to the photograph of Wilson and me on the wall.

So that's how the afternoon goes until Tía finally thanks everyone for coming. The kids start to go home, carrying extra pastries out the door on paper plates and napkins.

Miss McDaniels stands up to leave, too. She pats Lolo's hand, although he's "resting his eyes," as Abuela explains. Then she walks over to Tía Inés and introduces herself as "Jennifer McDaniels from Seaward Pines Academy."

"Hello, Miss McDaniels. Thank you for coming today."

Tía knows all about her, of course, but she doesn't let on about my complaints. Instead, she drapes her arm around my shoulder and pulls me close.

"Well, the truth is, I wanted to bring this invitation to you in person. It's from our headmaster, Dr. Newman."

Miss McDaniels hands Tía a fancy envelope from her purse. It has the gold and red Seaward Pines crest in the corner.

"For me?" Tía says.

What in the world would Dr. Newman want to write to

Tía about? I wonder. So, I stay put near Tía and read along with her.

> *Dear Ms. Suárez,*
>
> *It is with great interest that I recently read of your new youth program that focuses on Latin dance.*
>
> *As you may know, every spring, Seaward Pines Academy hosts an annual celebration of cultural heritage called One World Week. In past years, we have been privileged to host art groups and speakers from around the world.*
>
> *This year, we would like to focus on our own community. As such, we'd like to extend an invitation for you and your students to perform on April 30.*
>
> *I realize this is very late notice, but we are hopeful that your schedule can accommodate our request.*

Please make arrangements with Ms. Jennifer McDaniels in our main office at the number below. She will answer any questions you might have about our facilities and other logistics.

Sincerely yours,
Dr. Robert J. Newman III

Tía looks at her in surprise. "This is very nice of Dr. Newman, but we've only just opened," she says. "We won't be ready to perform for months."

Miss McDaniels stands straighter. I can read her face from here. It's the Ram Depot all over again. Nothing is going to stop her.

"The event is still several weeks away," she says. "And if it helps, we are prepared to offer a stipend of three thousand five hundred dollars for your performance."

Tía cocks her head to listen again. "Did you say 'three thousand five hundred dollars'?"

Miss McDaniels nods. "Actually, we may have some costume budget to add as well. I will check with our Theater Department to be sure."

Tía looks at all of us. Abuela, who has been eavesdropping with Mami and Papi, perks up right away.

Although she hasn't said so, I'm pretty sure Abuela would love the chance to make costumes out of something sturdier than papier-mâché.

"Are you sure?" Tía says. "These are children dancing, not a professional company like you usually have."

"Very sure," Miss McDaniels says. "We've had wonderful shows for our students over the years. But it has come to our attention that maybe our approach has missed the point of One World Week entirely. It isn't really about students watching a performance for an hour or eating new foods for a week. We want them to respect and get to know one another better in our own school community."

My stomach squeezes. Tía turns to me and whispers, "What do you think? It won't be easy, and I can't do it without you."

I look over at Lena and Hannah, who are nodding like crazy behind Miss McDaniels. I know for sure they'll help. But they won't be the problem. People might tease us about our costumes or if our music is all en español. They might laugh that we're holding hands and standing close as we move. Who needs that? Plus, it's going to be a lot of work.

Still, there's over three thousand smackers on the

table, so I channel *Peterson's Guide to Building Your Business,* chapter 14, "Making a Deal," and get right to the negotiations.

"It's an interesting offer, miss," I say, "but I need to be released from my extra community service to make it happen. There are lots of details in a show like this, you know. And I *am* doing it for the school."

Mami looks like she'd like to hit me with a chancleta, but Papi is next to her, trying hard not to grin.

Miss McDaniels doesn't so much as blink. "That's quite a request," she says coolly as she plots her next move. "However, I might be willing to agree to your terms on one condition—that you're part of the performance."

"Me?" The idea of swishing my bottom from side to side in front of the whole school starts a cold sweat down my back.

"Though it would be a significant sacrifice, I hope it's one you'd make for your school—and your family." She's got me in her clutches. "Are we agreed?" she asks.

Tía gives me a careful look. "You don't have to," she whispers, squeezing my hand. "I know it's hard."

But I'm Team Suárez and we don't back down. So, I take a step closer to Tía and say, "I'll do it."

"Dr. Newman will be very pleased to know this,"

Miss McDaniels says as they shake on the deal. "I'll send over the paperwork next week." She grabs her purse and puts on her sunglasses. "Thank you all for a most lovely afternoon."

If I didn't know her better, I would swear she does a little cha-cha step as she reaches the door.

CHAPTER 47

I CALL A SECRET MEETING at the Ram Depot early that Monday morning. The front office is still dark when we get there, and Mr. Vong has to unlock the doors for us.

Darius and Lena arrive first. Then Hannah and Edna show up and, of course, Wilson.

"Thanks for coming," I say, and make room on the floor for us to sit in a circle. When I look around, though, my mouth rusts closed.

Darius leans toward me. "Deep breaths."

Edna, never much of a morning person, watches me for a couple of exhales and loses it. "Are we here to watch you hyperventilate like Darth Vader?" she says. "Out with it. What's so important that I had to sacrifice thirty minutes of sleep?"

"Go easy . . ." Hannah warns her. "Take your time, Merci."

So, I take the plunge and explain what Hannah and Lena already know. I need more dancers for the show—specifically, them. I go over the whole plan: three weeks of rehearsals every day after school, costumes that Abuela is already designing, and then the big performance.

When I'm done, Darius cracks his knuckles loudly. "In front of the whole school?"

"We'll all be together up there," Lena says gently. "I can be your partner."

Edna picks at her shiny loafer, thinking. "Do we all get to pick who we dance with?"

I nod.

She looks pleased. "Vicente, then, and I'm in."

Hannah blushes a deep red.

"You can dance with him," I say, "but he's eighteen, just so you know."

"So?"

"So, he can already grow a full beard."

"We're just dancing," Edna says, shrugging. "Plus, people say I look older."

I glance at Wilson. He's been the quietest of all of us. He's staring at his shoes.

"I know that some people might laugh," I say. "I can't stop them, and that's going to stink."

Edna leans in, eyes narrow. "They *won't* laugh if we're good, like I intend to be."

Wilson is still thinking.

"If you don't want to do it, I understand," I say.

But Wilson makes a face at me. "Didn't you say that other people don't get to decide what's fun to do?"

My heart starts to race. "I did."

Wilson shrugs. "OK, so it looks like I'm your partner, woadie. But I'm bringing goalie gloves for protection." He wiggles the fingers I crushed last time.

The lights in the halls start to flicker on. A few teachers unlock their doors as kids begin to arrive for early morning tutoring.

I put my hand in the middle of our circle the way we sometimes do in soccer. Hannah and Lena stack their hands right away. Edna and Darius join, too. Wilson adds his last. I look at them all, a light feeling rising inside of me. It's like Team Suárez at home, except this is another team that I'm building out here on my own.

"We shake it," I say.

And all their voices come back as one. "We shake it!"

CHAPTER 48

"FIVE MORE MINUTES," TÍA TELLS us as she sweeps up some of the crumbs we've left on the studio floor. For the past few rehearsals, Tía has been bringing us Cuban sandwiches from the bakery, so we can eat together and do our homework before we start all that business of one-two-three, *this* way, one-two-three, *that* way. With only a week to go until we perform, I have blisters on top of blisters. At night, I hear the songs in my head. J.Lo. Marc Anthony. Pitbull. Celia Cruz and all those old-school sounds that Abuela said we needed, too.

Hannah asks, "Did you guys hear that Banana escaped from Miss Kirkpatrick's tank last night?" She closes her math book with a bang and shoves it in her backpack.

"Who's Banana?" a kid named Gilberto asks. He's one of the dancers from the same school as Stela, along with a girl named Emeli and her brother, Adrien. At first, it was a little weird having us all together, but now we just concentrate on getting our steps right.

"Our snake at school," I tell him, shuddering. "She's a ball python."

"An albino, too, so she's bright yellow and white and pretty." Lena scrolls through her camera and finds a picture of Banana in her tank, all coiled and sleepy.

Emeli's eyes get wide. "¡Ay! Gross!"

"Tell me about it," I say. Personally, I only like thinking about Banana behind glass. I mean, she's five feet long, which is only an inch shorter than me if I were lying right next to her, God forbid.

Darius decides to speak up today. "Banana eats frozen mice every couple of weeks. You have to feed her with tongs in case she thinks your hand is a mouse, too."

Stela slides closer to me.

"Can we talk about something else, please?" I ask. Every time I think about Banana slithering around loose, I get scared. The only thing that seems more terrifying is dancing in front of people.

Edna caps her pen and stretches. "Well, it's old news, anyway," she says. "Mr. Vong found it curled up behind a toilet in the everyone bathroom at lunchtime. I heard him radio Miss McDaniels in the office."

"I may never pee in that bathroom again," I say.

Darius and Wilson crack up.

Emeli takes a bite of her cookie and tells us her class has a fish tank with eight blue tetras that swim as a school. Adrien's teacher keeps a guinea pig named Twitch.

"He bites if you hold him too tight," he says.

"All right, if we're done with homework and pet stories, let's get some practice in," Tía tells us. "Abuela is going to finish fitting your costumes today, too. When it's your turn, head to the back room." She checks her list. "Hannah, you're first. The rest of you, time to warm up."

Hannah squeals and dashes off to the back room, where Abuela has her try on a shiny green skirt and a wrap for her hair with sequins. The rest of us push our backpacks to the edge of the room and take off our shoes and socks for another go at the four dances we're going to perform. Wilson keeps his brace on to move easier.

I try to put on my game face. I like doing homework together and talking about stupid stuff. But when it comes to doing what I'm not good at, like dancing, I'm not so confident.

"*Uff!*" Wilson grunts when I stomp on him again.

Tía stops the music because we've caused a pileup. I drop my hands in disgust.

"I can't do it!" I say.

"Don't you hear the music?" Edna asks.

Tía steps forward just before I answer. "Why are we here?"

"To make bank," I say bitterly.

"To have fun," she corrects. "And to show some dances and music that kids at your school might want to learn—¡y punto! This is about dancing from the heart, Merci. No offense, but nobody here is ready for the conservatory." She looks pointedly at Edna.

But I still know that I'm going to make the show look terrible. If people laugh at us, it's going to be on me.

"Merci!" Abuela calls me for my fitting. A blessing.

Last week Mami drove Abuela all the way down to Miami to get the best deal on some fabrics that are the color of tropical fruits. I picked a color called Prussian blue, like my favorite oil pastel. Abuela made it into a skirt that twirls as I dance. The wrap for my hair ends in a twisted knot near my temple. The boys have it easy, in my opinion. They wear plain black pants and guayaberas in colors that match their partners' outfits.

I stand on a crate in the dressing room, listening to the others and watching through a crack in the door. Edna and Vicente are the best at merengue, which is why they'll have a solo. Abuela drapes my skirt on me and marks it with chalk and pins.

"Are people going to see my underwear if I spin in this

thing?" I pluck at the rows of ruffles that she's planning to attach to the fabric.

Abuela takes the pins out of her mouth. "I'm going to stick you if you keep moving. And why all this worrying? Don't you have faith in my design skills? I already told you, I'm not making you look cartoonish." She means the pictures we googled of men shaking maracas and wearing big ruffled sleeves. The women wore pineapples in their hair pieces. I almost cried.

"It's not that."

"¿Entonces qué?"

"I just don't understand what's wrong with wearing dark pants and a T-shirt or something? We don't normally dress like this, not even when we dance."

"Merci, these are not everyday clothes. These are costumes. Now, what's really wrong?"

"I'm a terrible dancer," I say. "I'm just not like you and Lolo."

"Ah." She slides the first pin in place and kisses my cheek. "You are like you, Merci. And that's enough. Now, stand still, niña, so I can concentrate. I promise, you'll look so spectacular, no one will care how you dance."

CHAPTER 49

ON THE MORNING OF OUR show, Tía is waiting in the driveway for me. The twins are strapped in back, completely hidden behind a sea of skirts, next to Vicente, who came extra early with Simón. They're going to help drive the other kids to Seaward. Axel makes an opening in the fabric and sticks out his tongue at my "Buenos días."

"Stop playing with them," Tía snaps. "The costumes are going to be in tatters for the show."

"Did anyone complain about them missing school?" I ask, buckling in. Tía wrote a note to get special permission for the twins, Stela, and the other kids who don't go to Seaward to perform with us today.

"Be serious, Merci. Their teacher looked like I'd handed

her a million dollars." She checks her rearview mirror to make sure she can see past the costumes and pulls out of the driveway, nice and slow.

The Millicent B. Kiegel Theater has a big fountain in front and a brass plaque of the lady's face that it's named after in the lobby. Vicente stops pushing the bellman's cart that Mr. Vong left for us long enough to try to read the words. He doesn't say much, but I know what he and some of the other kids must be thinking. Everything looks strangely perfect and unreal, like a movie set. The flowers that are planted by color and size. The fieldstone walkways and stone benches. The palms without a single dried frond drooping down. Even the bikes filling the racks, sparkling and colorful as candies. He stops for a minute and looks through the window toward the sports fields glinting in the sun.

"This way," I say.

I lead us all past the box office and stanchions. The theater has red velvet seats to match the curtains. Tiny microphones hang from the ceiling, and there's a control booth at the very back of the auditorium. I show the twins the trapdoor in the stage floor where the Ghost of Christmas Past popped through last year. I point out where a whole orchestra can play so no one can see them at all.

When we make it to the dressing rooms, Tía looks around and lets out a long whistle, her fingers trailing along the lights on the mirrored makeup stations. The twins hide behind the screens that are for fast costume changes, but Tía's worried eyes are on me. Until this very second, I haven't seen her look unsure, but now I see a break in the calm, like maybe she finally understands why it's hard to feel like we can perform in a place like this.

She walks over to me and takes my hand, though. "Todo bien," she whispers bravely. "This is going to be fine. It's coming from our hearts."

I nod, even though my stomach flutters as she sits me down to start on my hair. The morning announcements begin, and I hear the muffled lines of the Pledge of Allegiance. Tía combs my curls, and I close my eyes, trying to calm down with every stroke. When she's done, she knots my hair in a bun and tucks the blue hair wrap in place. It has only the tiniest feathers. Then she puts blush on my cheeks and eye shadow on my lids. She puts her own gold hoops in my ears. I barely recognize my reflection when she's done.

"¡Bellísima! You look like a professional," she says, just as the others start to arrive. Then she goes in search of Stela and Emeli.

Lena, Edna, and Hannah crowd around my chair. The

boys are with Vicente in the dressing room next door.

"Merci! You look amazing!" Lena says.

"You too," I say. Her spiky hair is smoothed flat into a slick bob that's tucked behind her ears. And she's not the only one who looks different. Hannah's straight black hair is fastened into a long braid along her back, and her cheeks are already dusted with glittery blush and glued-on rhinestones near her eyes. Edna is still wearing her uniform, but her face is the fanciest of all. She's wearing red lipstick, eyeliner, and even long eyelashes that look like little spiders sitting on her face.

Soon, there's a knock on the backstage door. It's Mr. Ellis, with Jason in tow.

"Miss Suárez?" he says to Tía. "I'm Mr. Ellis, Merci's science teacher. I'm here to help with the technology check today." He puts his hand firmly on Jason's shoulder. "And this student will be helping me with lights."

We all look at Jason warily, especially Edna, who glares at him through her false eyelashes. The word *sabotage* darts around my brain like a squirrel.

Mr. Ellis adds, "I'll be with him the whole time."

From backstage, we can hear the sound of the students filing into their seats. All of our parents are in the front row, according to Wilson, who is peeking from the wings, like we're not supposed to, and giving us reports. I sneak next to him and spot Lolo and Abuela right in the middle next to Mami and Papi. Simón is also there, wearing his best shirt and holding a small bouquet of flowers, which must be for Tía. It has always been Lolo and Papi who've given flowers in our family. But now, I guess, Simón is part of that, too.

A big screen has been lowered and there's our name and logo in gigantic projected letters:

THE SUÁREZ SCHOOL OF LATIN DANCE

The slides scroll to pictures of the studio and of Lolo and Abuela dancing all those years ago. Then come pictures that Tía must have taken on the sly as we've rehearsed these last few weeks.

Miss McDaniels steps out of the darkness and startles us. She hands Tía a wireless mic and shows her how to clip it on.

"Everyone is seated, so we are ready to get started. I'll introduce you, Miss Inés Suárez, and then you can introduce the program."

Then she turns to look at all of us. It's like she's taking a mental picture. Hannah with her glittery cheeks. Edna in her red skirt that matches the scarf at Vicente's neck, looking every bit as old as she claims she does. The twins in their white outfits match Stela's. Emeli, Gilberto, and Adrien in yellows and oranges. Lena and Darius in daring purple. Finally, she looks at me and Wilson and smiles. My skirt cascades like a waterfall from my waist, and the top is beaded in a peacock blue. "I am very pleased that you are sharing your gift with our school. Thank you, everyone."

"Places, please," Tía whispers, and then she blows us a kiss and follows Miss McDaniels to the wings.

The curtain is still drawn closed as we take our spots behind it. I hear Dr. Newman asking everyone to settle down. The hum in the auditorium dies completely, and then he thanks his sponsors.

When Miss McDaniels takes over, my ears start to buzz, and that's when my feet turn to lead. All I want is for the trapdoor to open in the stage floor so I can get swallowed up.

But too soon, Tía is speaking, thanking everyone for coming. It's almost time.

"This morning, we'll be doing several dances for you . . ."

"I can't," I whisper, breaking my pose. Sweat drips along down my back. "You guys go on."

The younger kids look at me, suddenly seeming

unsure. Stela and Gilberto turn to me with worried looks, too. So, Wilson takes me by the hand before I can run away, and now it's his turn to squeeze my hand too tight. I notice his palms are also a little clammy.

"Let go," I say.

"My mom told me to just look out at the back of the auditorium," he says. "You can't see anybody back there."

"I—I just can't."

Edna walks over and takes me by the shoulders. "Well, you're going to dance anyway. This was your idea, Merci Suárez, remember? Sigue bailando, no matter what. No one is going to know there's a mistake except us. And we already forgive you."

I blink hard as she takes her place again, my eye swerving inward. "Breathe," I hear Lena whisper as the applause for Tía fades.

Then, before I can bolt, the curtains finally part to reveal us.

There's a gasp as we stay frozen in our poses against a brightly lit background. We look like silhouettes, like maybe we're not real. Abuela's costumes are spectacular for the shapes they make in the dark. Then the lights lift slowly, and kids start pointing and saying some of our names as they recognize us on the stage. I don't move a muscle, staring at the back of the auditorium where everything disappears, just like Wilson said. All I see are the blazing lights above us and the eye of Jason's spotlight pinning me into place.

For a second I shift my glance to the only faces I want to see clearly right now. Lolo and Abuela are holding hands in the front row, watching. Even from here, I can see that Lolo's smile fills his whole face, as if he's about to open the most wonderful surprise. Abuela has those happy tears of hers.

The first chords of merengue music start, and I hear Tía in the wings, clapping out the beat: five, six, seven, eight . . .

Everyone starts to move. Even me.

I slide up and back, pretending I have Papi's old T-shirt under my feet. I turn when I have to and wait for a beat when I mess up a little bit, watching. I keep smiling when Wilson steps on my skirt by accident, and even when one of Edna's eyelashes drops on the floor as she's spinning with Vicente. It's just like she said. No one sees our mistakes. They see the costumes, hear the happy music, and feel our smiles.

We go off into the wings and watch the twins start the next number with their solo, and everyone cheers because of their cuteness, just like Tía promised they would. On cue, we come out to join them, all of us doing a cha-cha-cha.

And finally, when it's time to perform our last number, I hold hands with Wilson in front of everyone, and we dance our salsa as a pair, our four legs moving like two, our own way, without a single mistake.

I smile at the Cyclops of Jason's light, unafraid, trusting that Mr. Ellis is there, too, rooting for us. And with each song, I dance for Tía and Simón, for Lolo and Abuela, for Mami and Papi, for my friends who helped me, even for Edna, who needed a way to come in. I let the whole Merci open herself to Seaward Pines, even this special, once-in-a-while dancing one, who's inside me, too.

When our last dance is over, we are all out of breath and jittery with nerves. We join hands and go back out for our bows. My head wrap has slid down to my eyebrows. The twins' shirts are untucked. Edna looks like Popeye with only one eyelash, but she's got her hands tightly on Vicente's elbow. Darius keeps bowing over and over until Lena stops him. Hannah holds Stela on her hip, and they wave at the crowd along with Emeli and the others. Then Tía comes out to the stage and bows with us. Simón jumps up and presents her with the flowers. The whole time Wilson stands next to me, holding my hand in front of the whole world, and I am not feeling like I want to die.

Instead, I am smiling, wide like Lolo. The audience are on their feet, and they hoot and whistle for us all. And finally, when we curtsy and bow one last time, I can believe that all of me, even the parts that are new and I don't really understand, are going to be just fine today and one day and always.

ACKNOWLEDGMENTS

When I first discovered Merci Suárez as a character, I had no notion she would ever be the subject of a novel, much less launch a sequel. Merci debuted in "Sol Painting," as part of the middle-grade anthology *Flying Lessons and Other Stories*. I will be forever grateful to Ellen Oh and Phoebe Yeh, who were the first people to meet Merci in written form. Their enthusiasm and curiosity about her served as a launchpad for all that was to come.

Writing a second book for the Suárez clan felt like a big challenge, particularly after the success of *Merci Suárez Changes Gears*. I knew that Merci's story was not done at the end of that novel because she still had a lot to learn about herself in middle school.

I am so lucky to be surrounded by friends and colleagues who gave me the courage to write this next installment.

I owe a huge debt to Lamar Giles for his constant cheerleading and for allowing me to share the problems that came up during the drafting stage. His excellent ideas made this book much better, and his unshakeable faith in me helped me face the page on days when I would have rather watched Netflix.

A big thanks to Tanya Gonzalez of the Sacred Heart Center in Richmond, Virginia, and to the students in her after-school dance program. They allowed me to watch their rehearsals and shared their insights on the pros and occasional cons of performing folkloric dance.

As always, I want to thank Kate Fletcher, my editorial partner in crime for over a decade, who always makes my characters and their stories bloom.

A huge thanks to my entire Candlewick family, especially Phoebe Kosman, for championing this book and connecting me to readers. Thank you to Erin DeWitt, Maggie Deslaurier, Julia Gaviria, and Martha Dwyer for their care in fixing all my sloppy mistakes — and a special shout-out to Alex Robertson and Iraida Iturralde for their help in making sure that my usage en español was perfecto. Thanks to Pam Consolazio and artist Joe Cepeda for their care in designing the most beautiful book possible.

Thanks also to my assistant, Kerri Poore, for keeping my "book life" straight so that I could have time to compose.

And finally, as always, I want to thank my family—Javier, Cristina, Sandra, and Alex—for their love and support. They are, and always will be, the core of everything I am.